KINGS OF NOWHERE™

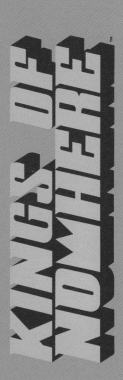

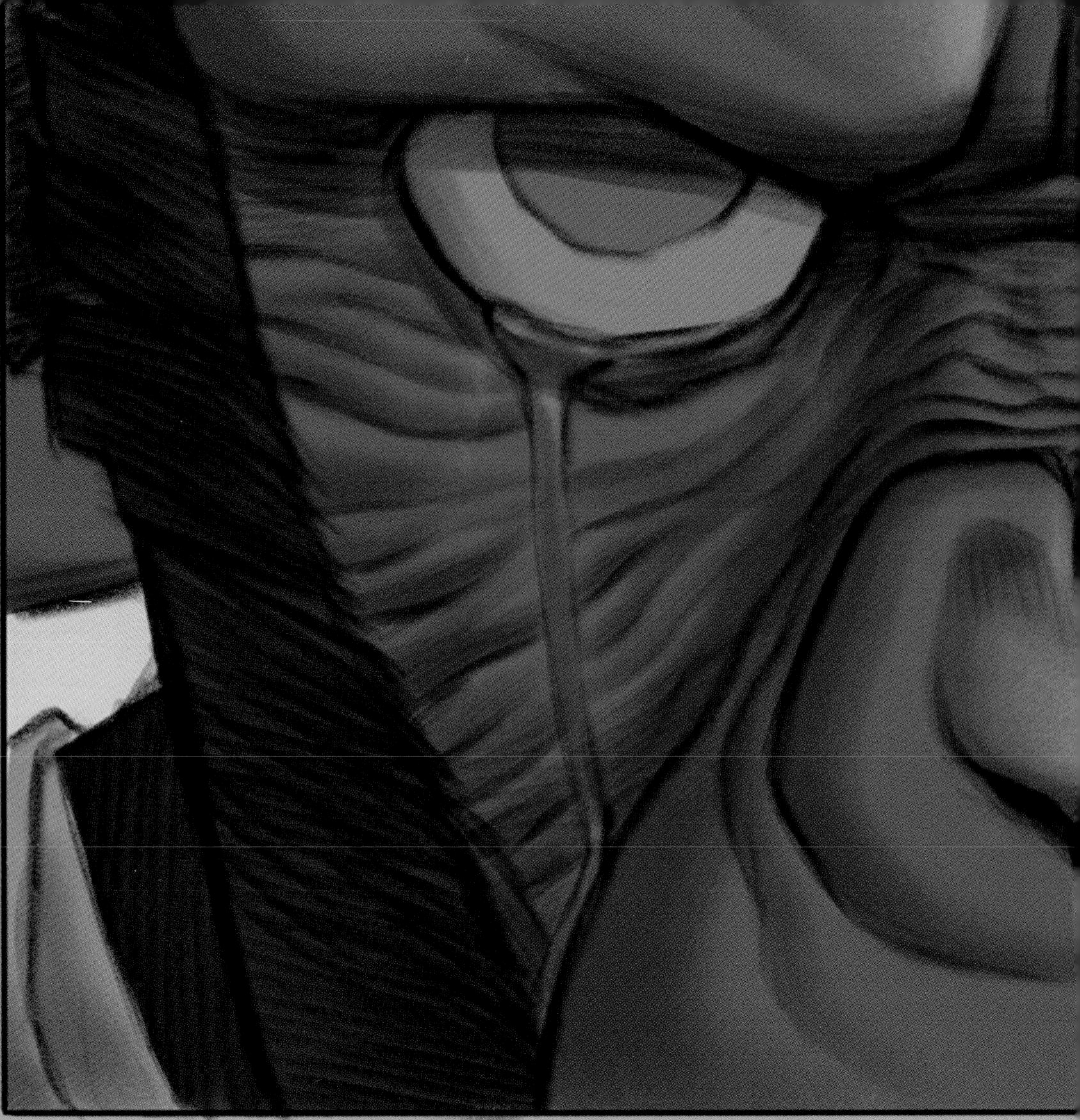
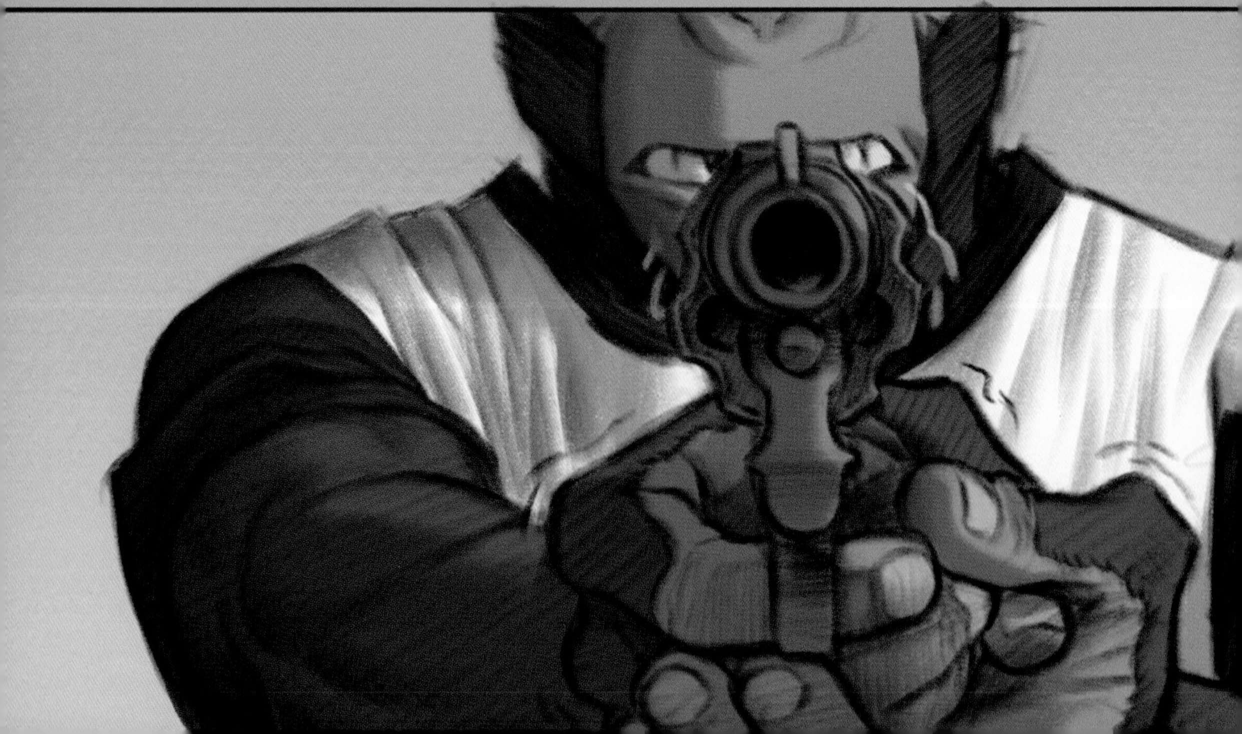

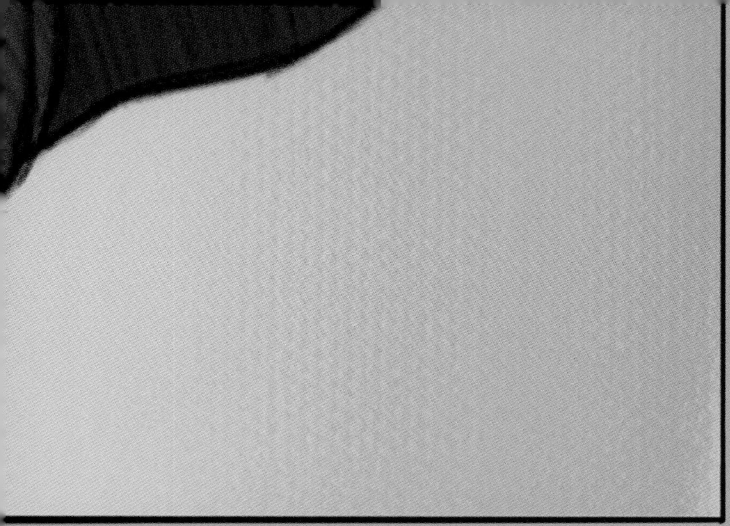

KINGS OF NOWHERE™

VOLUME 1

CREATED, WRITTEN, AND ILLUSTRATED BY
SOROUSH BARAZESH

DARK HORSE BOOKS

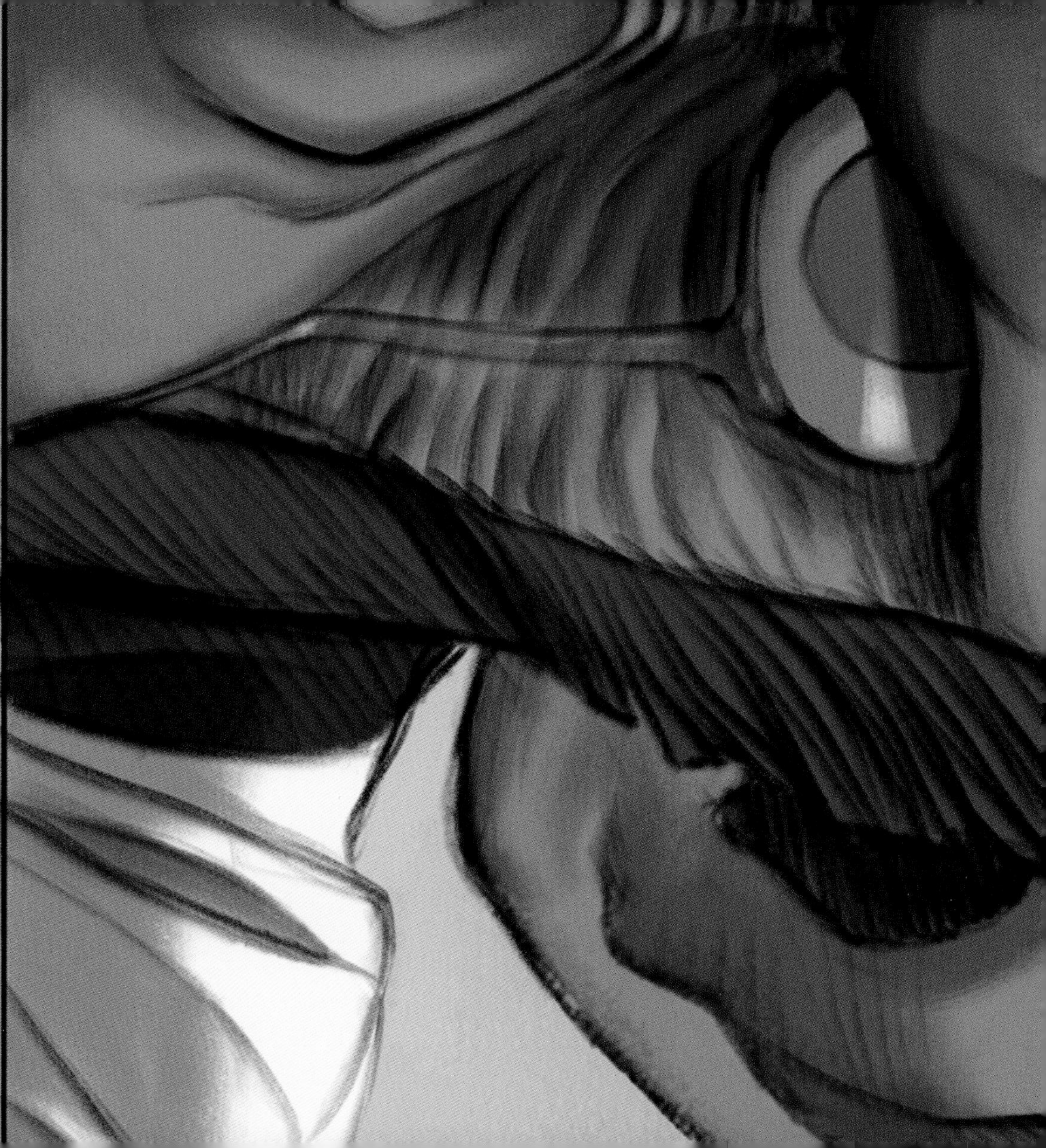

President & Publisher
MIKE RICHARDSON

Collection Editor
JUDY KHUU

Collection Assistant Editor
ROSE WEITZ

Collection Designer
JUSTIN COUCH

Digital Art Technician
ADAM PRUETT

KINGS OF NOWHERE VOLUME 1

Neil Hankerson Executive Vice President • Tom Weddle Chief Financial Officer • Dale LaFountain Chief Information Officer • Tim Wiesch Vice President of Licensing • Matt Parkinson Vice President of Marketing • Vanessa Todd-Holmes Vice President of Production and Scheduling • Mark Bernardi Vice President of Book Trade and Digital Sales • Randy Lahrman Vice President of Product Development and Sales • Ken Lizzi General Counsel • Dave Marshall Editor in Chief • Davey Estrada Editorial Director • Chris Warner Senior Books Editor • Cary Grazzini Director of Specialty Projects • Lia Ribacchi Art Director • Matt Dryer Director of Digital Art and Prepress • Michael Gombos Senior Director of Licensed Publications • Kari Yadro Director of Custom Programs • Kari Torson Director of International Licensing

Published by Dark Horse Books
A division of Dark Horse Comics LLC
10956 SE Main Street
Milwaukie, OR 97222

DarkHorse.com

To find a comics shop in your area, visit comicshoplocator.com

First edition: September 2022
Ebook ISBN 978-1-50673-324-1
Trade Paperback ISBN 978-1-50673-328-9

10 9 8 7 6 5 4 3 2 1
Printed in China

Library of Congress Cataloging-in-Publication Data

Names: Barazesh, Soroush, writer, artist.
Title: Kings of nowhere / Soroush Barazesh.
Description: Milwaukie, OR : Dark Horse Books, 2022-
Identifiers: LCCN 2022011814 (print) | LCCN 2022011815 (ebook) | ISBN 9781506733289 (v. 1 ; trade paperback) | ISBN 9781506733241 (v. 1 ; ebook)
Subjects: LCSH: Shapeshifting--Comic books, strips, etc. | Revenge--Comic books, strips, etc. | LCGFT: Action and adventure comics. | Fantasy comics. | Graphic novels.
Classification: LCC PN6733.B27 K56 2022 (print) | LCC PN6733.B27 (ebook) | DDC 741.5/971--dc23/eng/20220426
LC record available at https://lccn.loc.gov/2022011814
LC ebook record available at https://lccn.loc.gov/2022011815

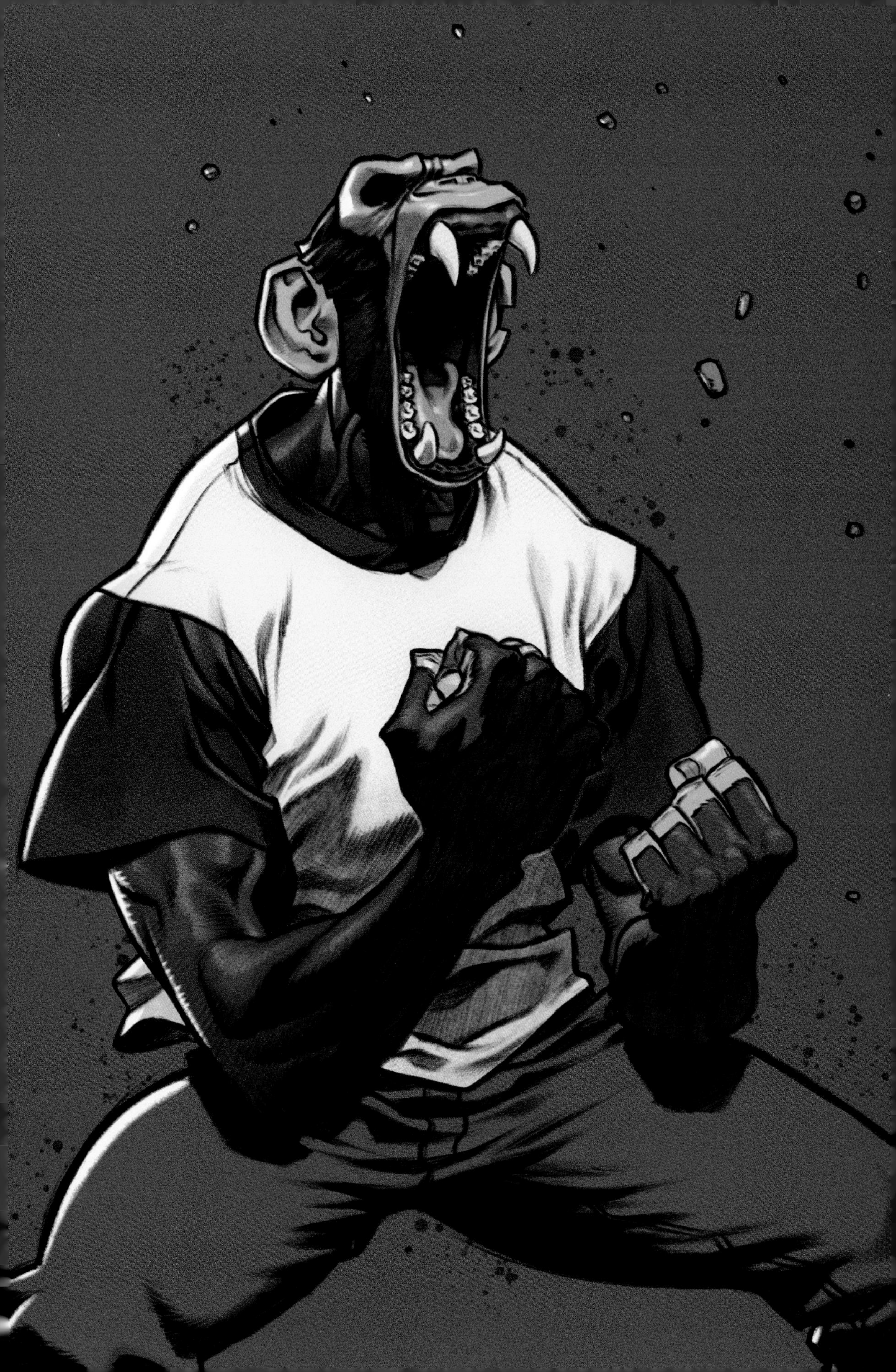

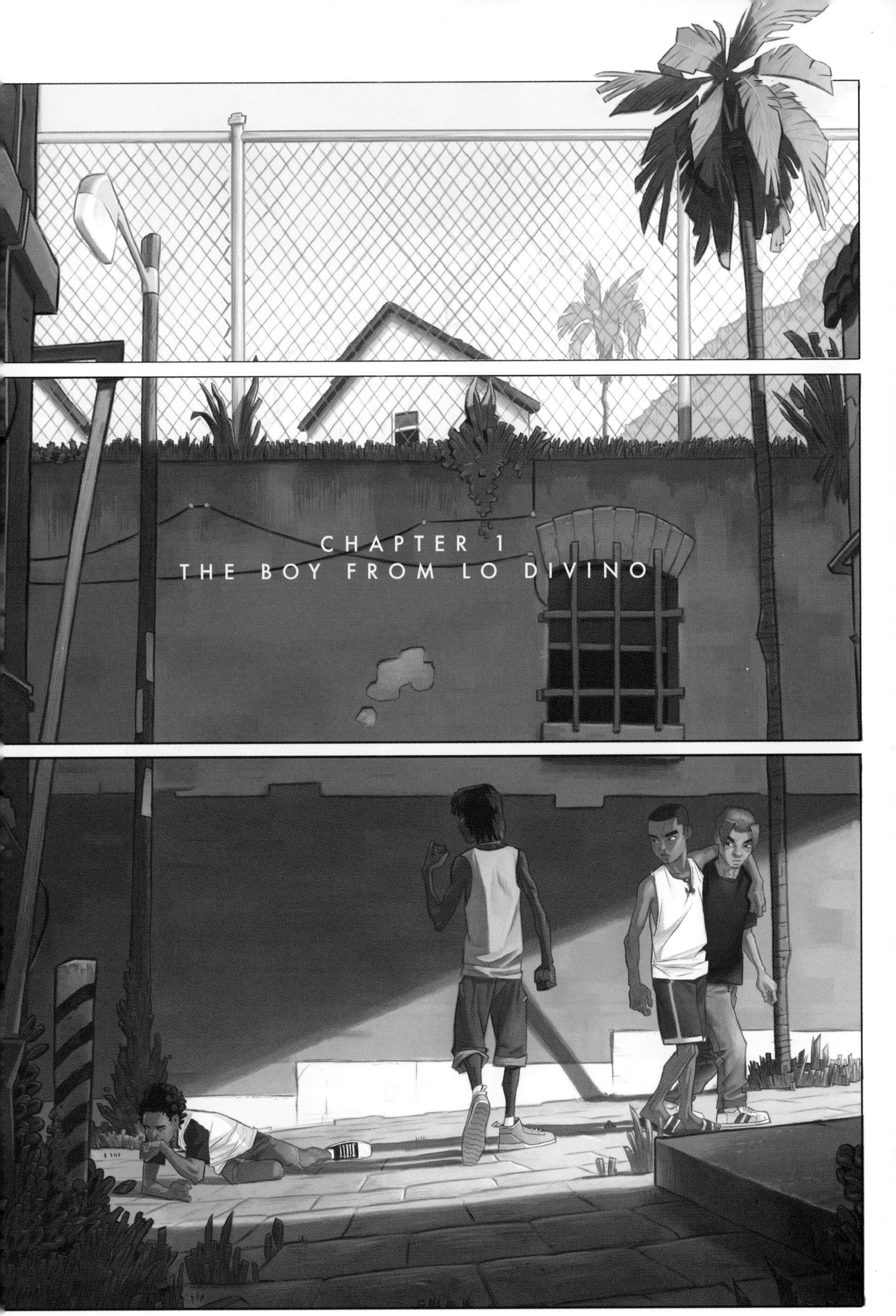
CHAPTER 1
THE BOY FROM LO DIVINO

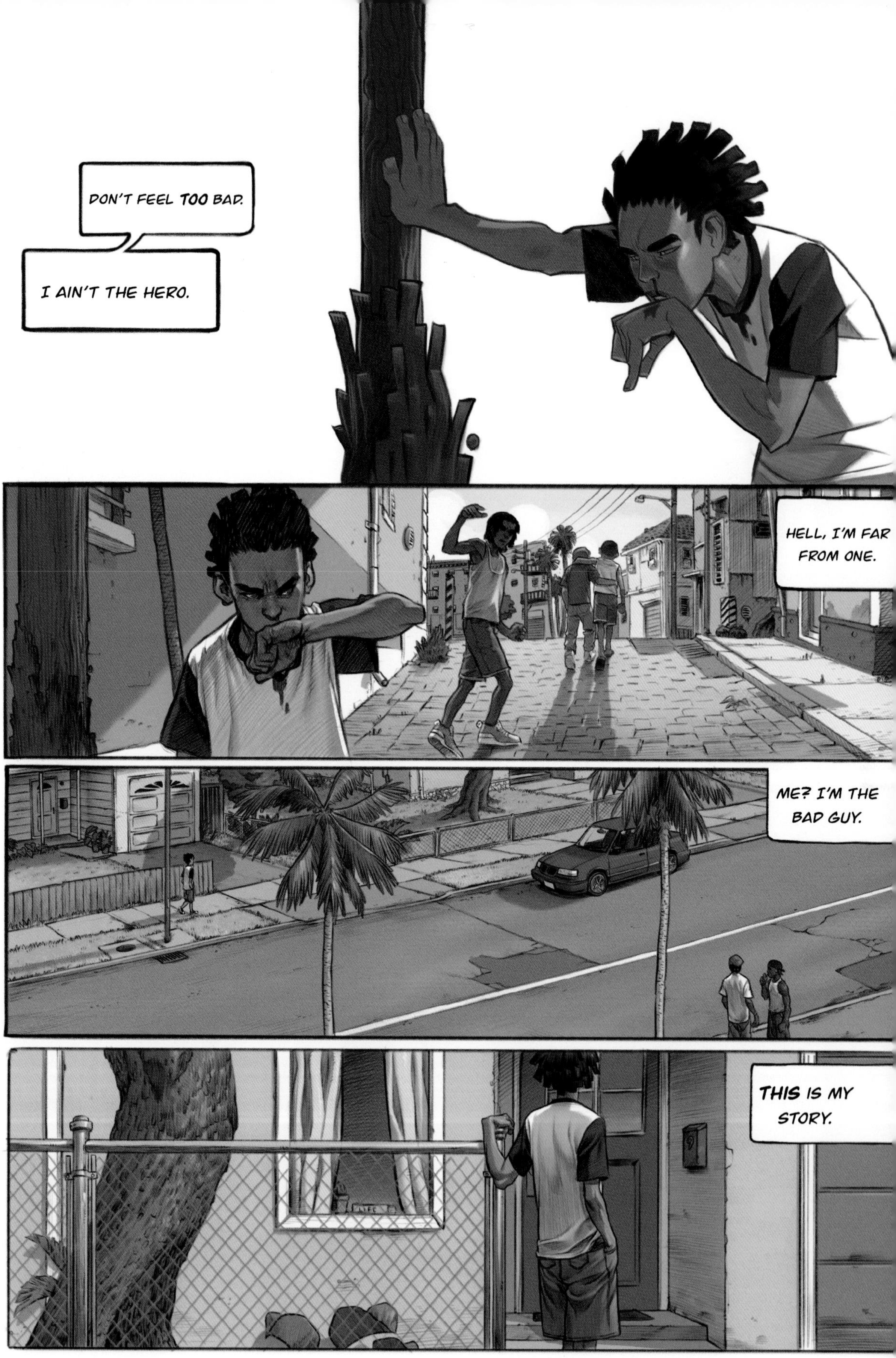
DON'T FEEL TOO BAD.
I AIN'T THE HERO.
HELL, I'M FAR FROM ONE.
ME? I'M THE BAD GUY.
THIS IS MY STORY.

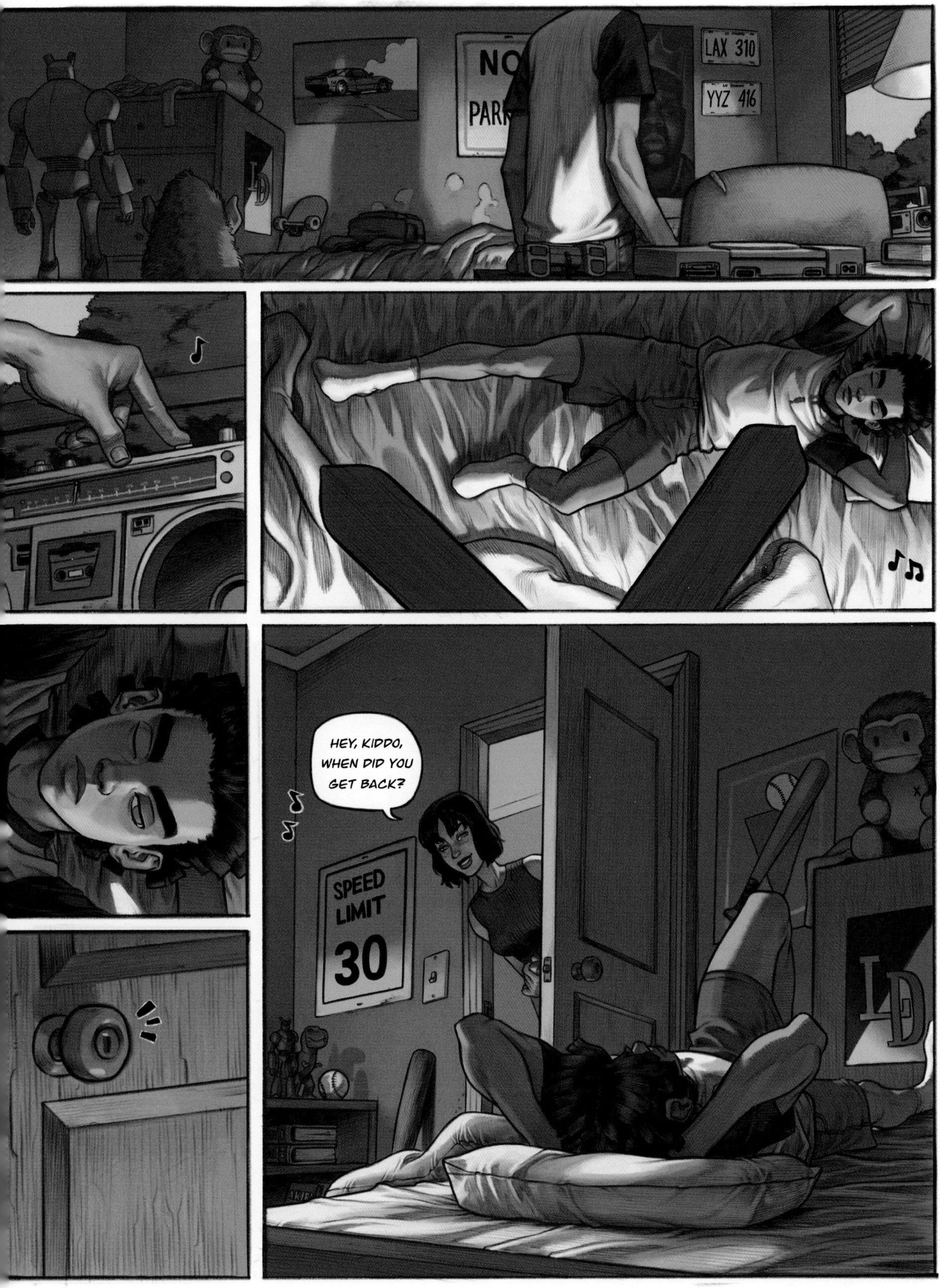
NO
PARK
LAX 310
YYZ 416
HEY, KIDDO, WHEN DID YOU GET BACK?
SPEED LIMIT 30

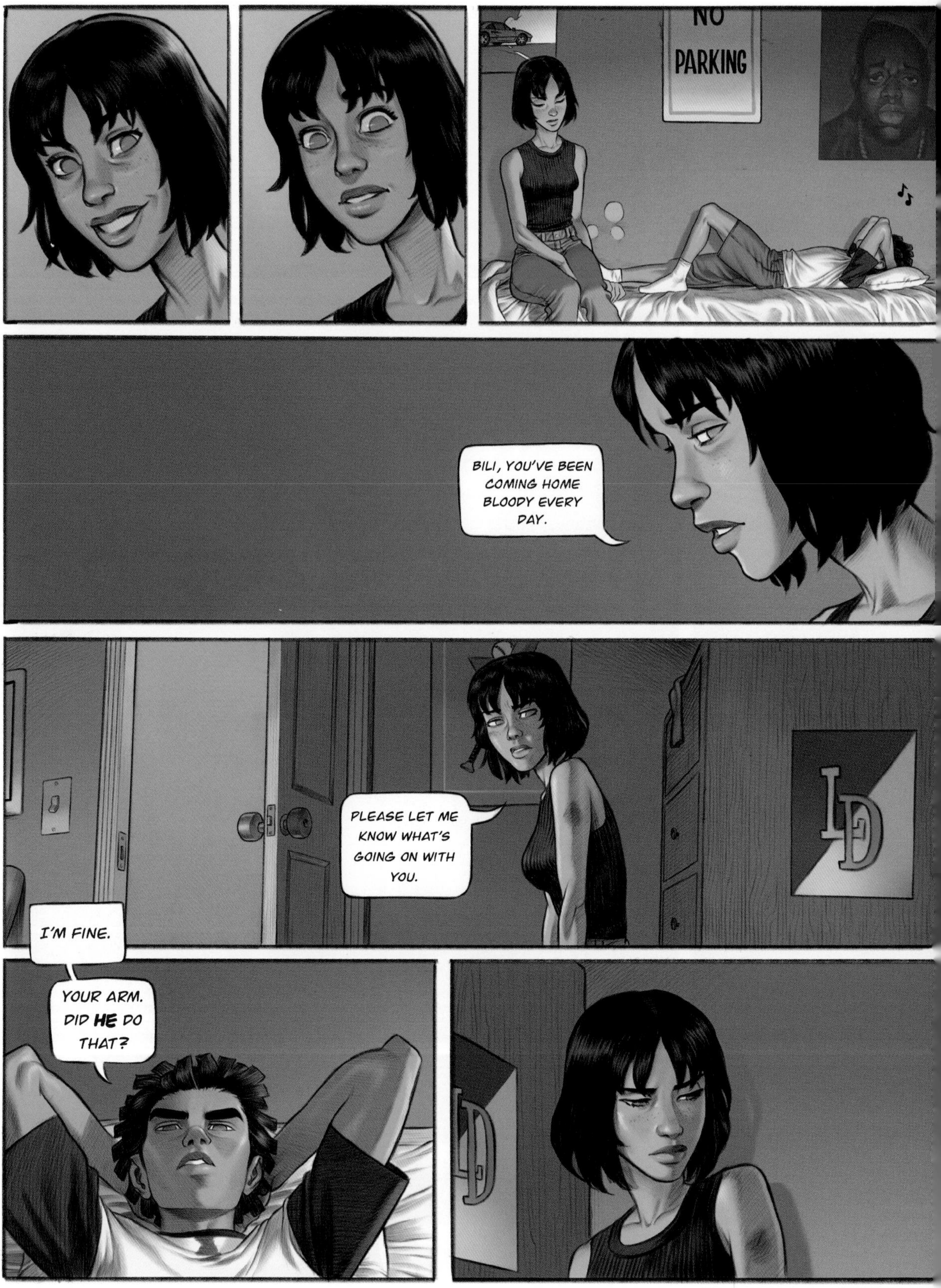
NO
PARKING
BILI, YOU'VE BEEN COMING HOME BLOODY EVERY DAY.
PLEASE LET ME KNOW WHAT'S GOING ON WITH YOU.
I'M FINE.
YOUR ARM. DID **HE** DO THAT?

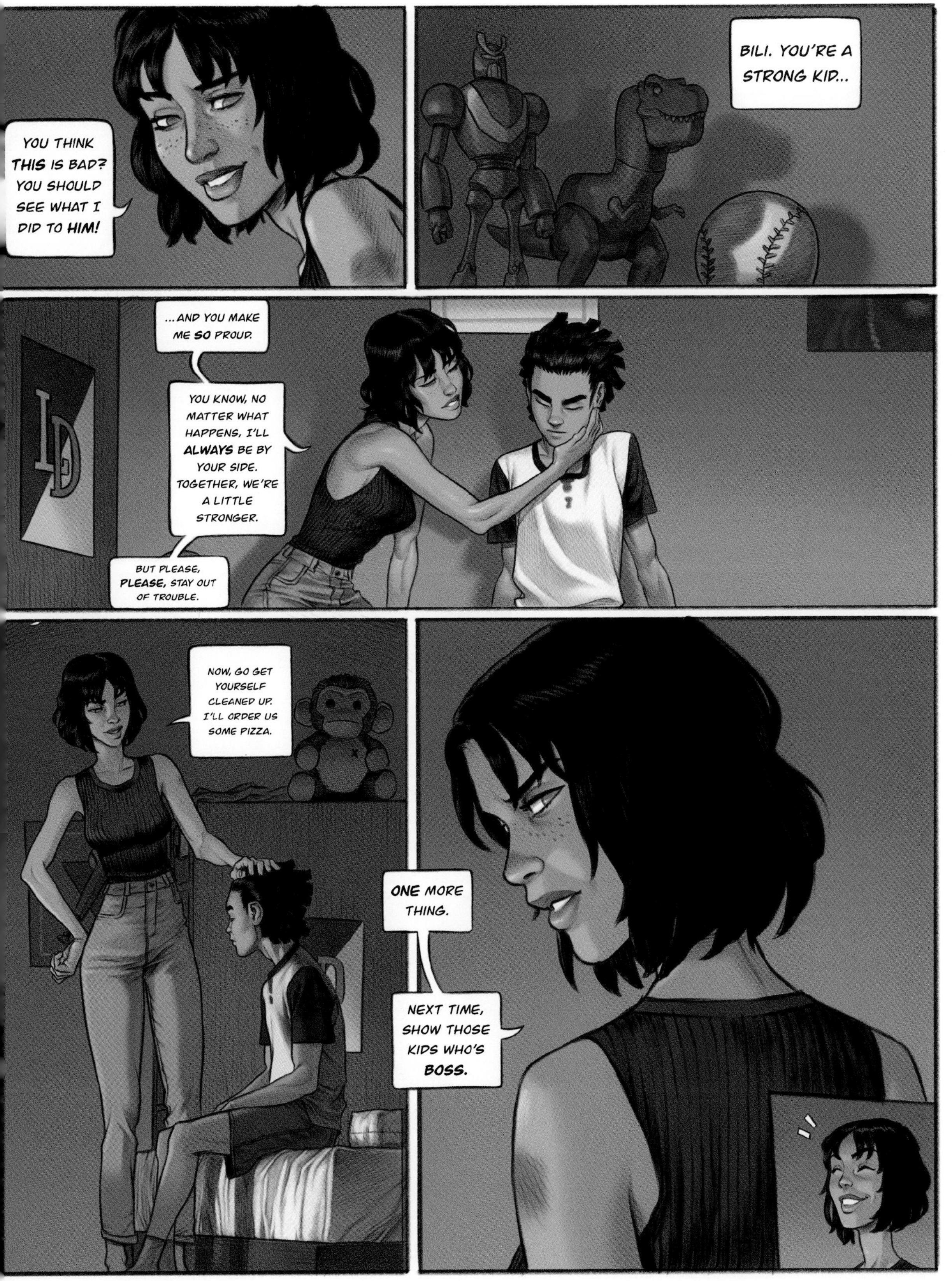
YOU THINK THIS IS BAD? YOU SHOULD SEE WHAT I DID TO HIM!
BILI. YOU'RE A STRONG KID...
...AND YOU MAKE ME SO PROUD.
YOU KNOW, NO MATTER WHAT HAPPENS, I'LL ALWAYS BE BY YOUR SIDE. TOGETHER, WE'RE A LITTLE STRONGER.
BUT PLEASE, PLEASE, STAY OUT OF TROUBLE.
NOW, GO GET YOURSELF CLEANED UP. I'LL ORDER US SOME PIZZA.
ONE MORE THING.
NEXT TIME, SHOW THOSE KIDS WHO'S BOSS.

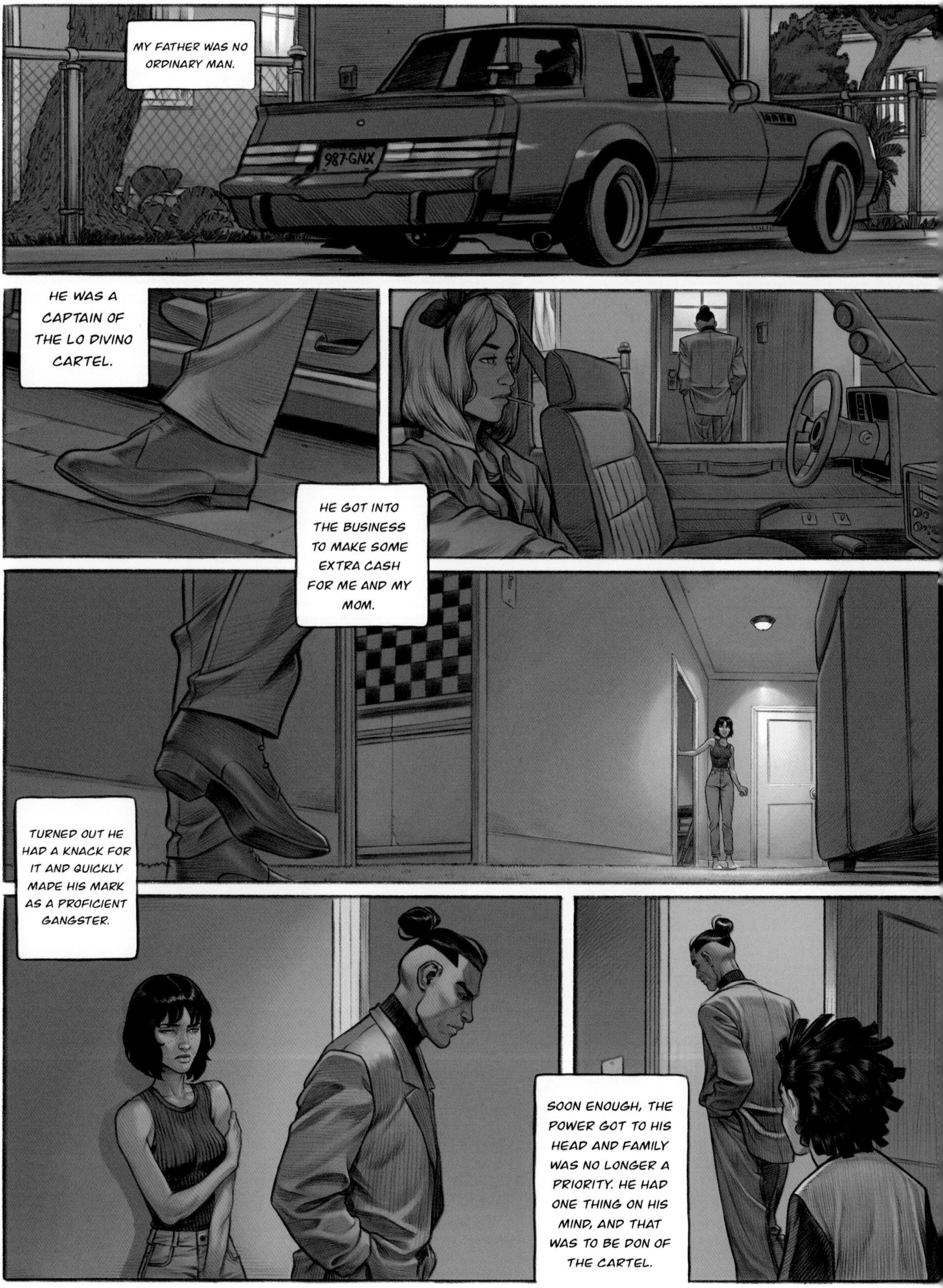
MY FATHER WAS NO ORDINARY MAN.
987·GNX
HE WAS A CAPTAIN OF THE LO DIVINO CARTEL.
HE GOT INTO THE BUSINESS TO MAKE SOME EXTRA CASH FOR ME AND MY MOM.
TURNED OUT HE HAD A KNACK FOR IT AND QUICKLY MADE HIS MARK AS A PROFICIENT GANGSTER.
SOON ENOUGH, THE POWER GOT TO HIS HEAD AND FAMILY WAS NO LONGER A PRIORITY. HE HAD ONE THING ON HIS MIND, AND THAT WAS TO BE DON OF THE CARTEL.

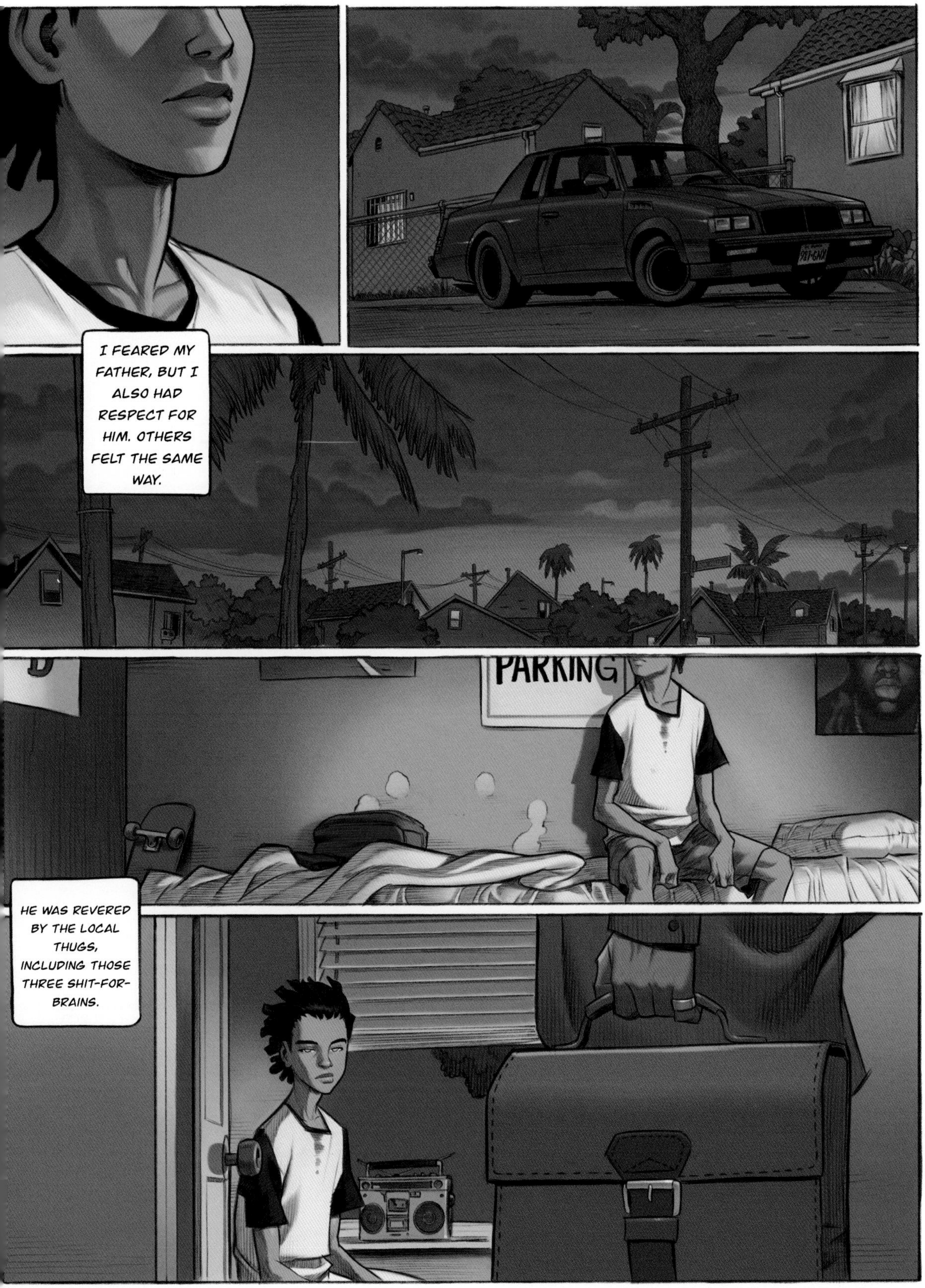
I FEARED MY FATHER, BUT I ALSO HAD RESPECT FOR HIM. OTHERS FELT THE SAME WAY.
PARKING
HE WAS REVERED BY THE LOCAL THUGS, INCLUDING THOSE THREE SHIT-FOR-BRAINS.

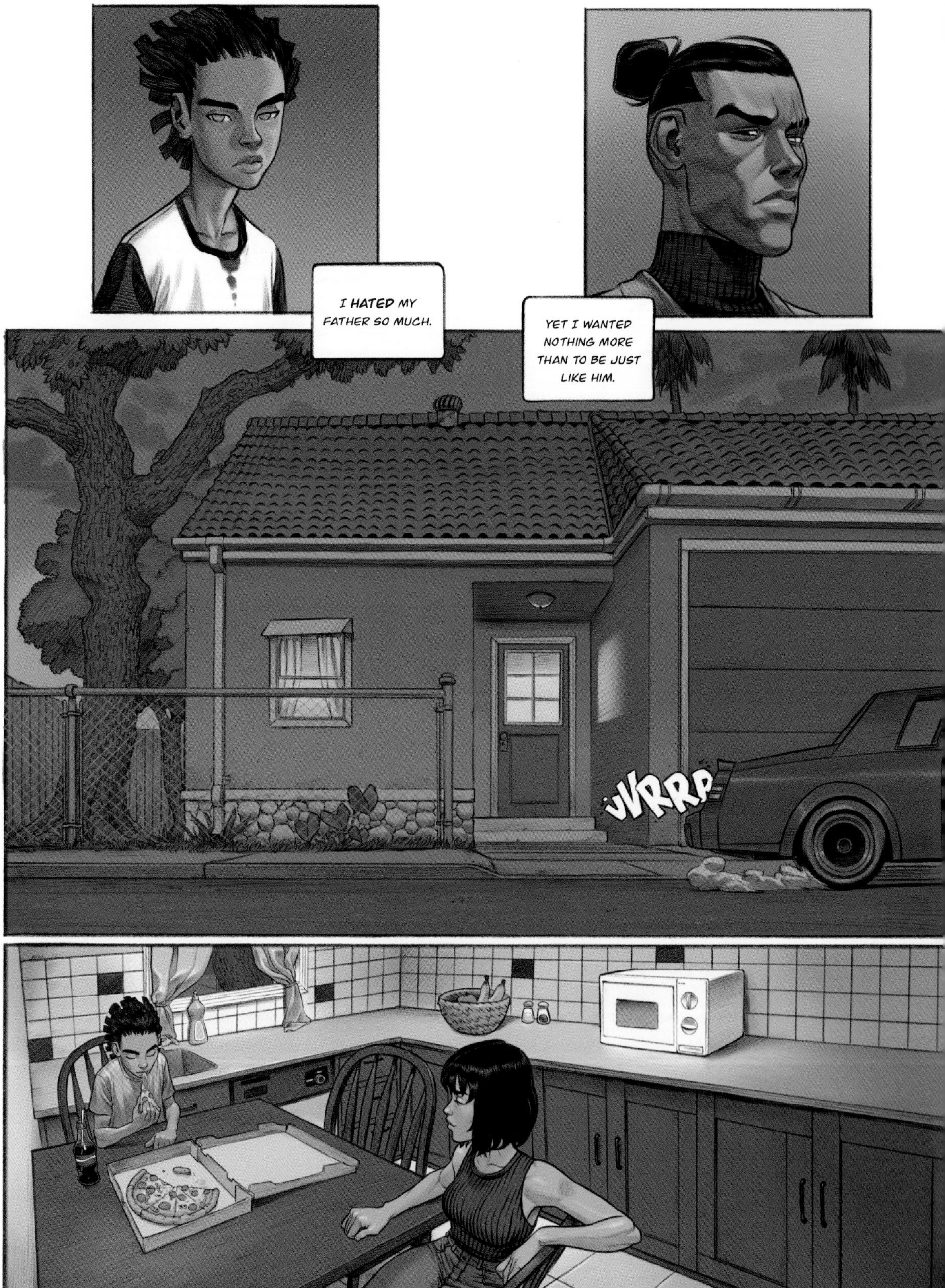
I HATED MY FATHER SO MUCH.
YET I WANTED NOTHING MORE THAN TO BE JUST LIKE HIM.
VVRRP

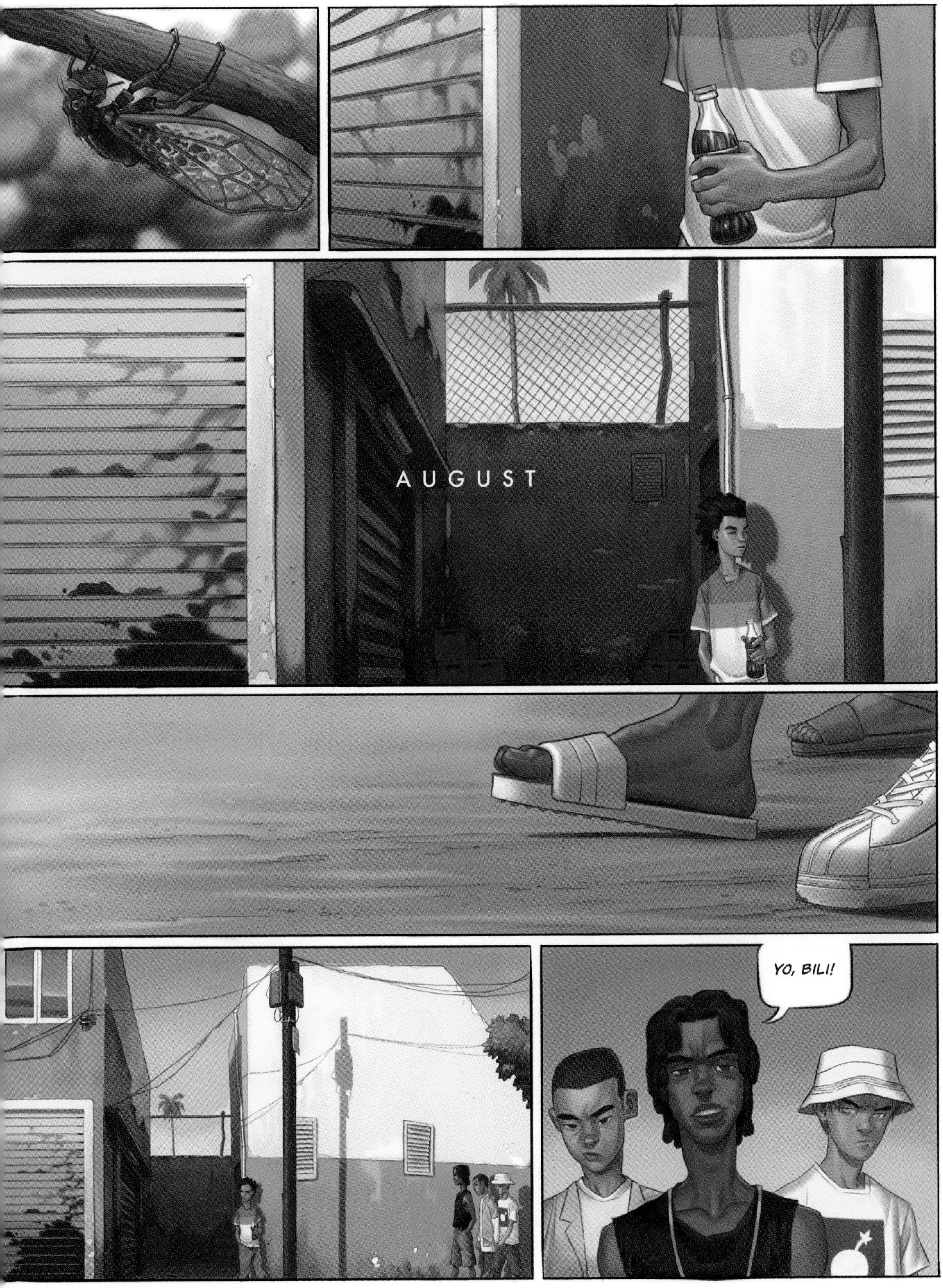
AUGUST
YO, BILI!

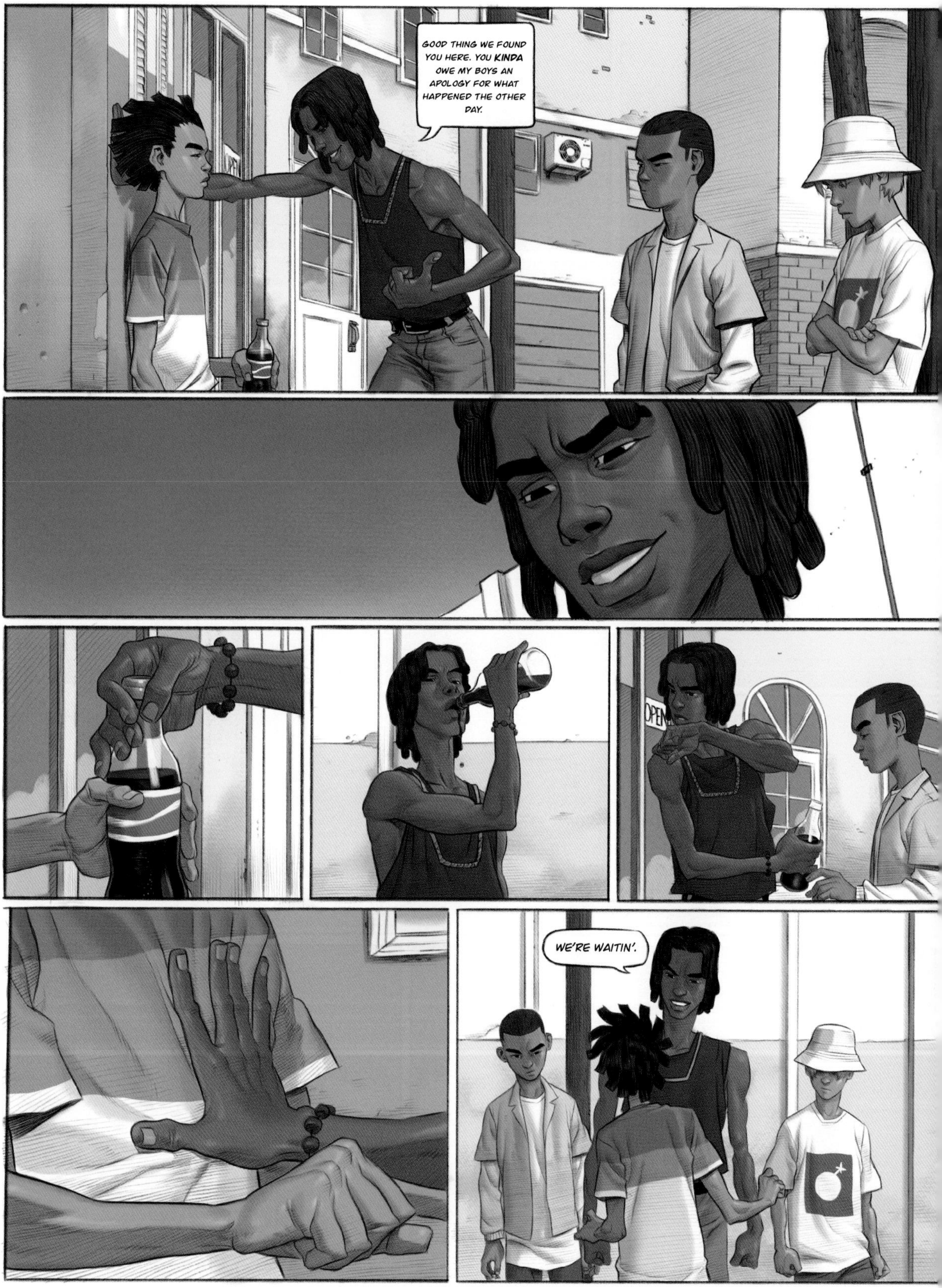
GOOD THING WE FOUND YOU HERE. YOU KINDA OWE MY BOYS AN APOLOGY FOR WHAT HAPPENED THE OTHER DAY.
OPEN
WE'RE WAITIN'.

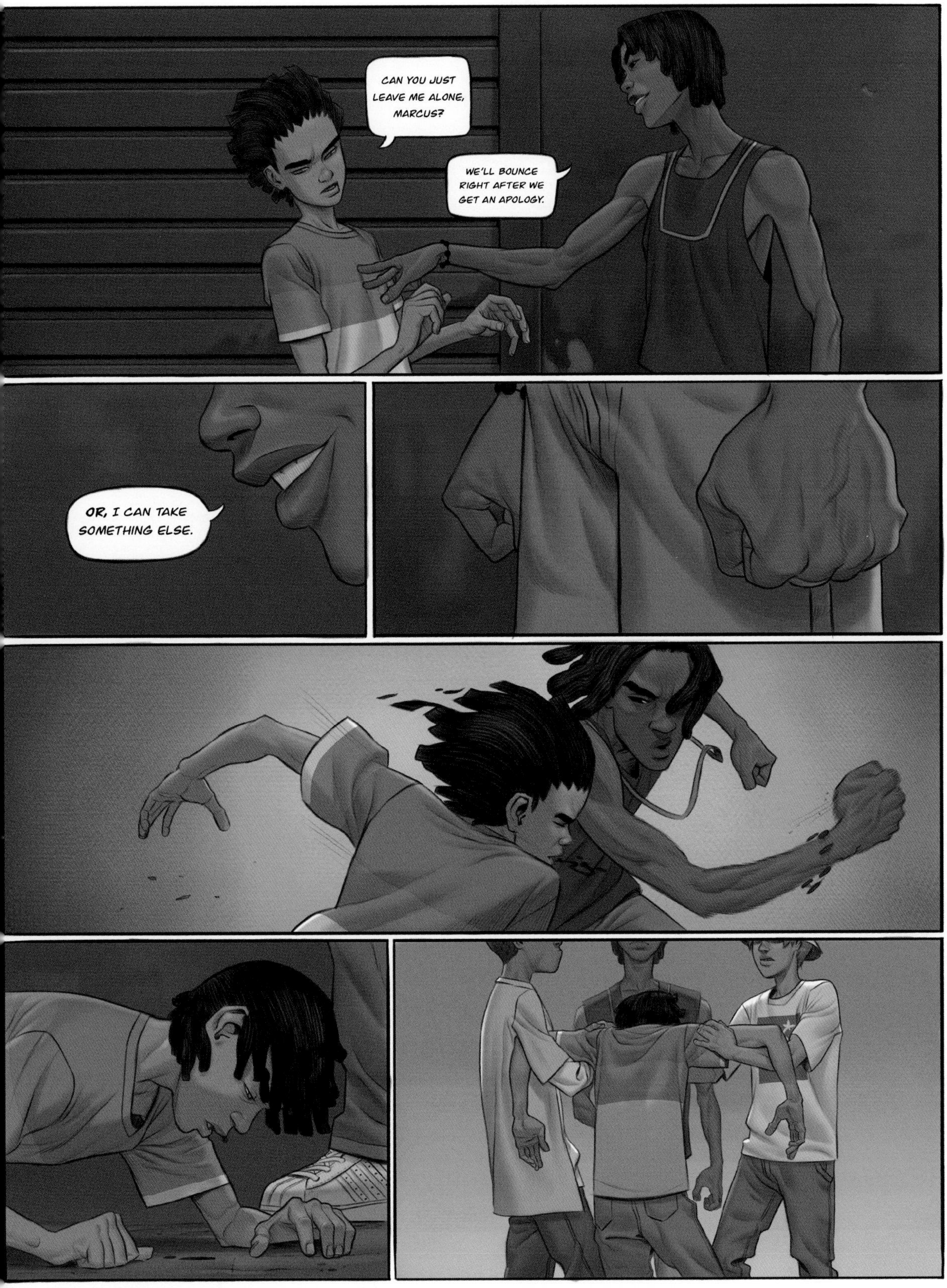
CAN YOU JUST LEAVE ME ALONE, MARCUS?
WE'LL BOUNCE RIGHT AFTER WE GET AN APOLOGY.
OR, I CAN TAKE SOMETHING ELSE.

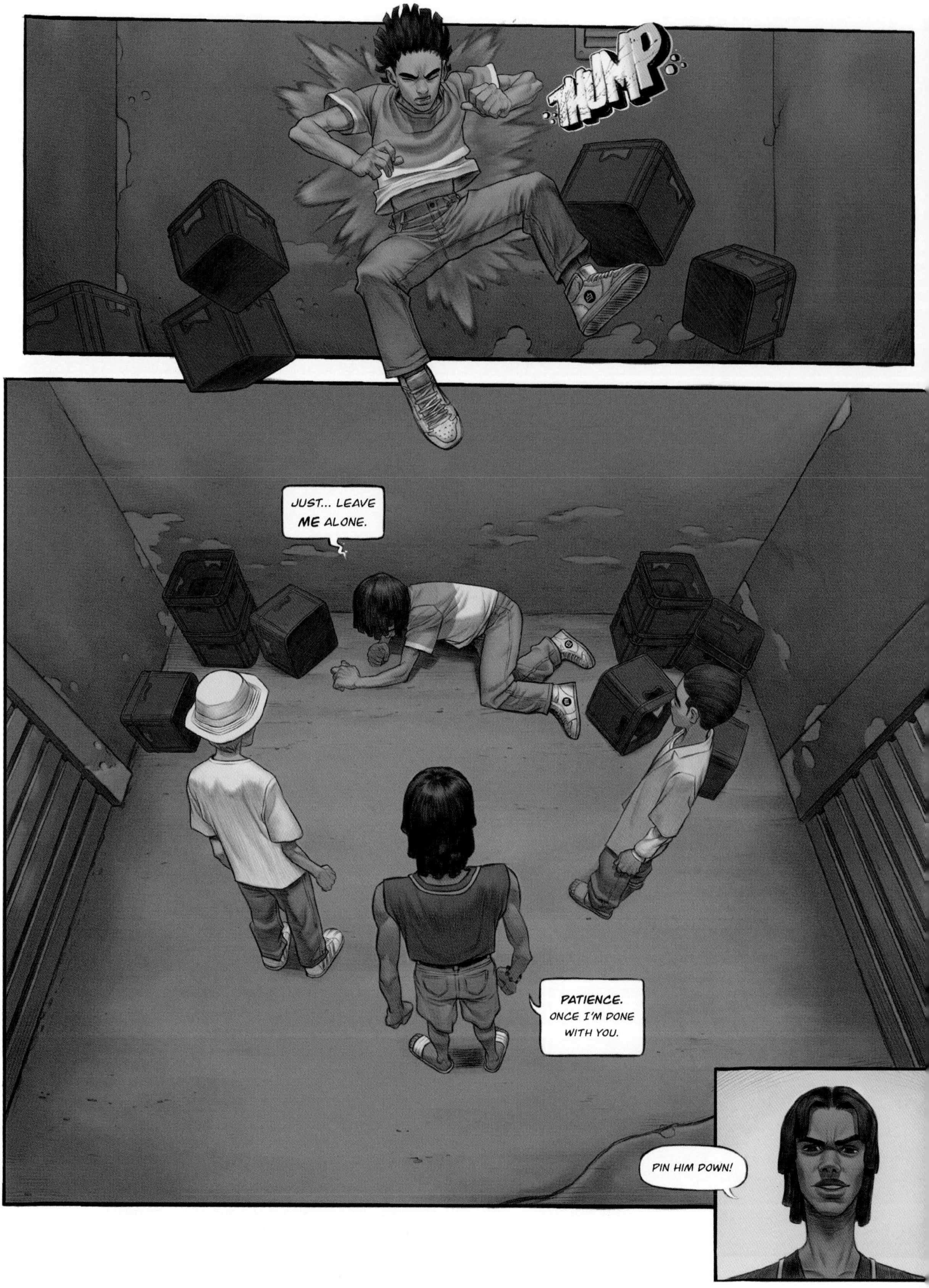
THUMP
JUST... LEAVE ME ALONE.
PATIENCE. ONCE I'M DONE WITH YOU.
PIN HIM DOWN!

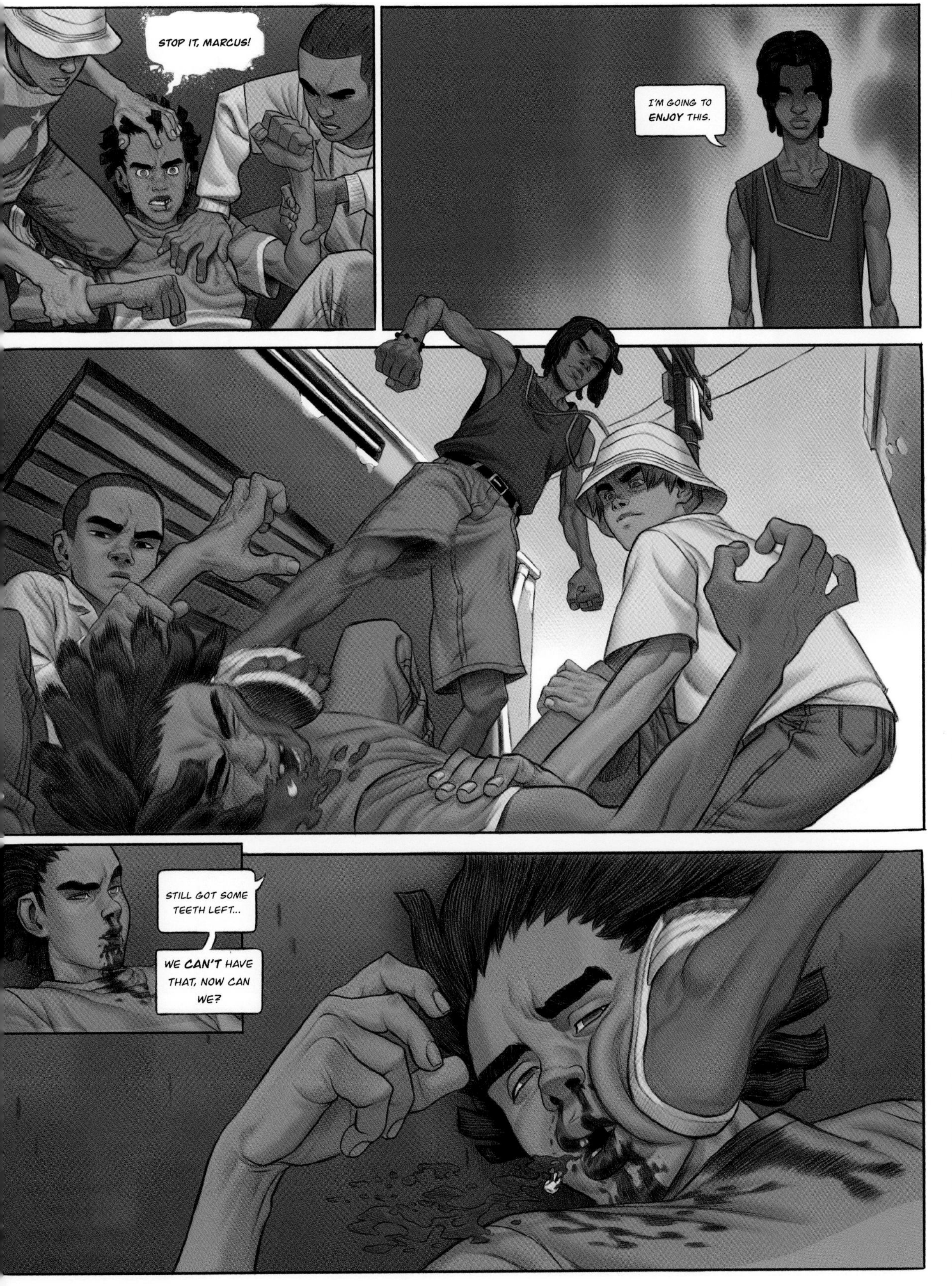
STOP IT, MARCUS!
I'M GOING TO ENJOY THIS.
STILL GOT SOME TEETH LEFT...
WE CAN'T HAVE THAT, NOW CAN WE?

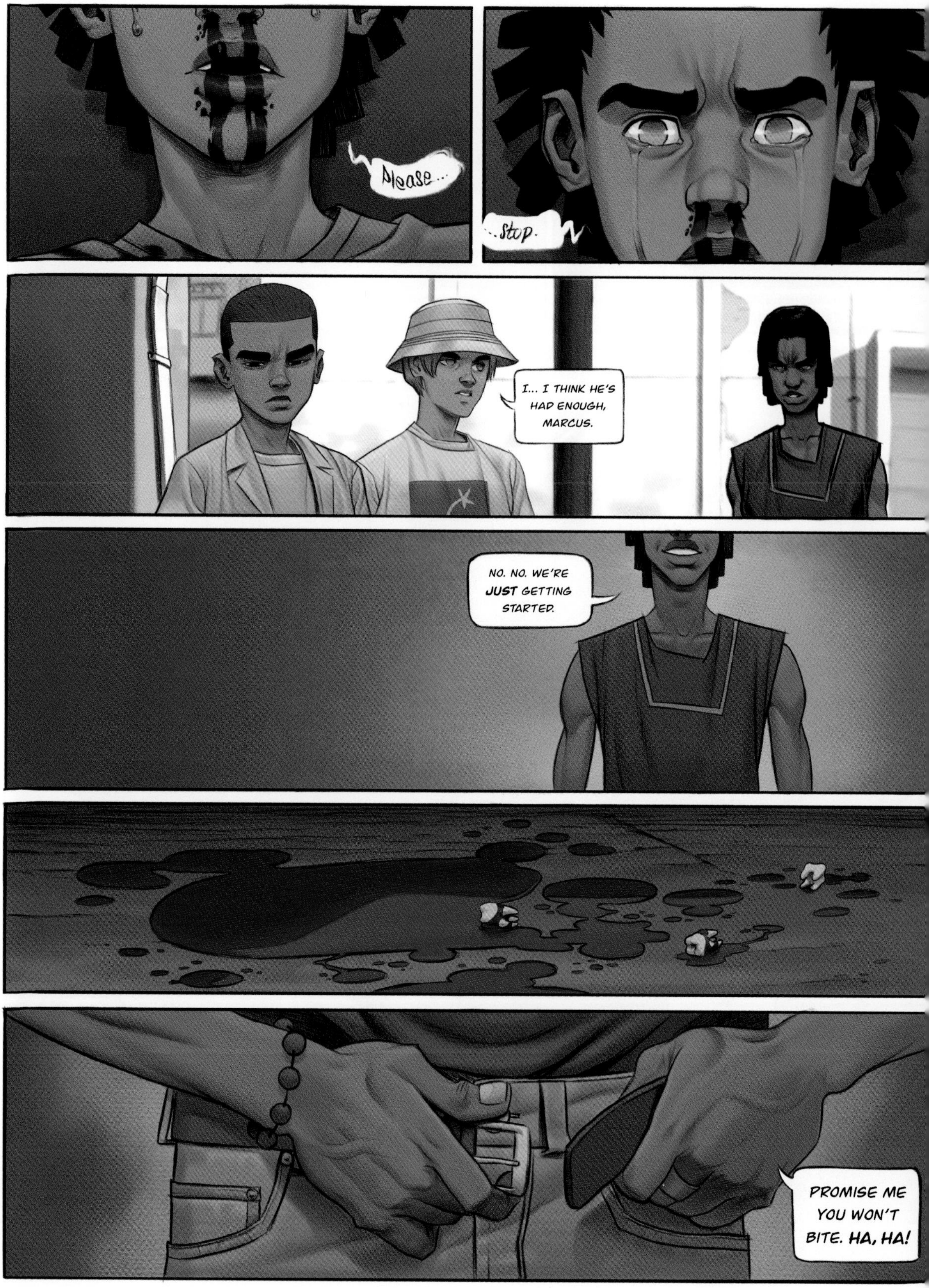
Please...
...stop.
I... I THINK HE'S HAD ENOUGH, MARCUS.
NO. NO. WE'RE **JUST** GETTING STARTED.
PROMISE ME YOU WON'T BITE. **HA, HA!**

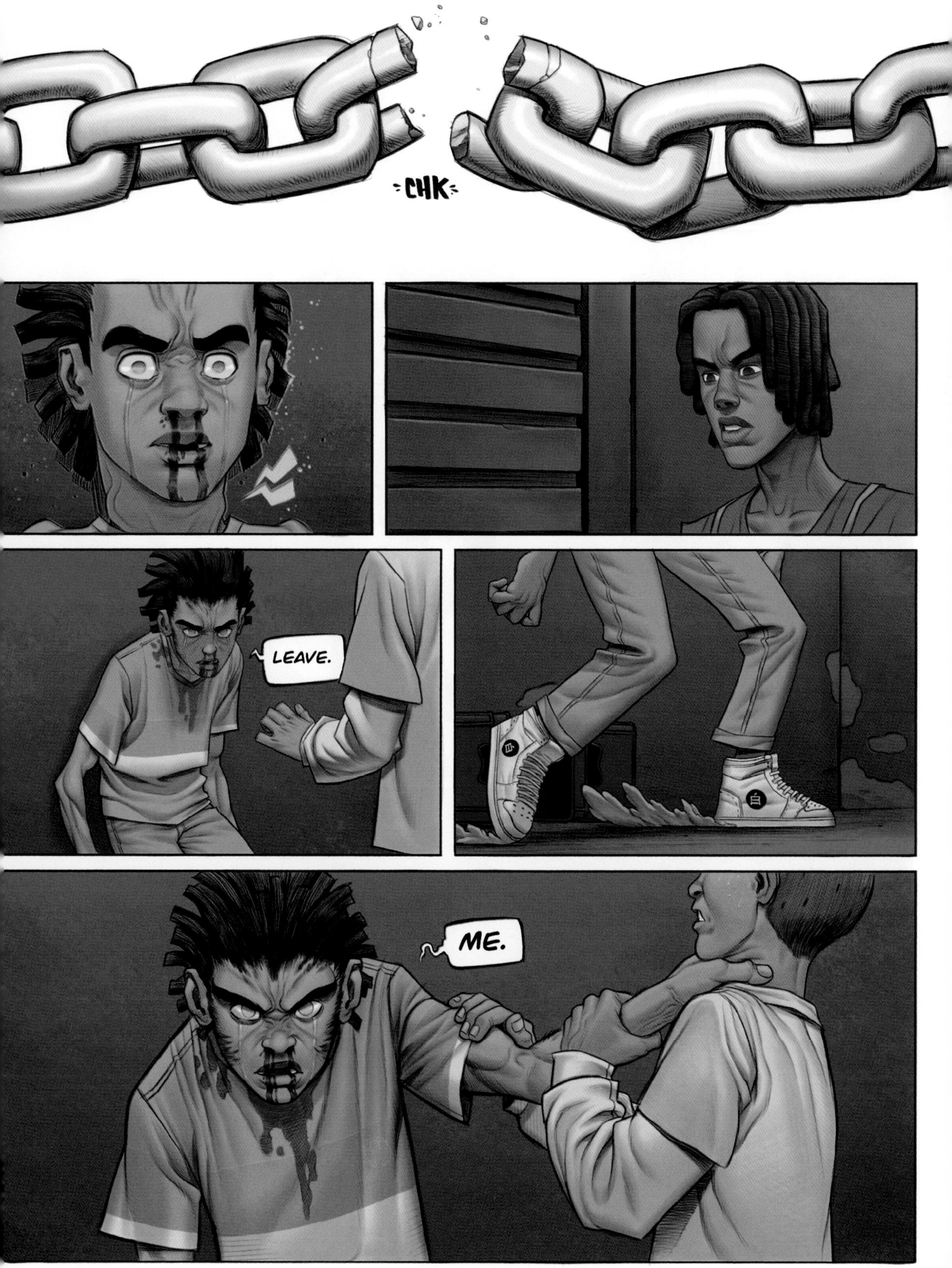
CHK
LEAVE.
ME.

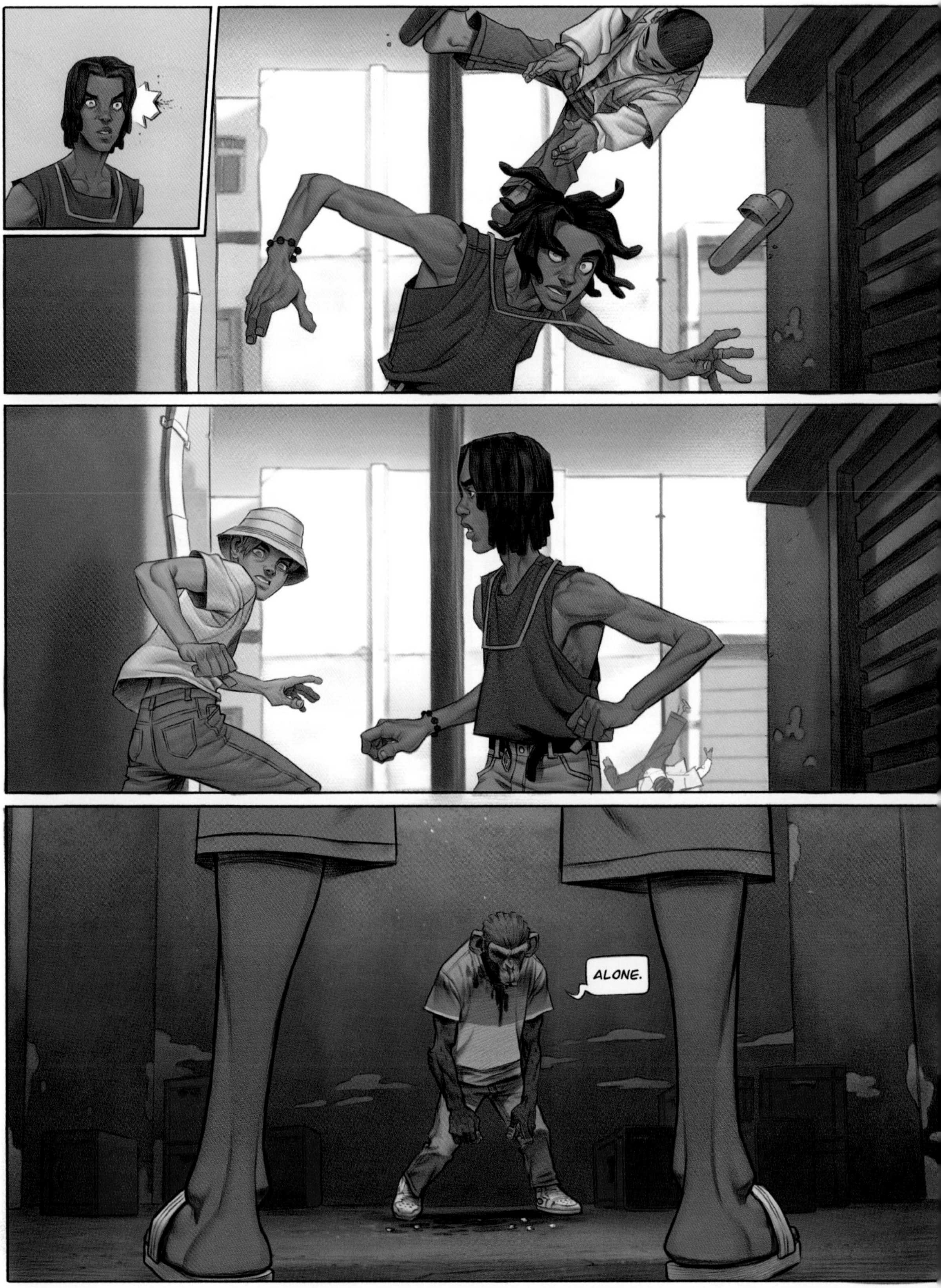
ALONE.

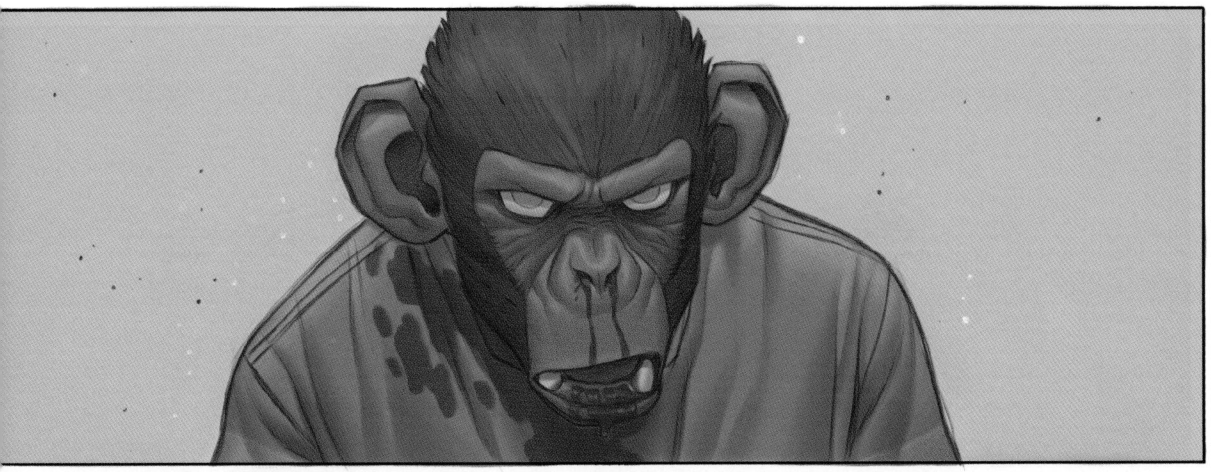

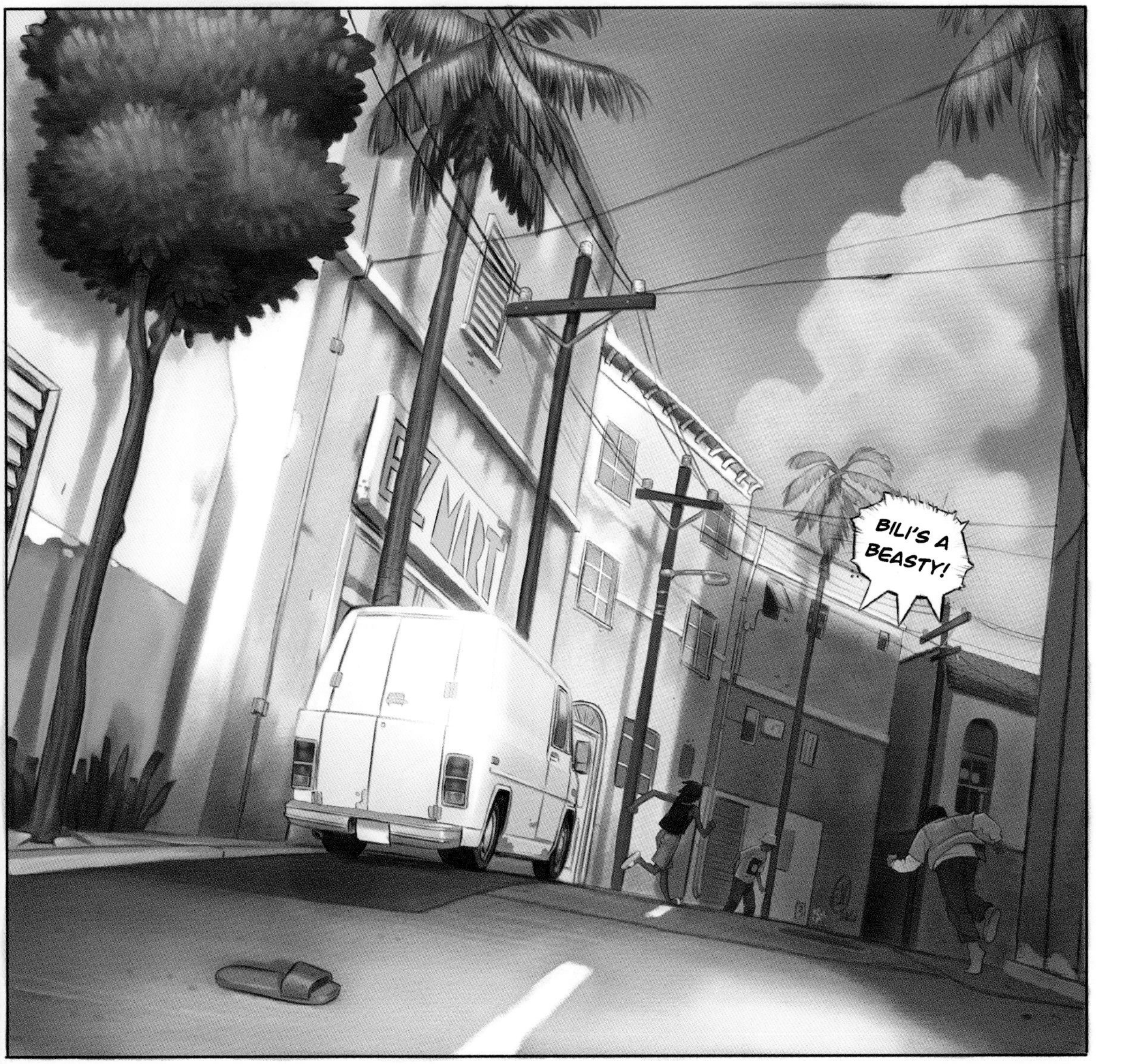
EZ MART
BILI'S A BEASTY!

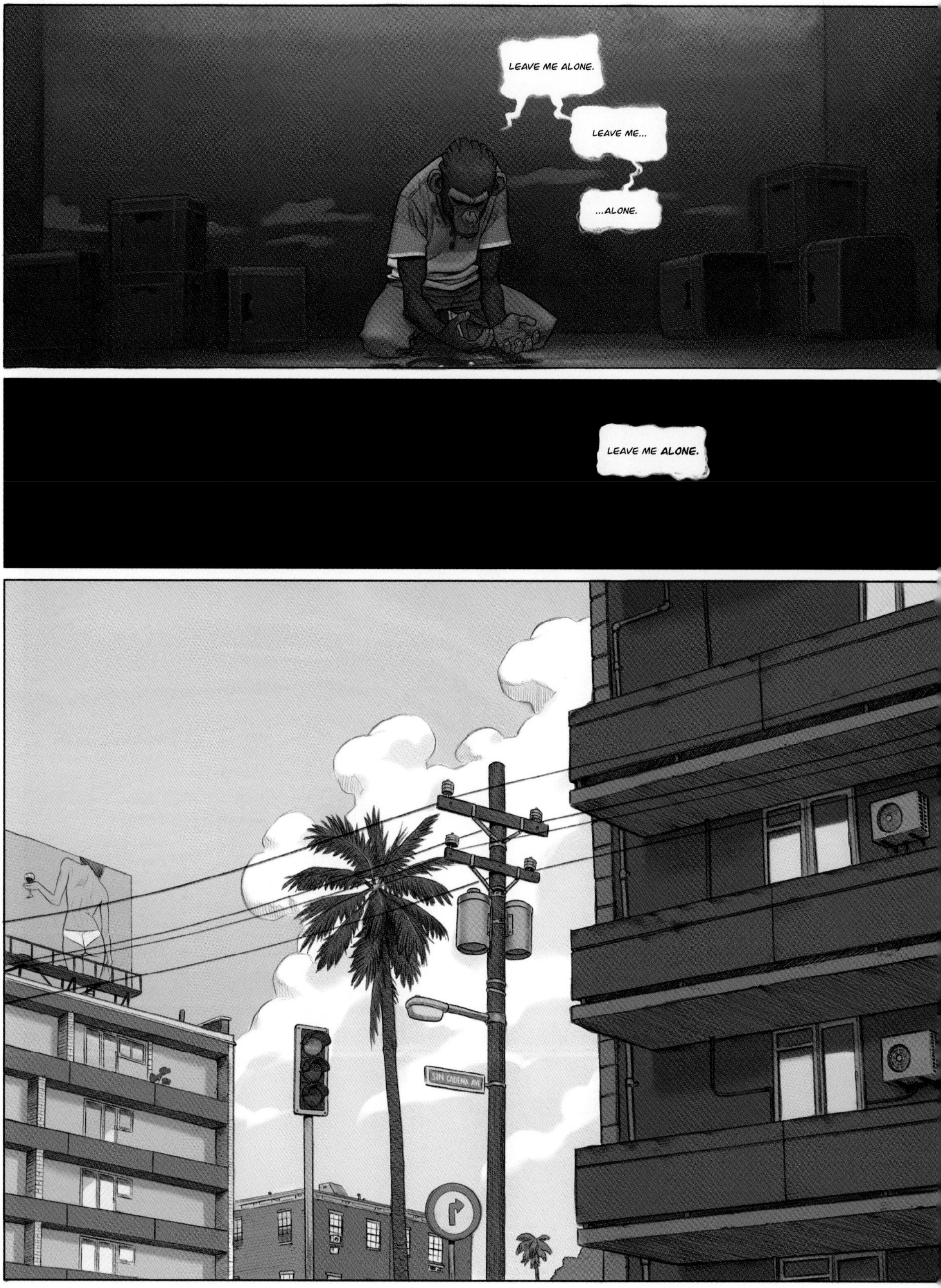
LEAVE ME ALONE.
LEAVE ME...
...ALONE.
LEAVE ME ALONE.
SIN CADENA AVE

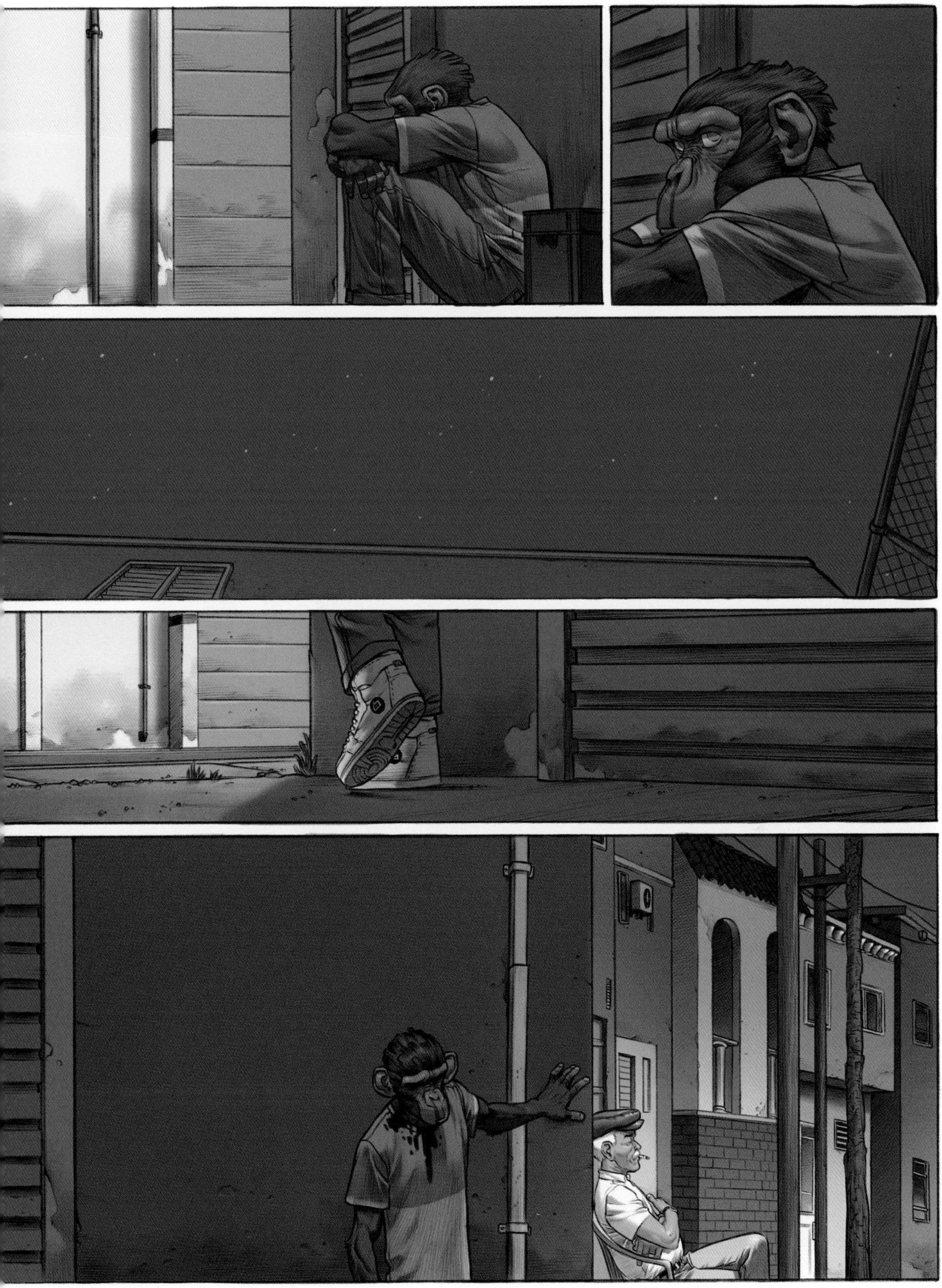

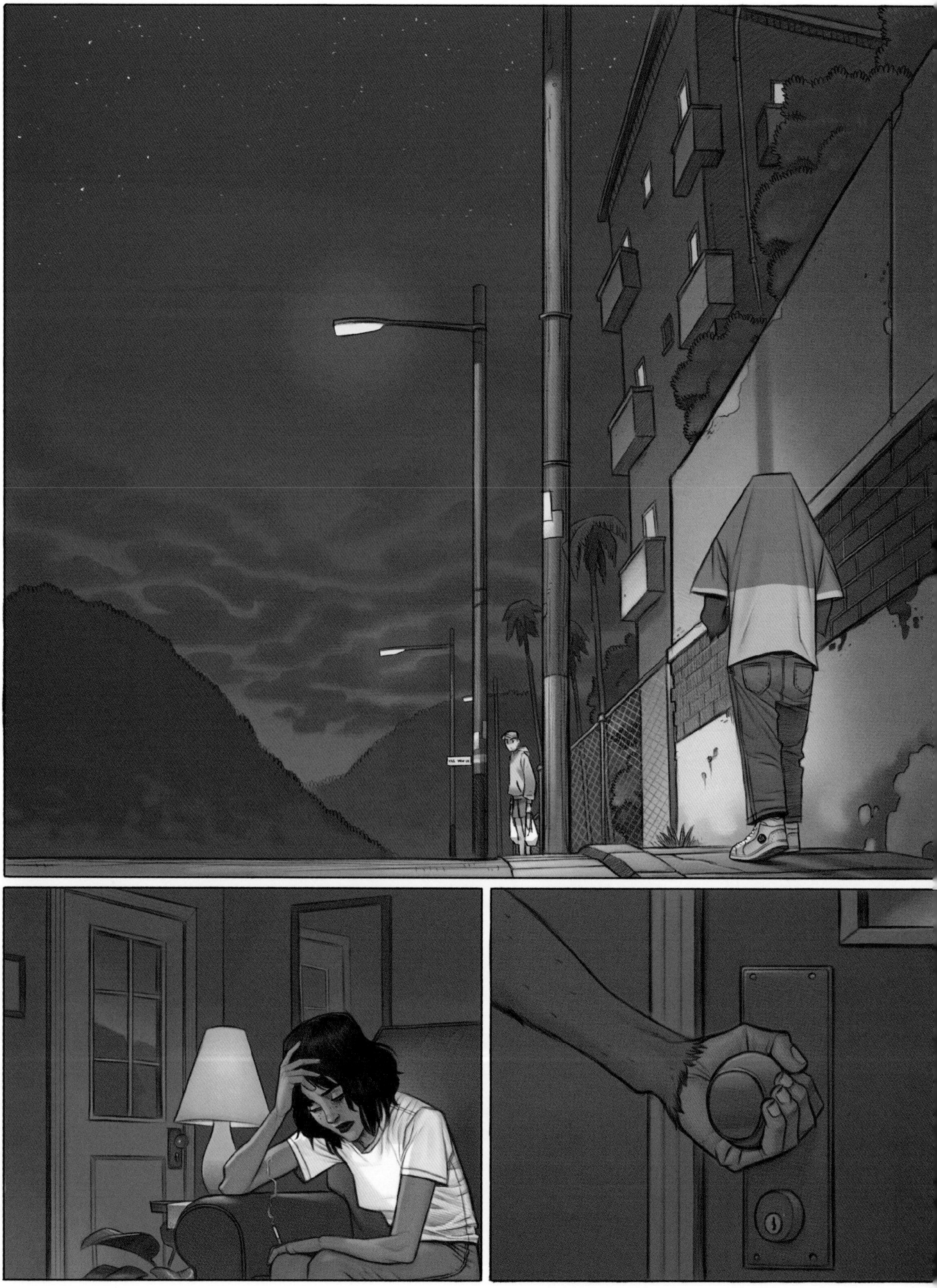

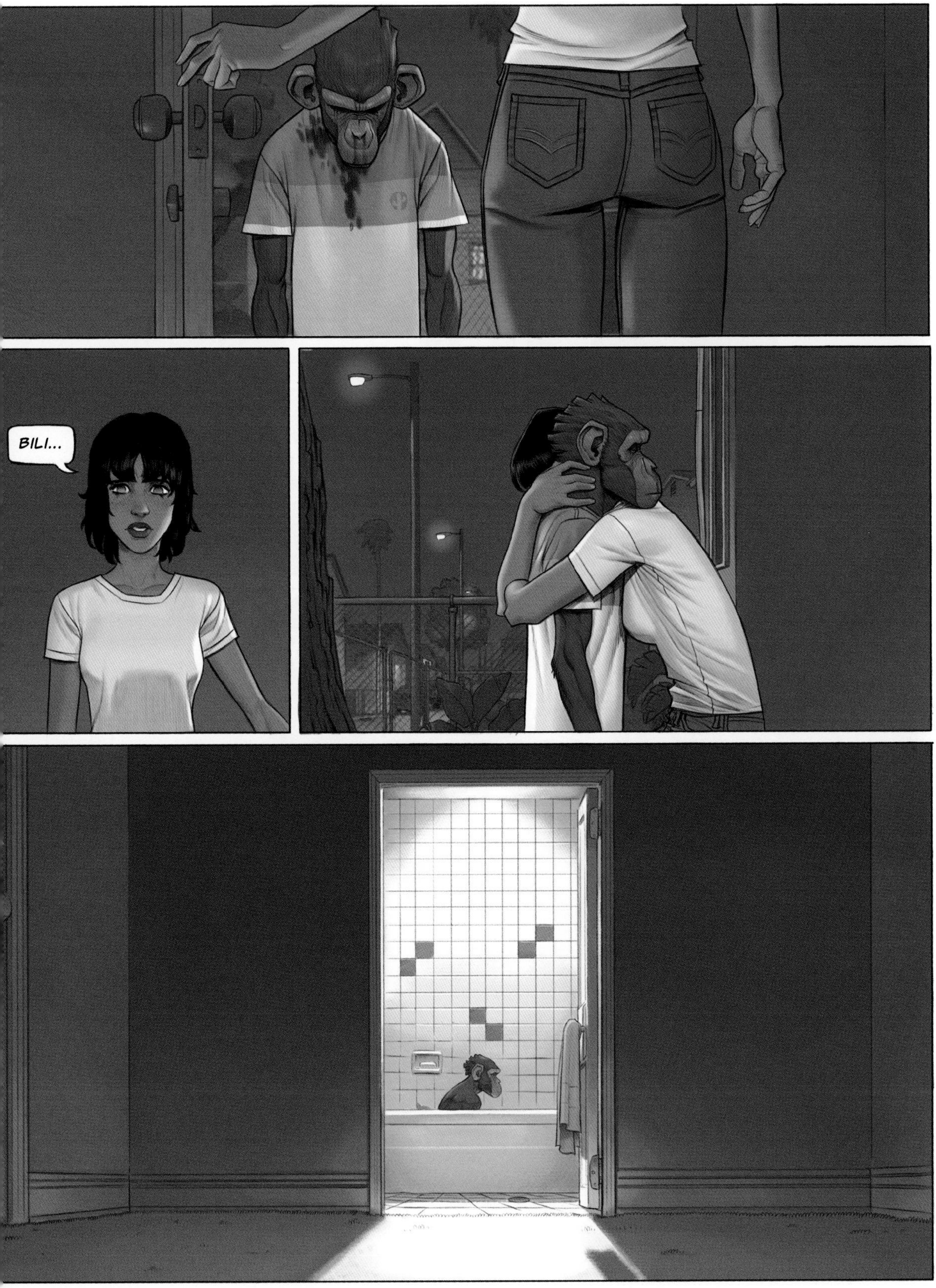
BILI...

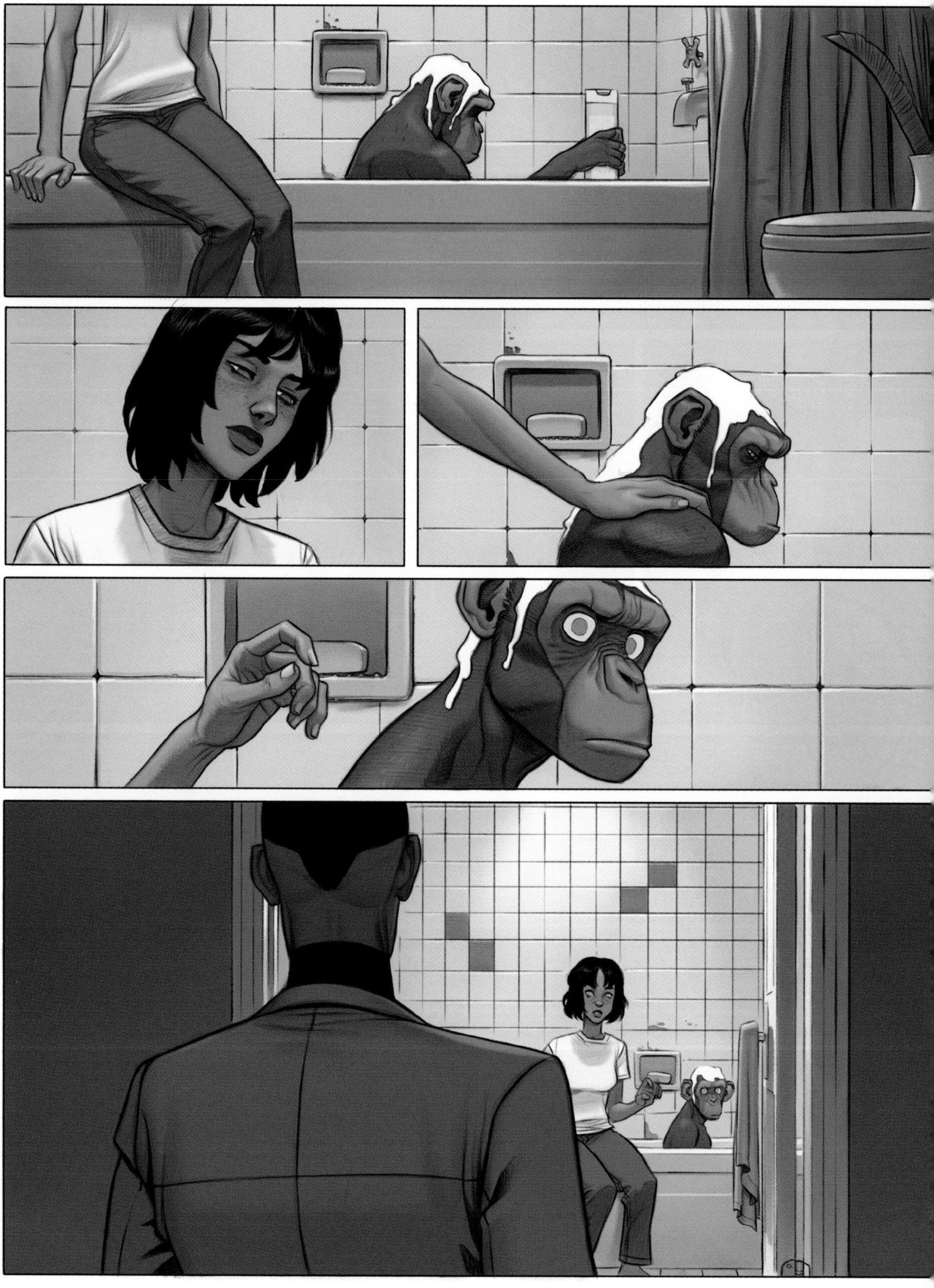

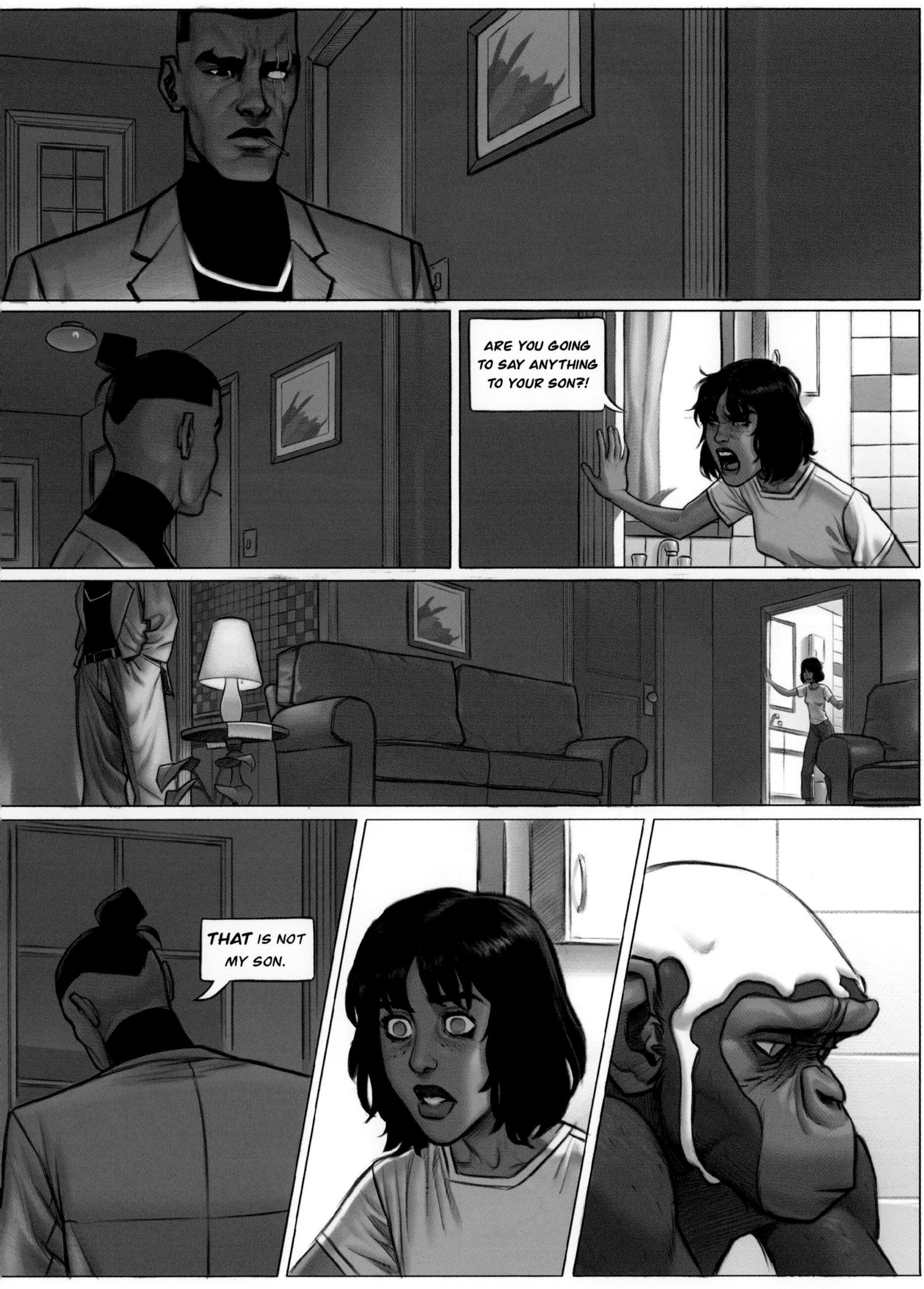
ARE YOU GOING TO SAY ANYTHING TO YOUR SON?!
THAT IS NOT MY SON.

SEPTEMBER

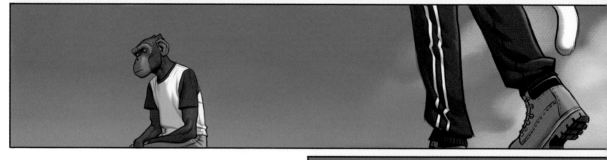

HERE.

'SUP, BILI. THE NAME'S HAMED.

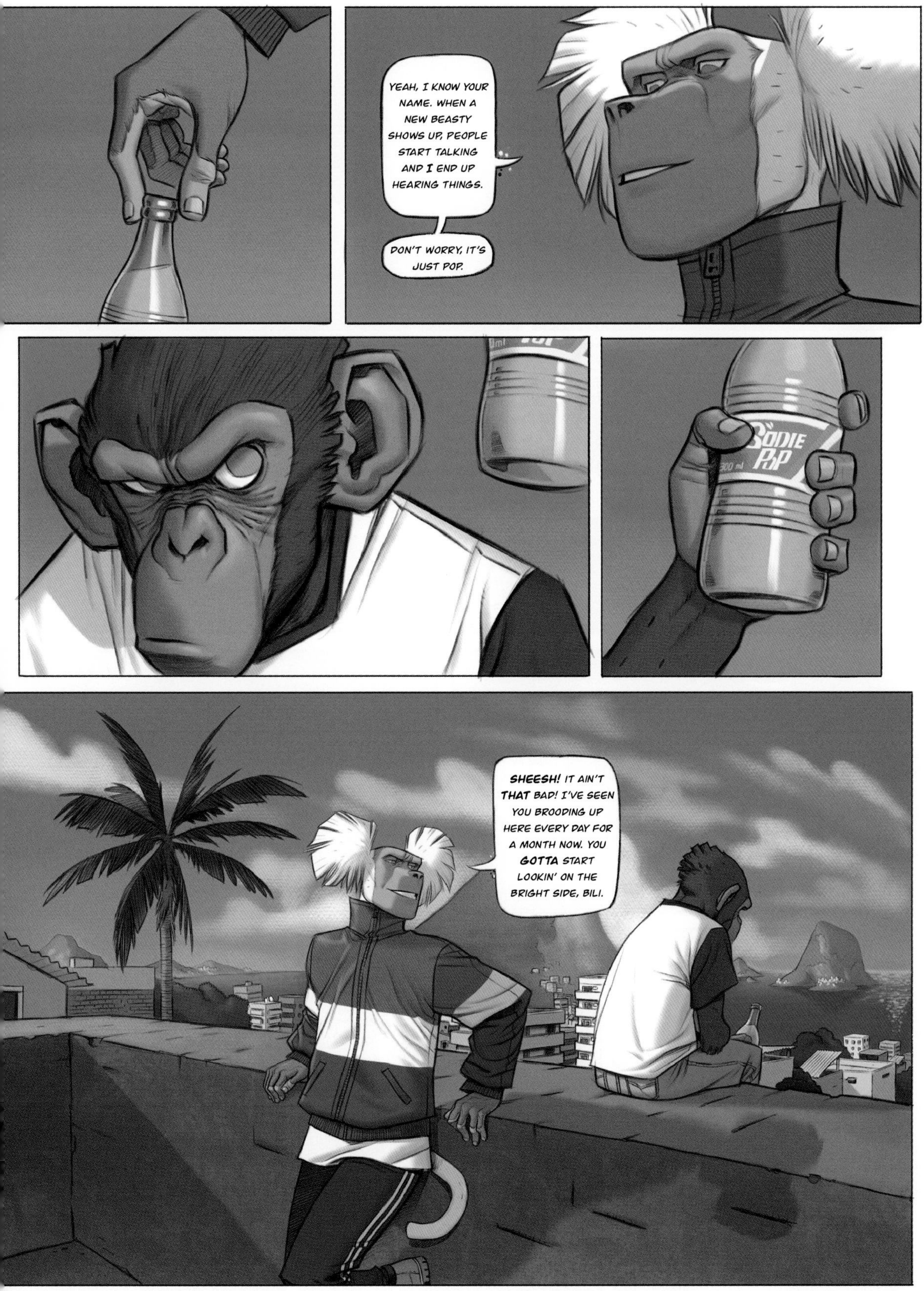
YEAH, I KNOW YOUR NAME. WHEN A NEW BEASTY SHOWS UP, PEOPLE START TALKING AND I END UP HEARING THINGS.
DON'T WORRY, IT'S JUST POP.
SODIE POP
300 ml
SHEESH! IT AIN'T THAT BAD! I'VE SEEN YOU BROODING UP HERE EVERY DAY FOR A MONTH NOW. YOU GOTTA START LOOKIN' ON THE BRIGHT SIDE, BILI.

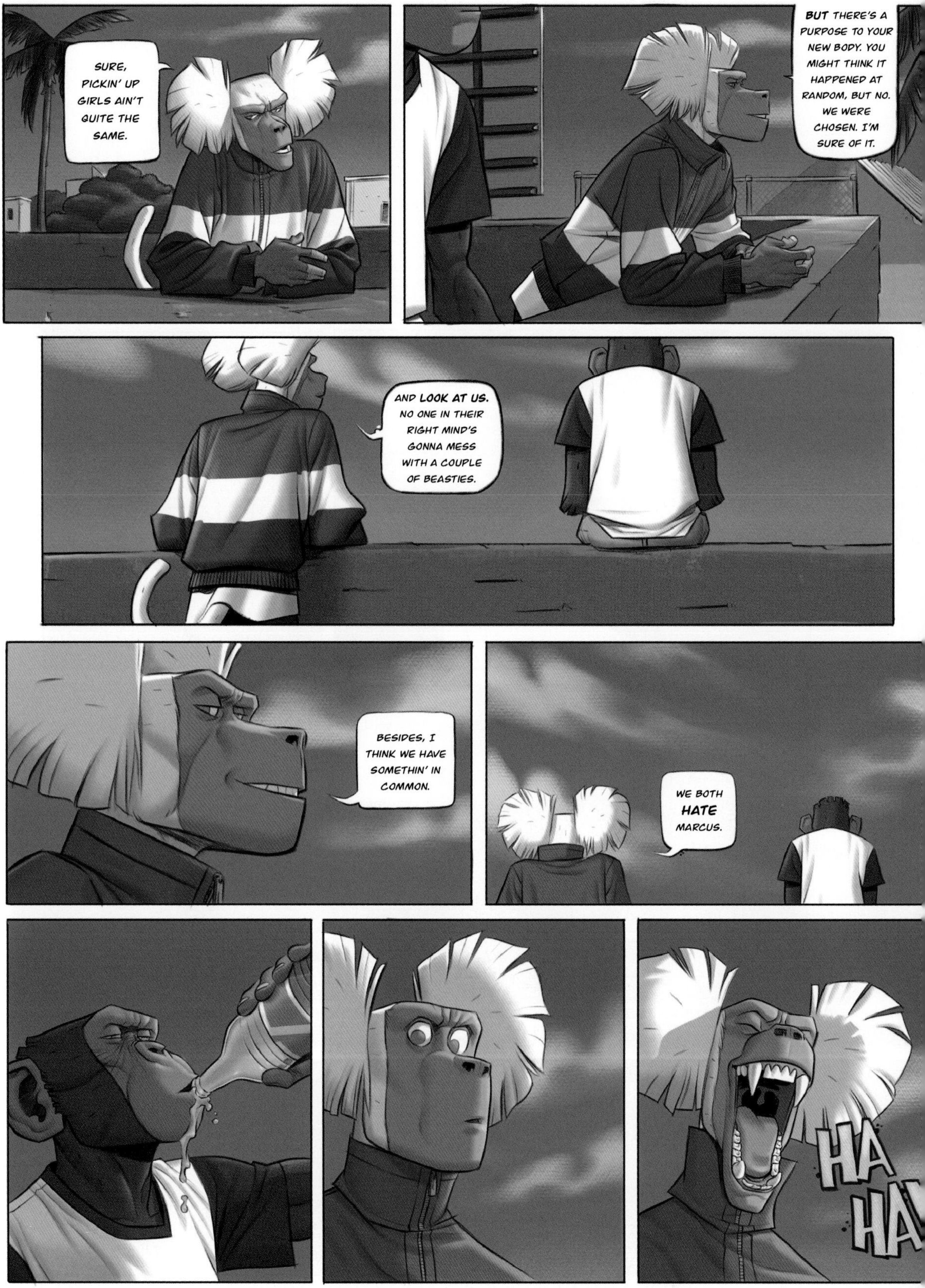
SURE, PICKIN' UP GIRLS AIN'T QUITE THE SAME.
BUT THERE'S A PURPOSE TO YOUR NEW BODY. YOU MIGHT THINK IT HAPPENED AT RANDOM, BUT NO. WE WERE CHOSEN. I'M SURE OF IT.
AND LOOK AT US. NO ONE IN THEIR RIGHT MIND'S GONNA MESS WITH A COUPLE OF BEASTIES.
BESIDES, I THINK WE HAVE SOMETHIN' IN COMMON.
WE BOTH HATE MARCUS.
HA HA

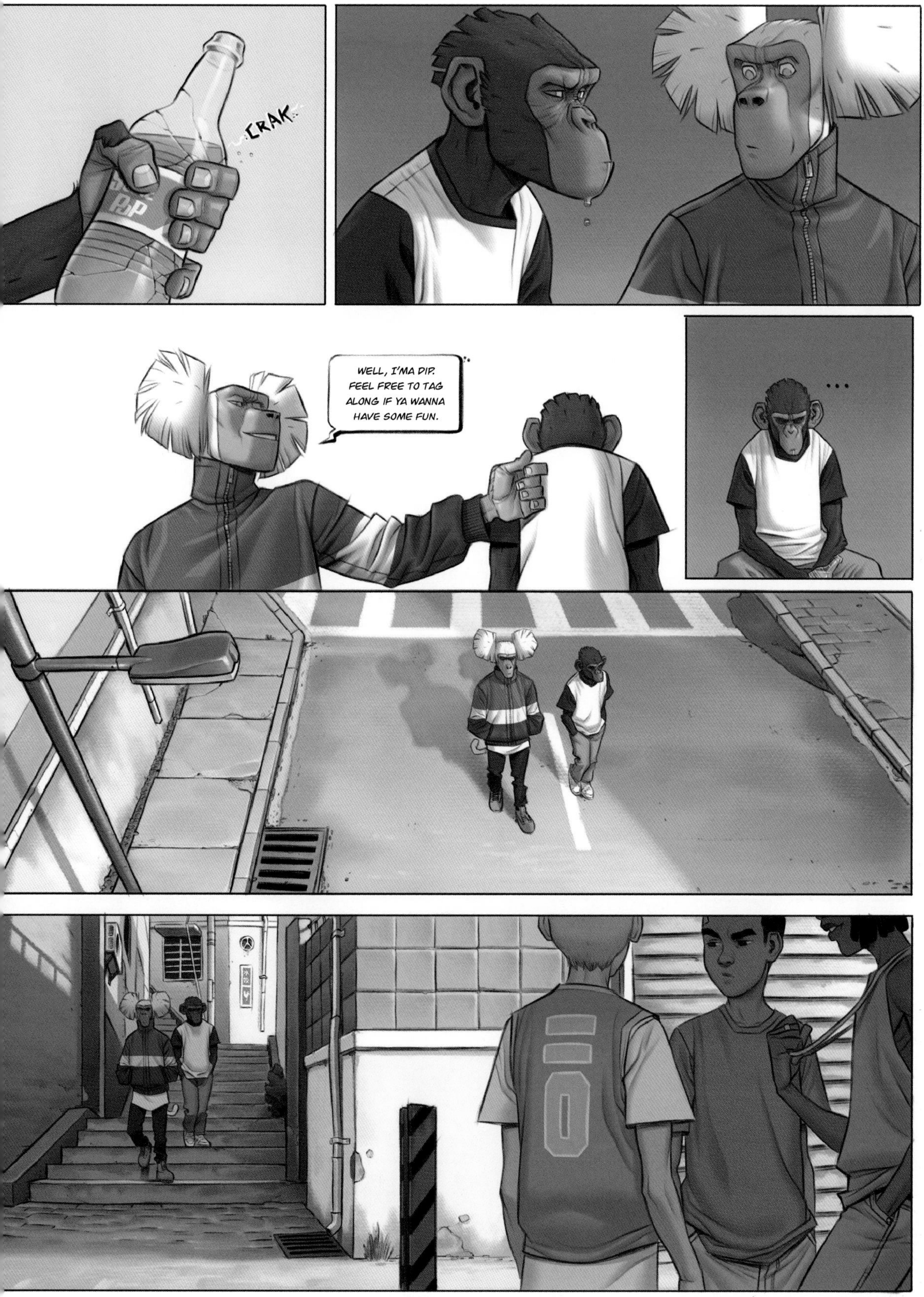
CRAK
WELL, I'MA DIP. FEEL FREE TO TAG ALONG IF YA WANNA HAVE SOME FUN.
...

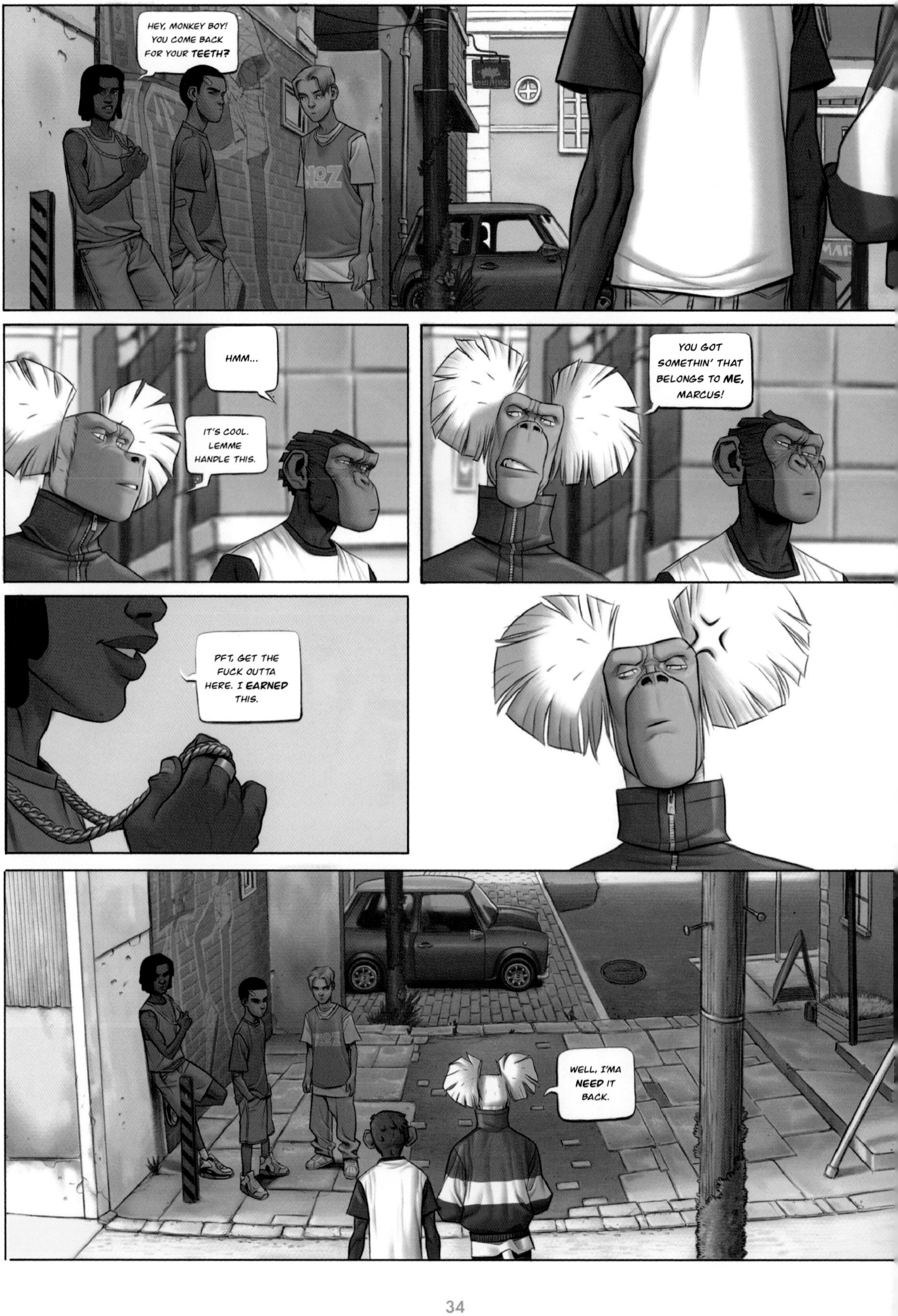
HEY, MONKEY BOY! YOU COME BACK FOR YOUR TEETH?
HMM...
IT'S COOL. LEMME HANDLE THIS.
YOU GOT SOMETHIN' THAT BELONGS TO ME, MARCUS!
PFT, GET THE FUCK OUTTA HERE. I EARNED THIS.
WELL, I'MA NEED IT BACK.

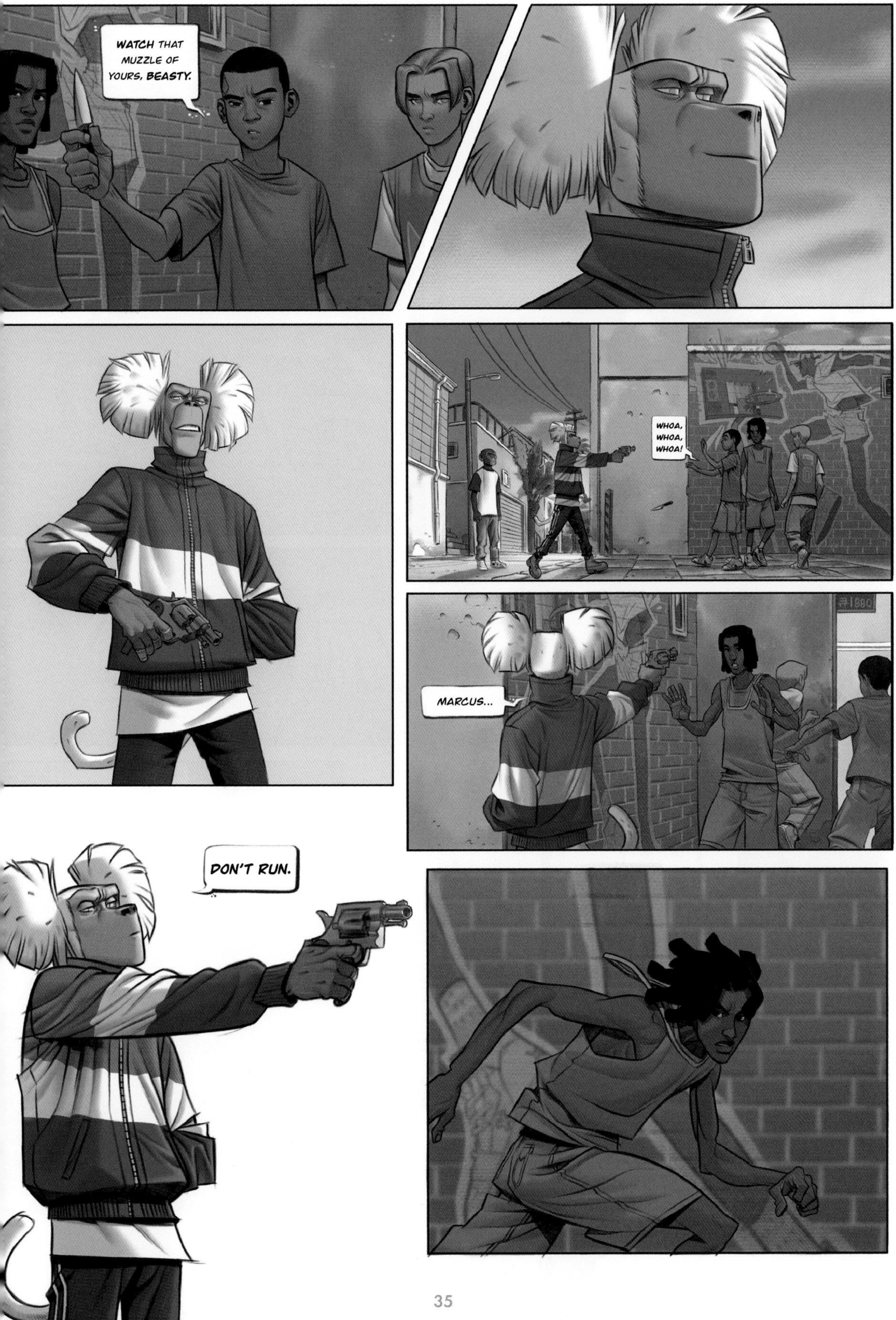
WATCH THAT MUZZLE OF YOURS, BEASTY.
WHOA, WHOA, WHOA!
MARCUS...
DON'T RUN.

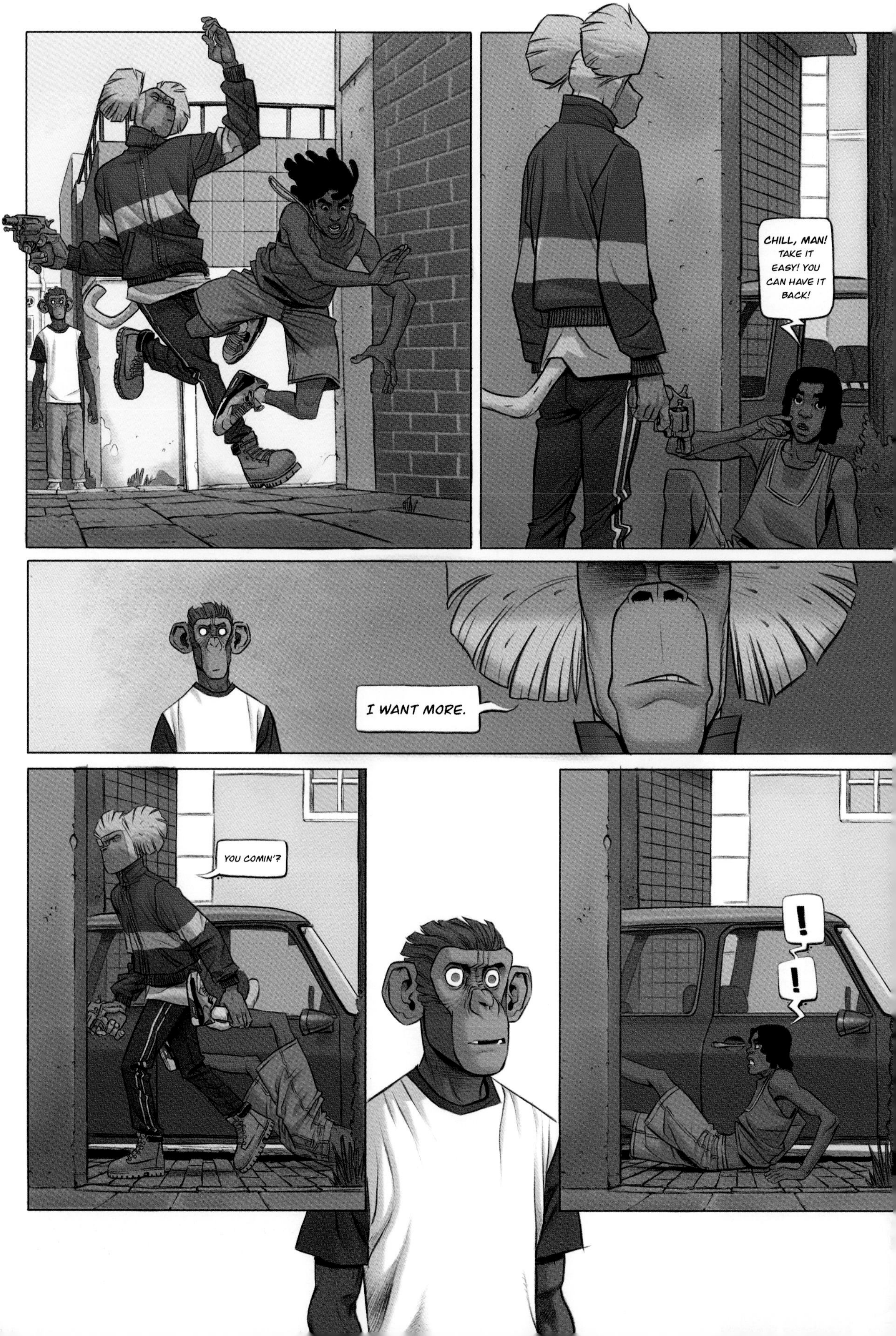
CHILL, MAN! TAKE IT EASY! YOU CAN HAVE IT BACK!
I WANT MORE.
YOU COMIN'?
!
!

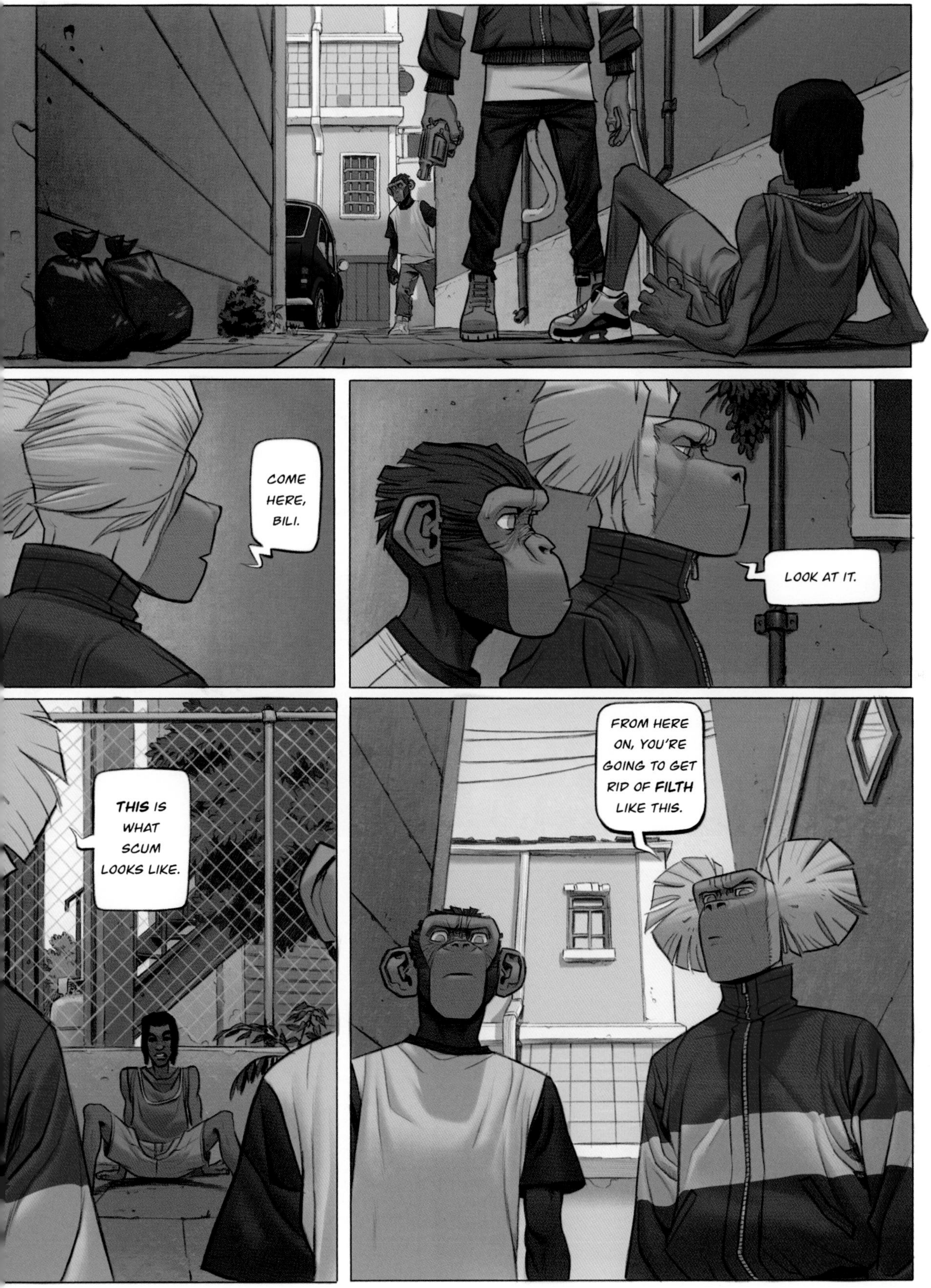
COME HERE, BILI.
LOOK AT IT.
THIS IS WHAT SCUM LOOKS LIKE.
FROM HERE ON, YOU'RE GOING TO GET RID OF FILTH LIKE THIS.

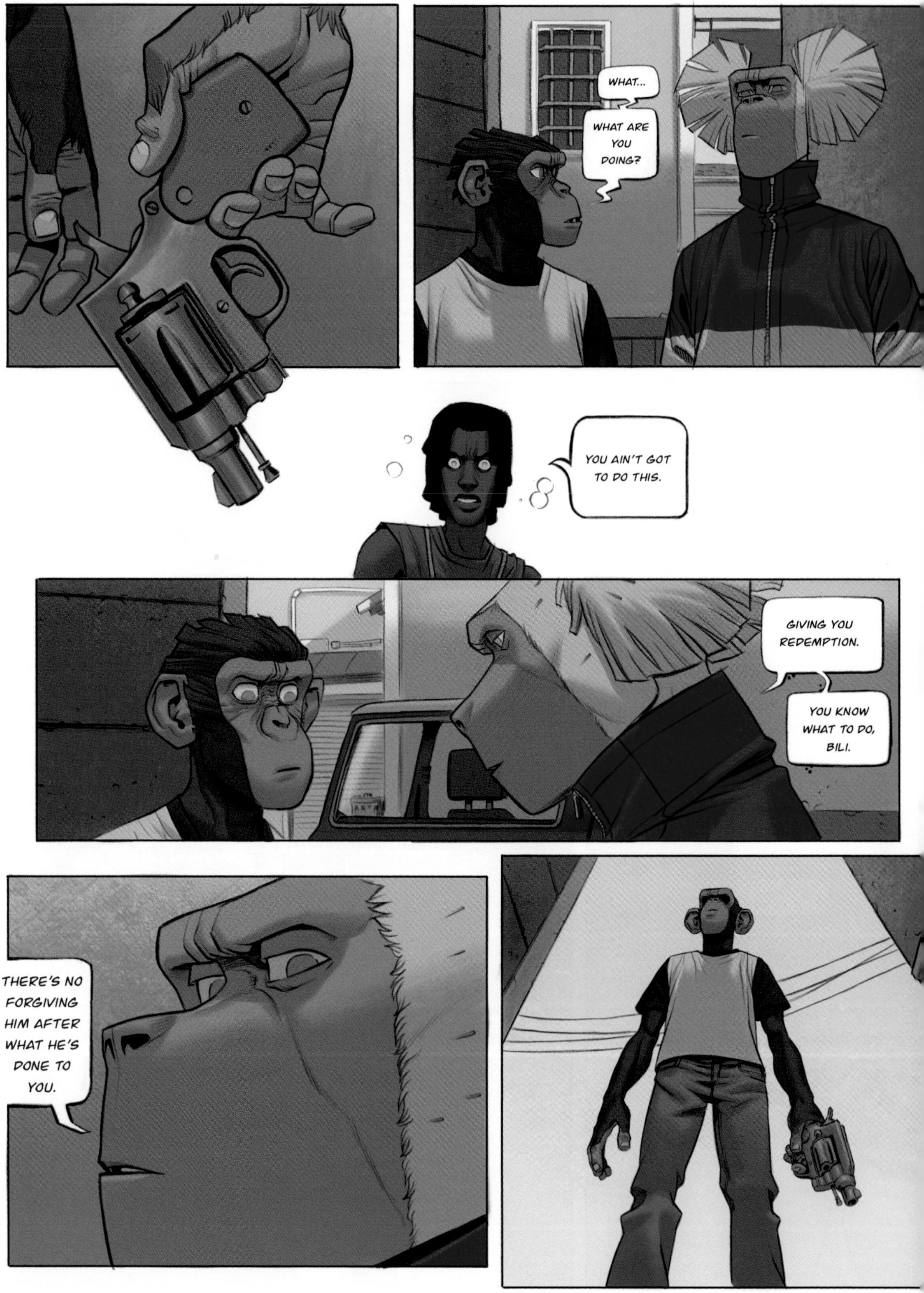
WHAT...
WHAT ARE YOU DOING?
YOU AIN'T GOT TO DO THIS.
GIVING YOU REDEMPTION.
YOU KNOW WHAT TO DO, BILI.
THERE'S NO FORGIVING HIM AFTER WHAT HE'S DONE TO YOU.

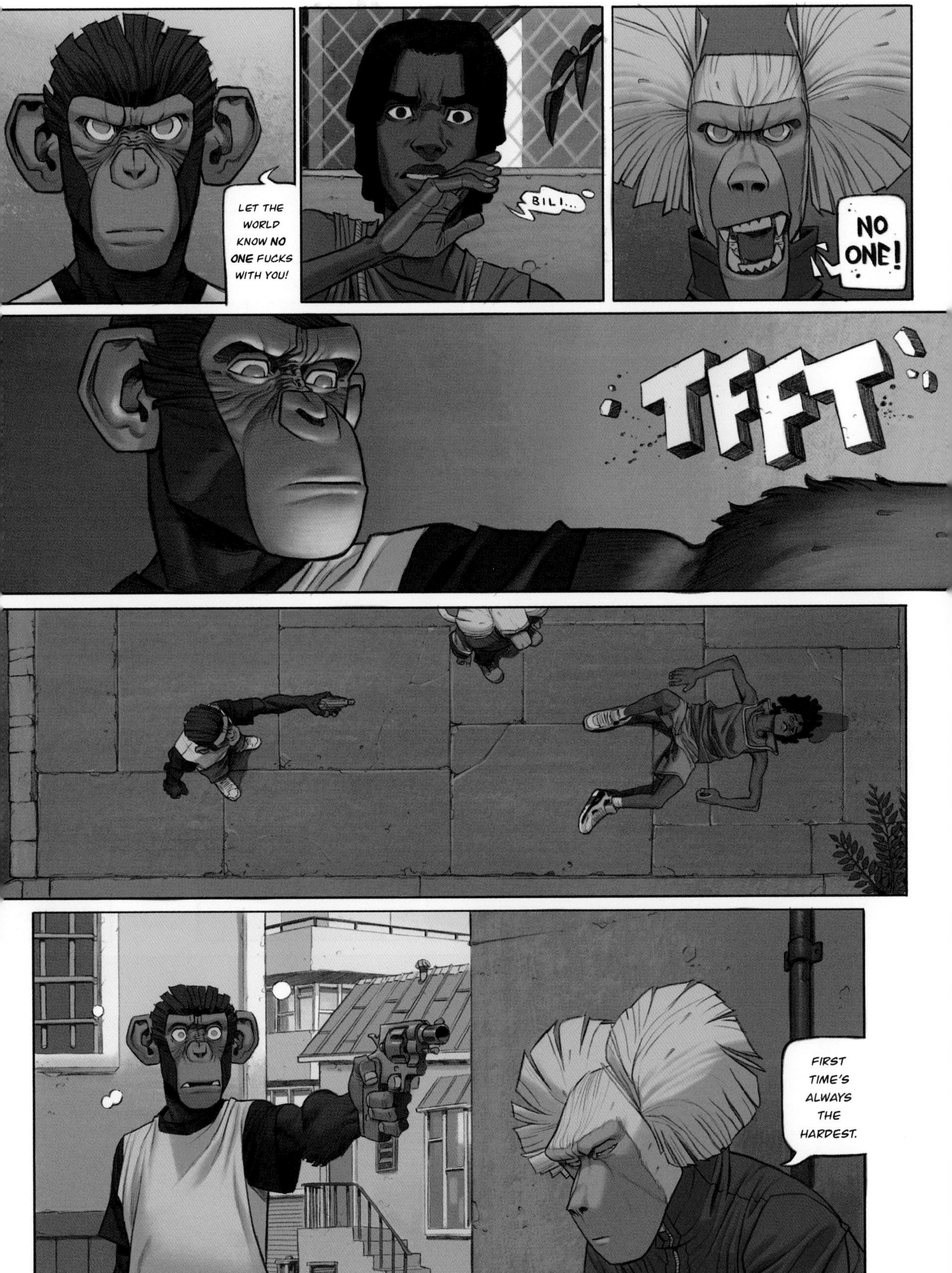
LET THE WORLD KNOW NO ONE FUCKS WITH YOU!
BILI...
NO ONE!
TFFT
FIRST TIME'S ALWAYS THE HARDEST.

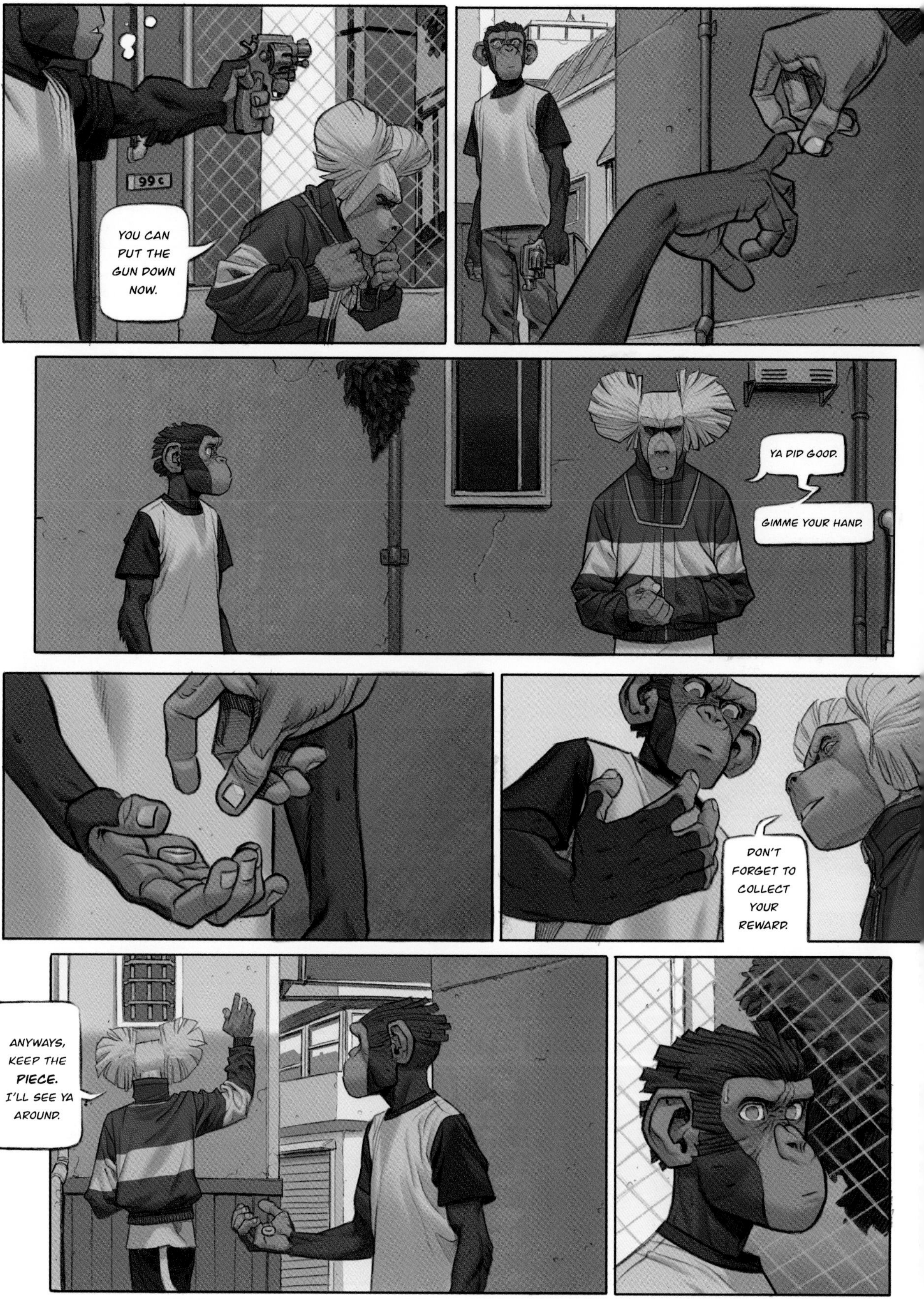
YOU CAN PUT THE GUN DOWN NOW.
99¢
YA DID GOOD.
GIMME YOUR HAND.
DON'T FORGET TO COLLECT YOUR REWARD.
ANYWAYS, KEEP THE PIECE. I'LL SEE YA AROUND.

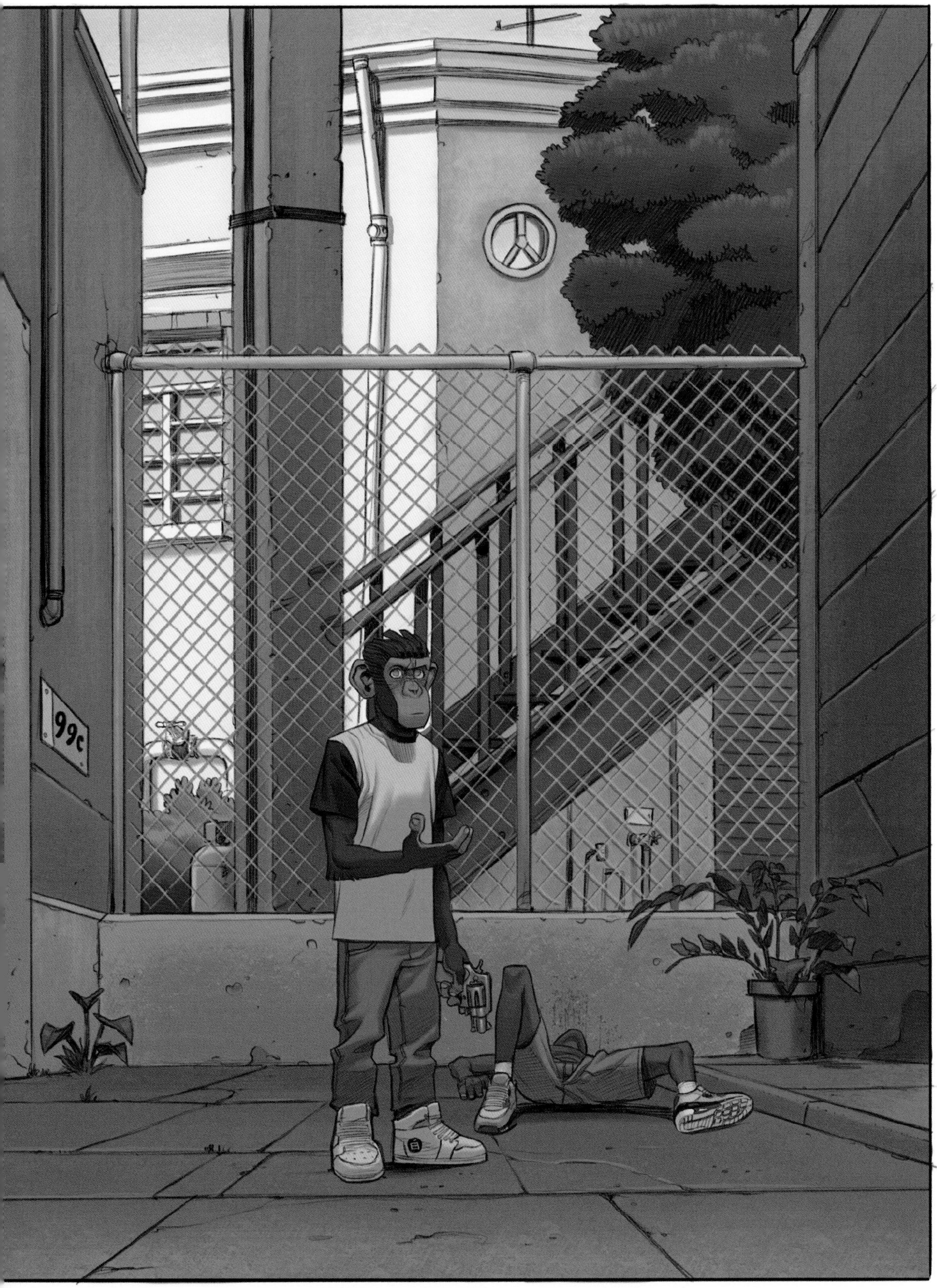
99¢

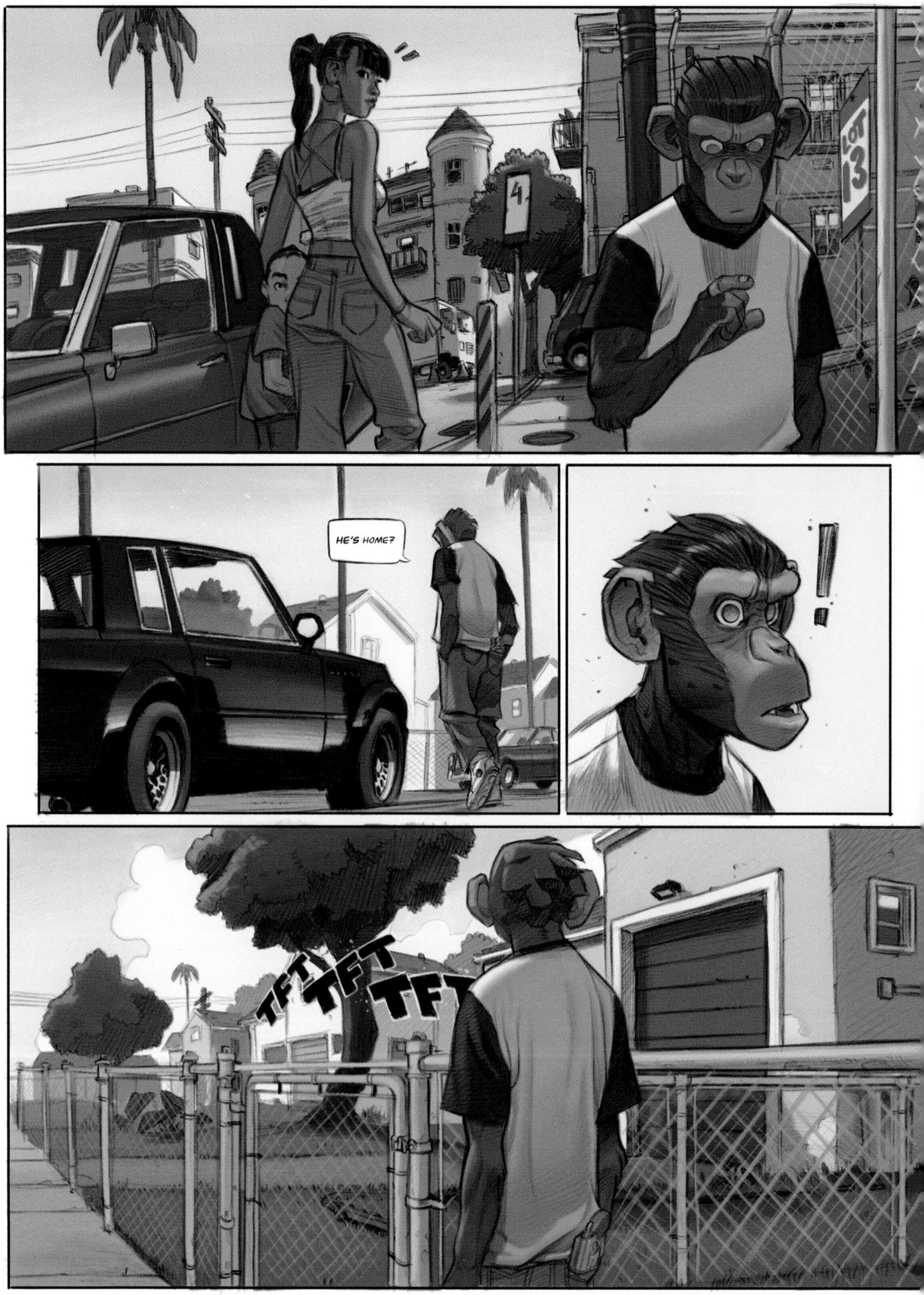
4
LOT 13
HE'S HOME?
!
TFT
TFT
TFT

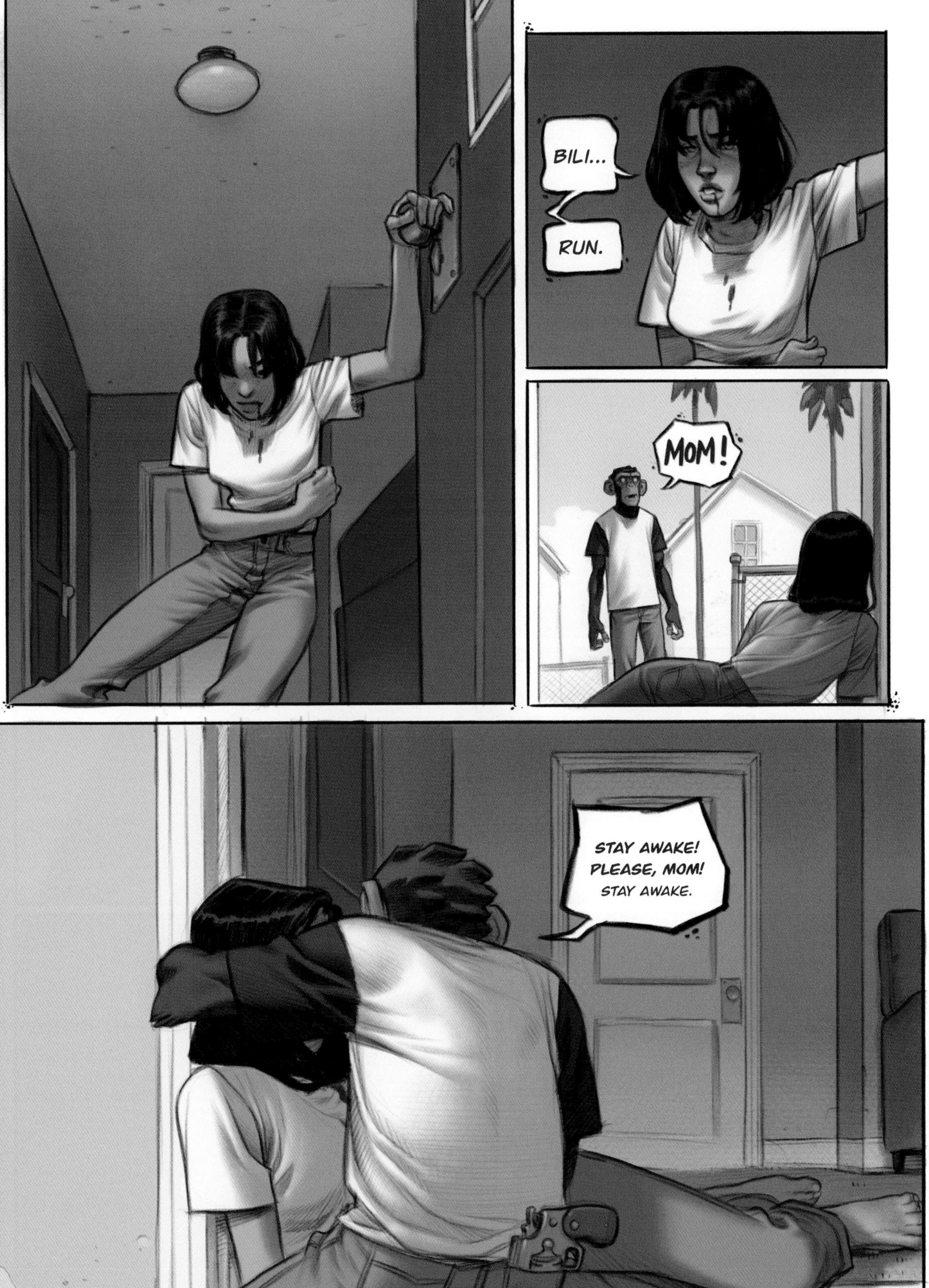
BILI...
RUN.
MOM!
STAY AWAKE!
PLEASE, MOM!
STAY AWAKE.

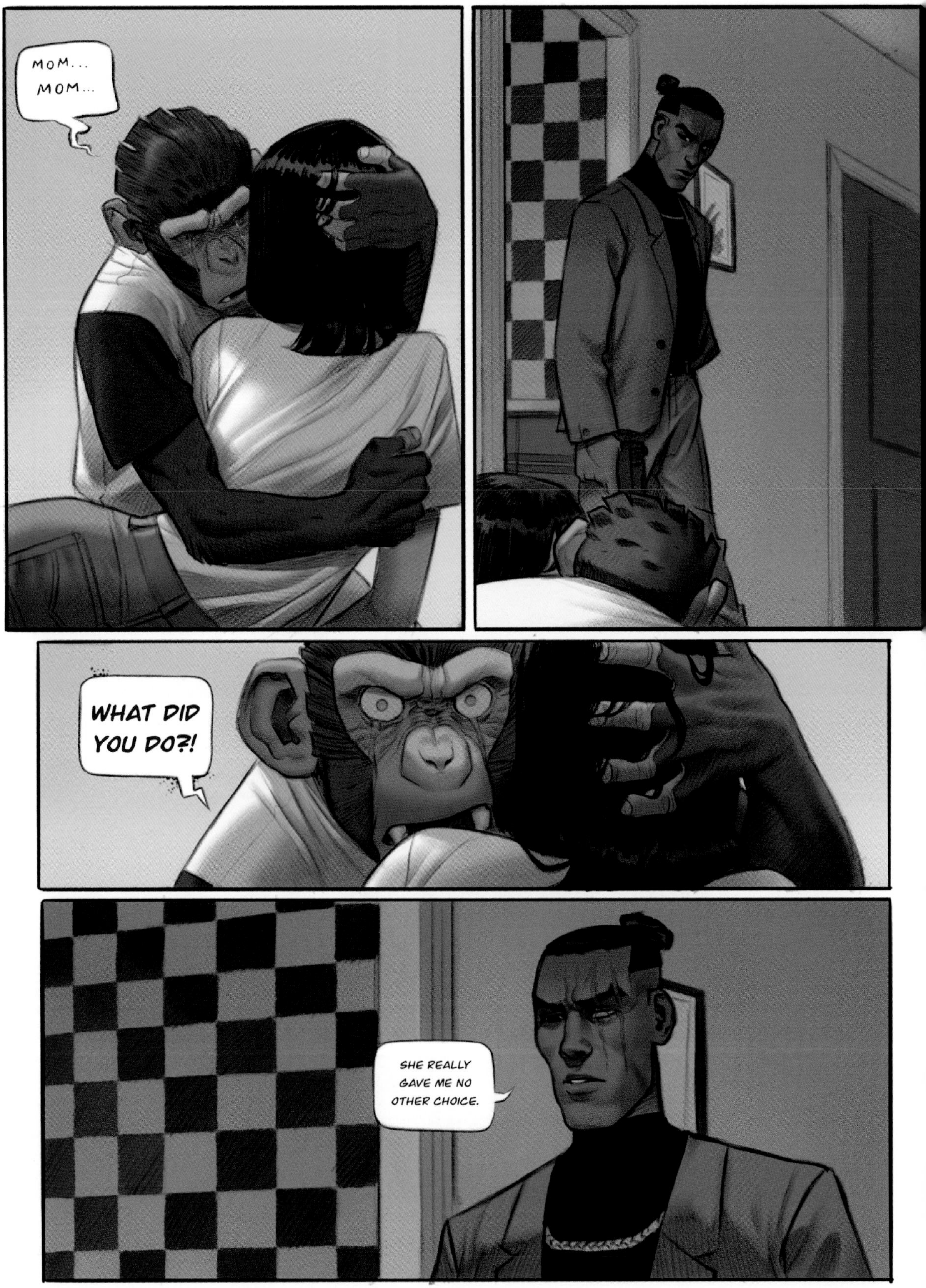
MOM...
MOM...
WHAT DID YOU DO?!
SHE REALLY GAVE ME NO OTHER CHOICE.

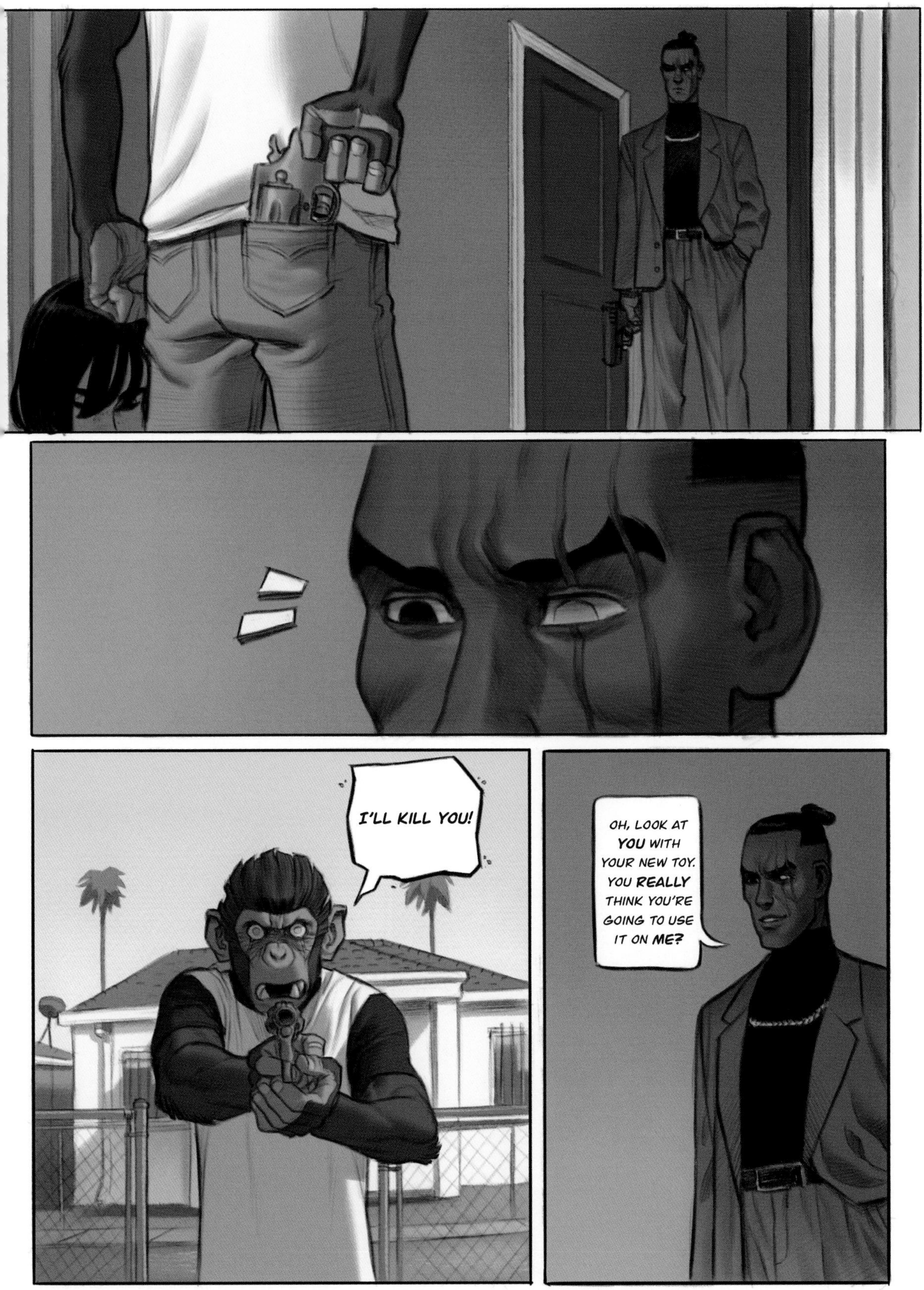
I'LL KILL YOU!
OH, LOOK AT YOU WITH YOUR NEW TOY. YOU REALLY THINK YOU'RE GOING TO USE IT ON ME?

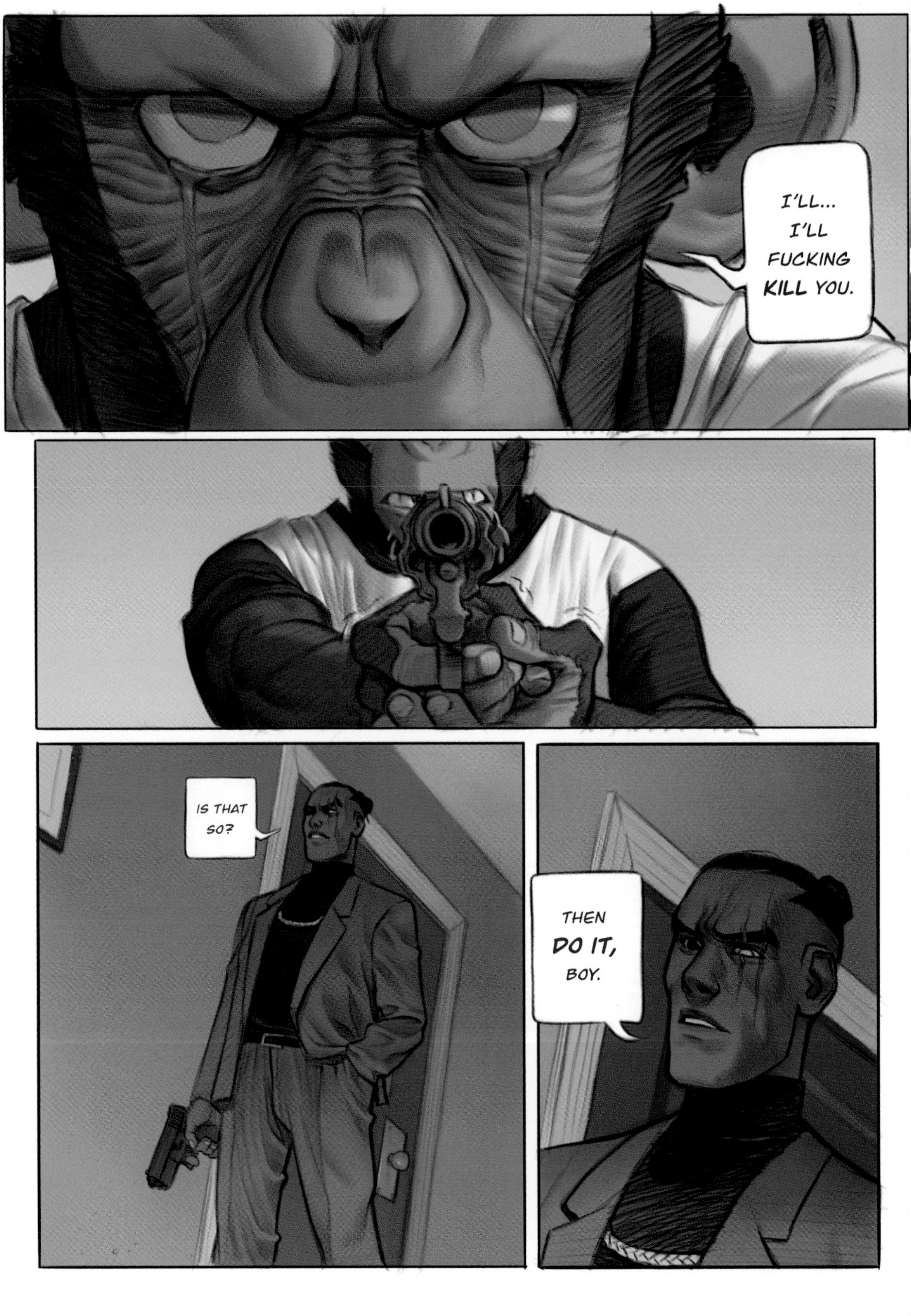
I'LL...
I'LL FUCKING KILL YOU.
IS THAT SO?
THEN DO IT, BOY.

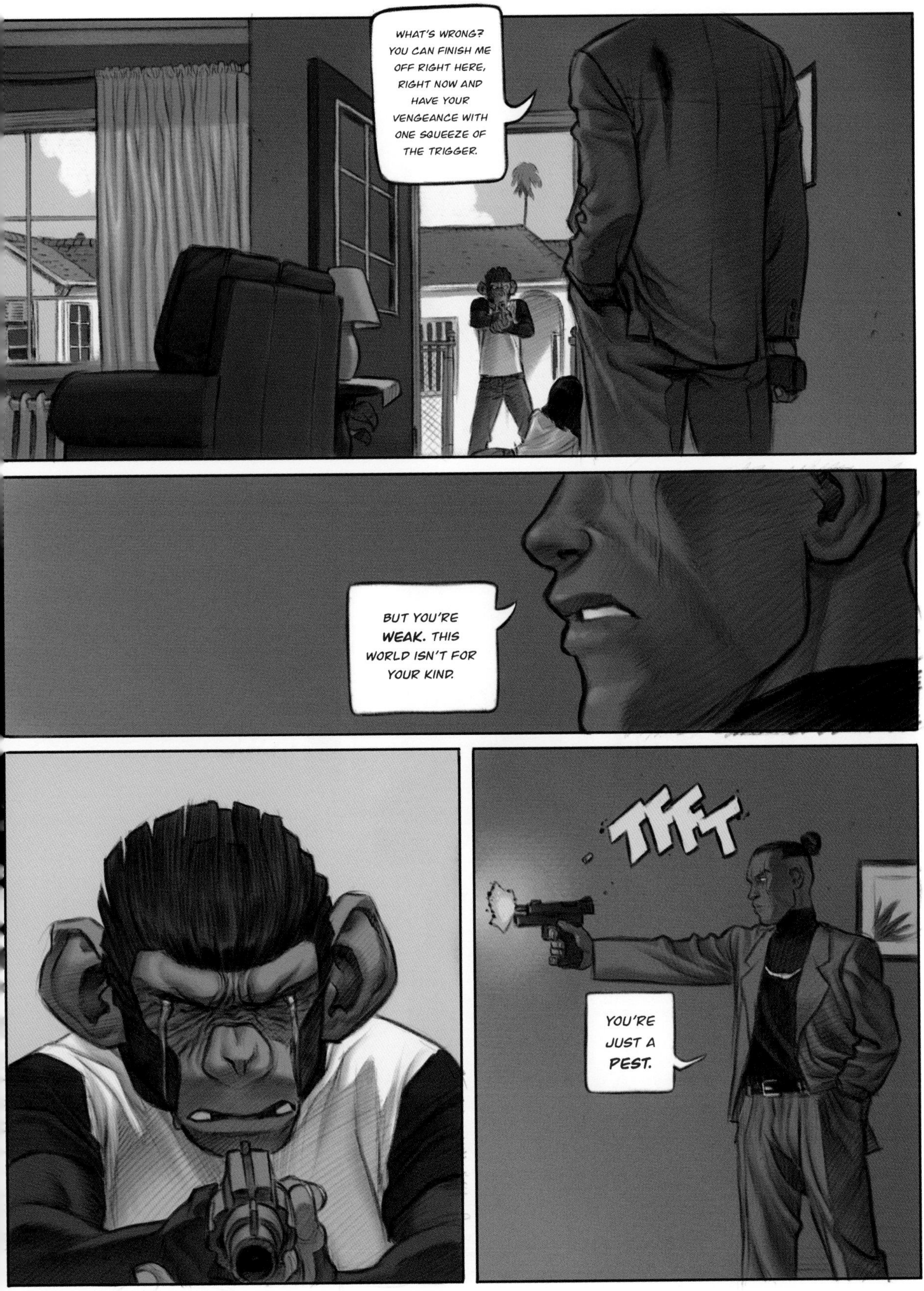
WHAT'S WRONG? YOU CAN FINISH ME OFF RIGHT HERE, RIGHT NOW AND HAVE YOUR VENGEANCE WITH ONE SQUEEZE OF THE TRIGGER.
BUT YOU'RE WEAK. THIS WORLD ISN'T FOR YOUR KIND.
TFFT
YOU'RE JUST A PEST.

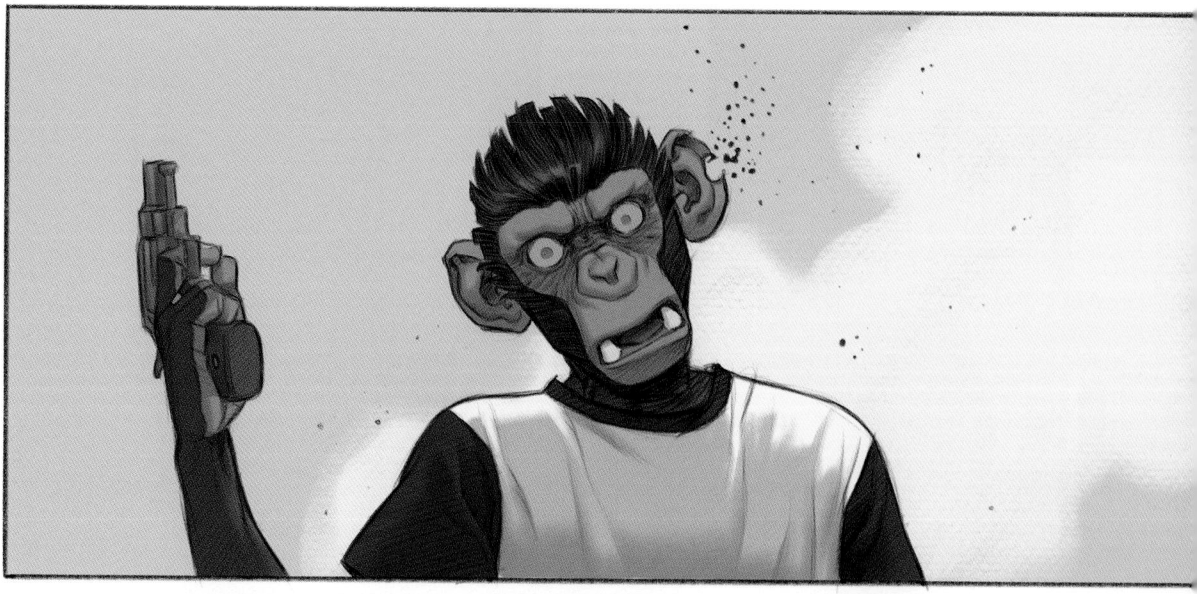

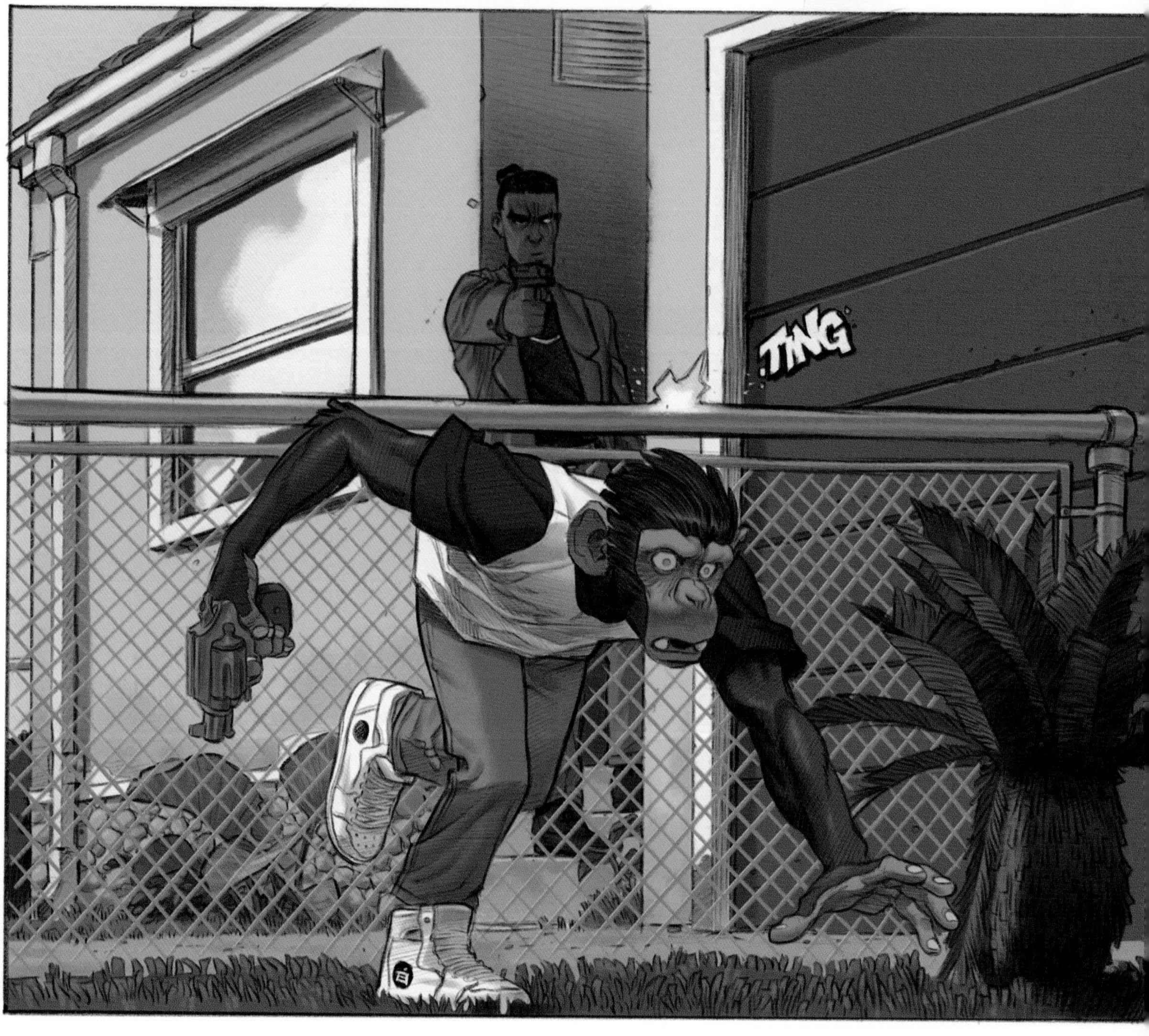
TING

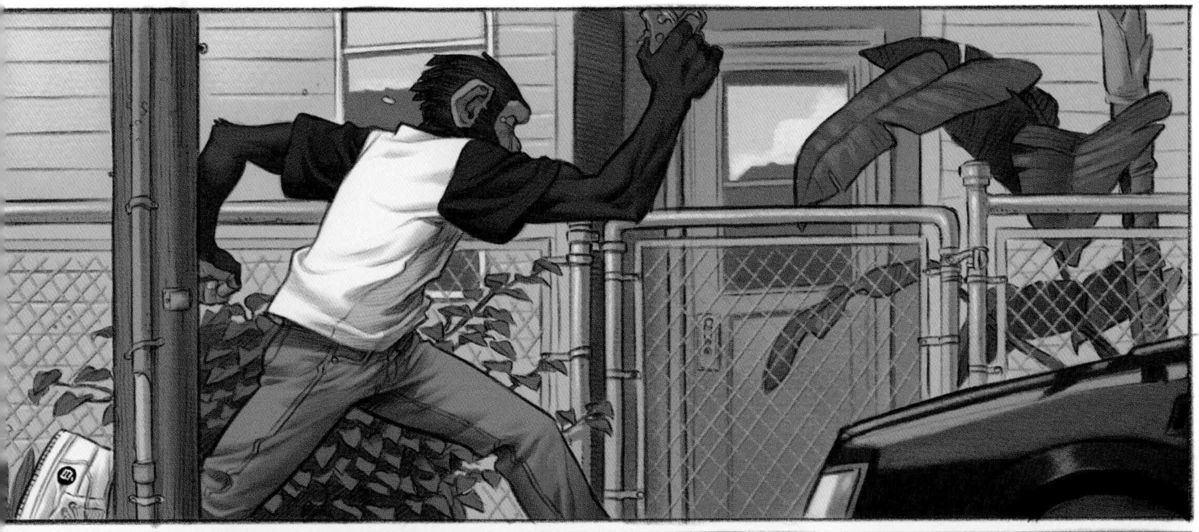

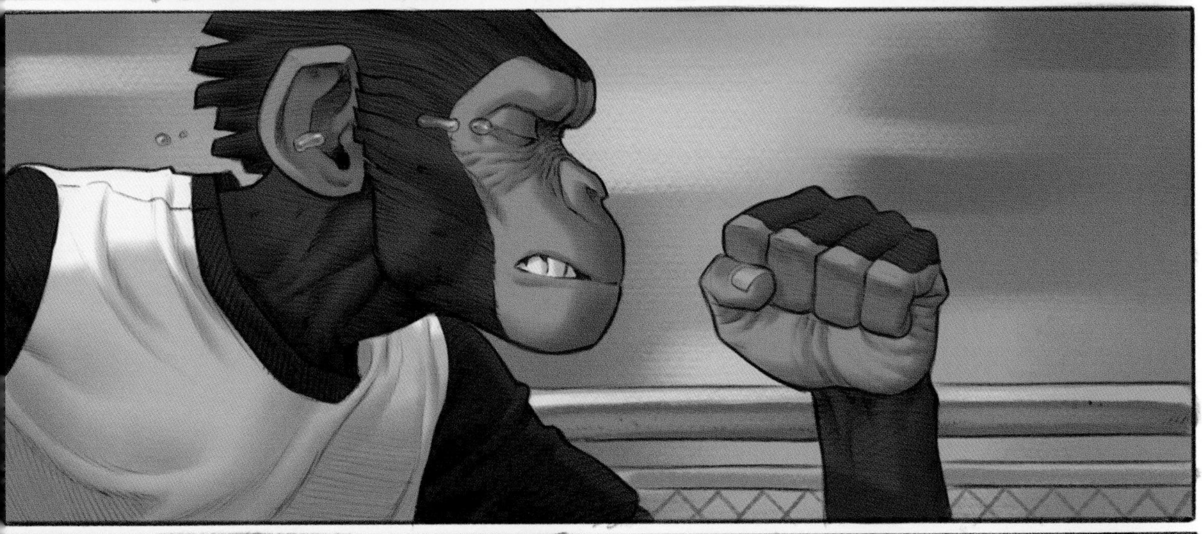

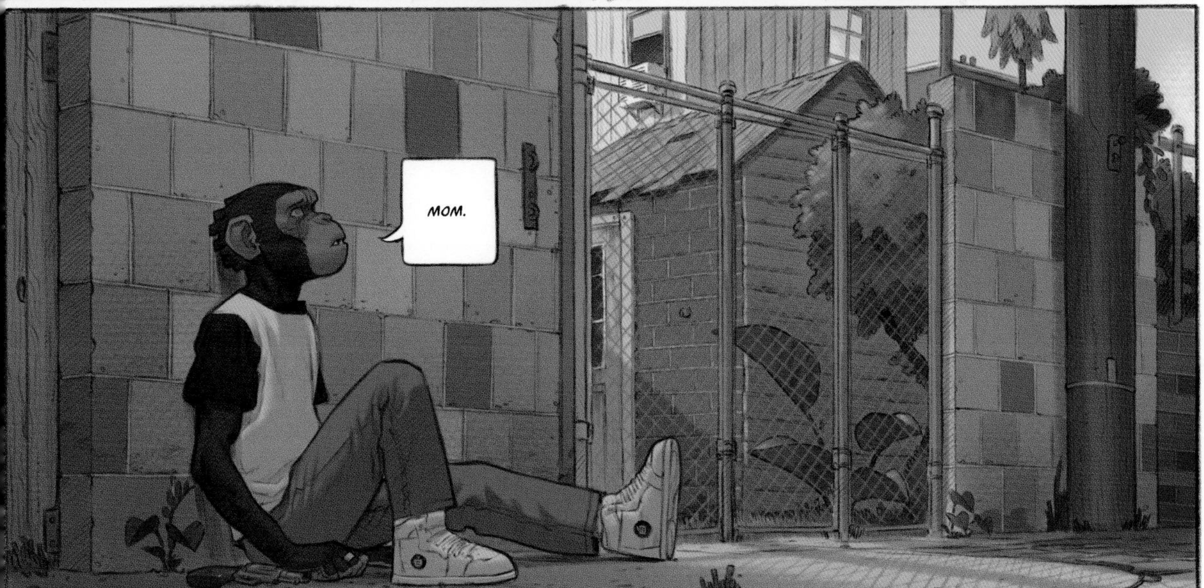
MOM.

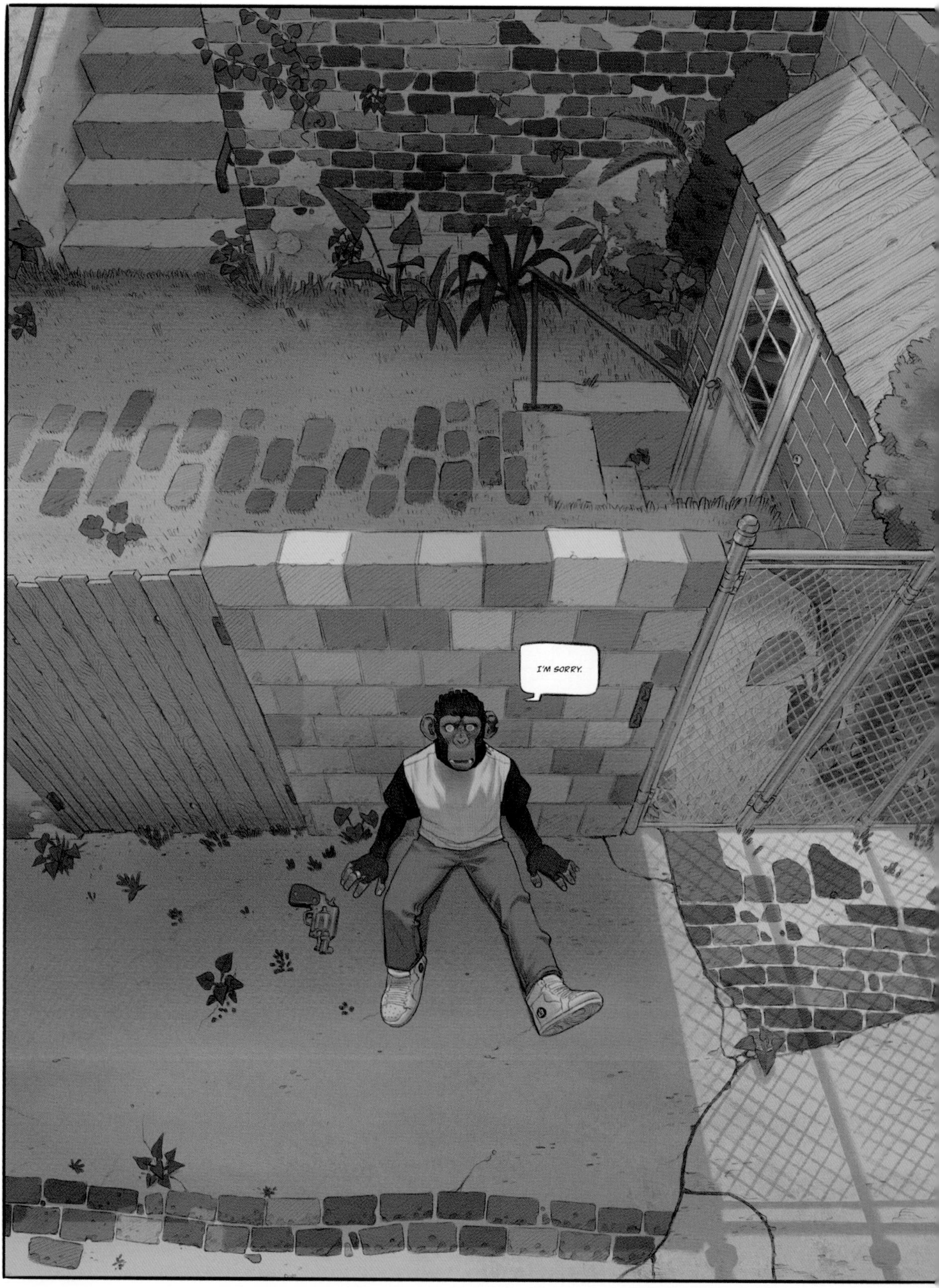
I'M SORRY.

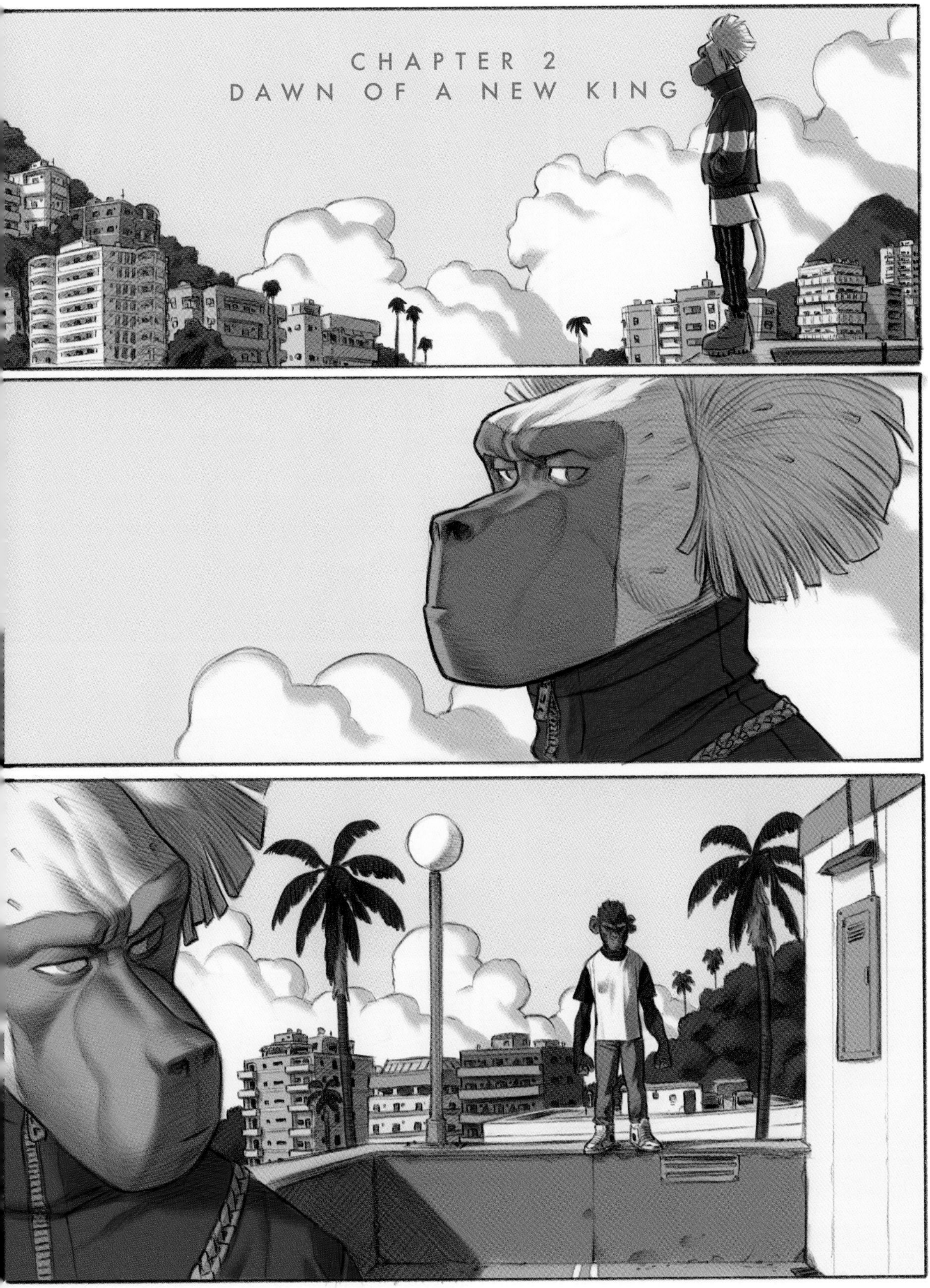
CHAPTER 2
DAWN OF A NEW KING

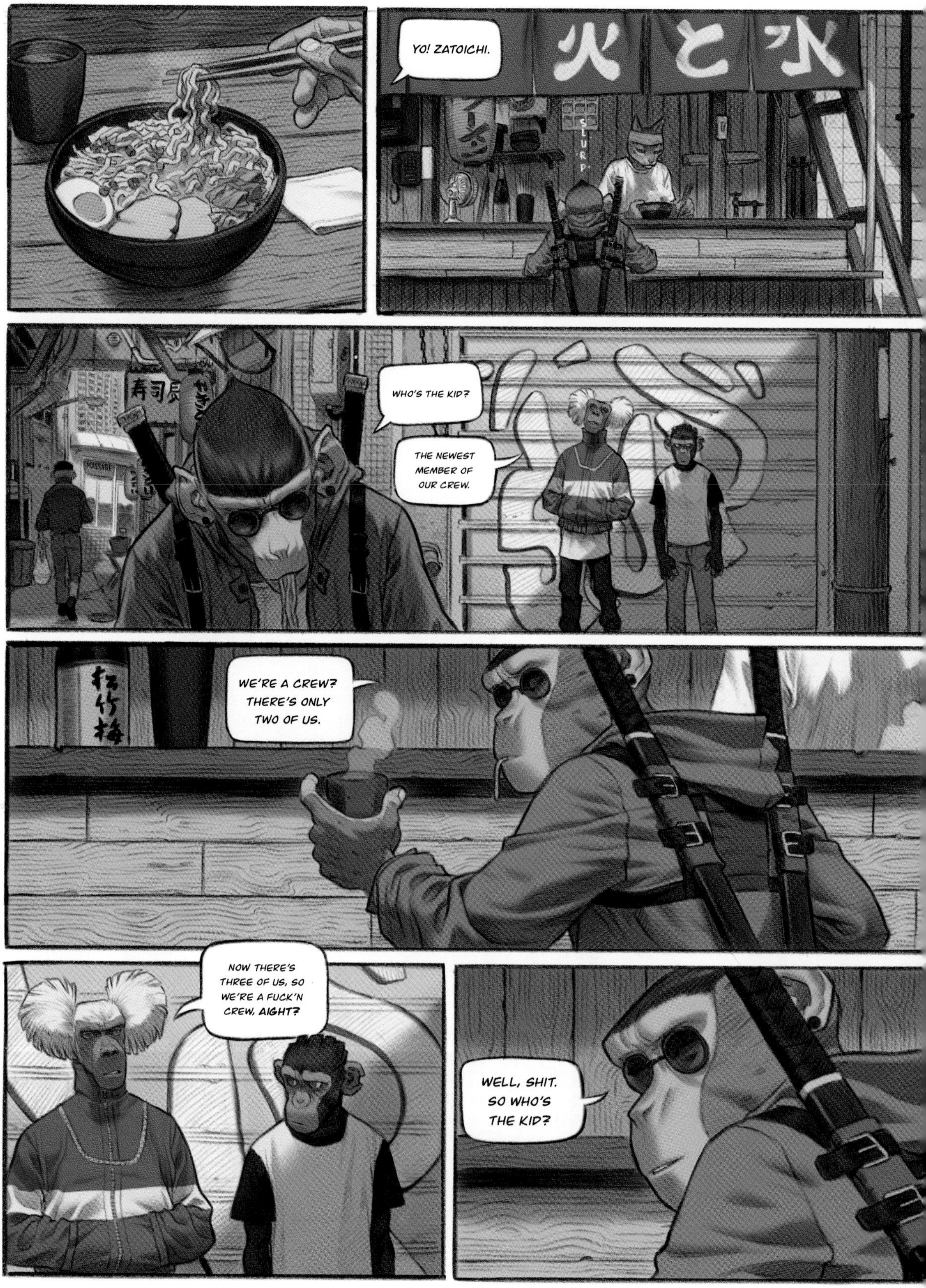
YO! ZATOICHI.
火と水
SLURP
寿司房
MASSAGE
WHO'S THE KID?
THE NEWEST MEMBER OF OUR CREW.
松竹梅
WE'RE A CREW? THERE'S ONLY TWO OF US.
NOW THERE'S THREE OF US, SO WE'RE A FUCK'N CREW, AIGHT?
WELL, SHIT. SO WHO'S THE KID?

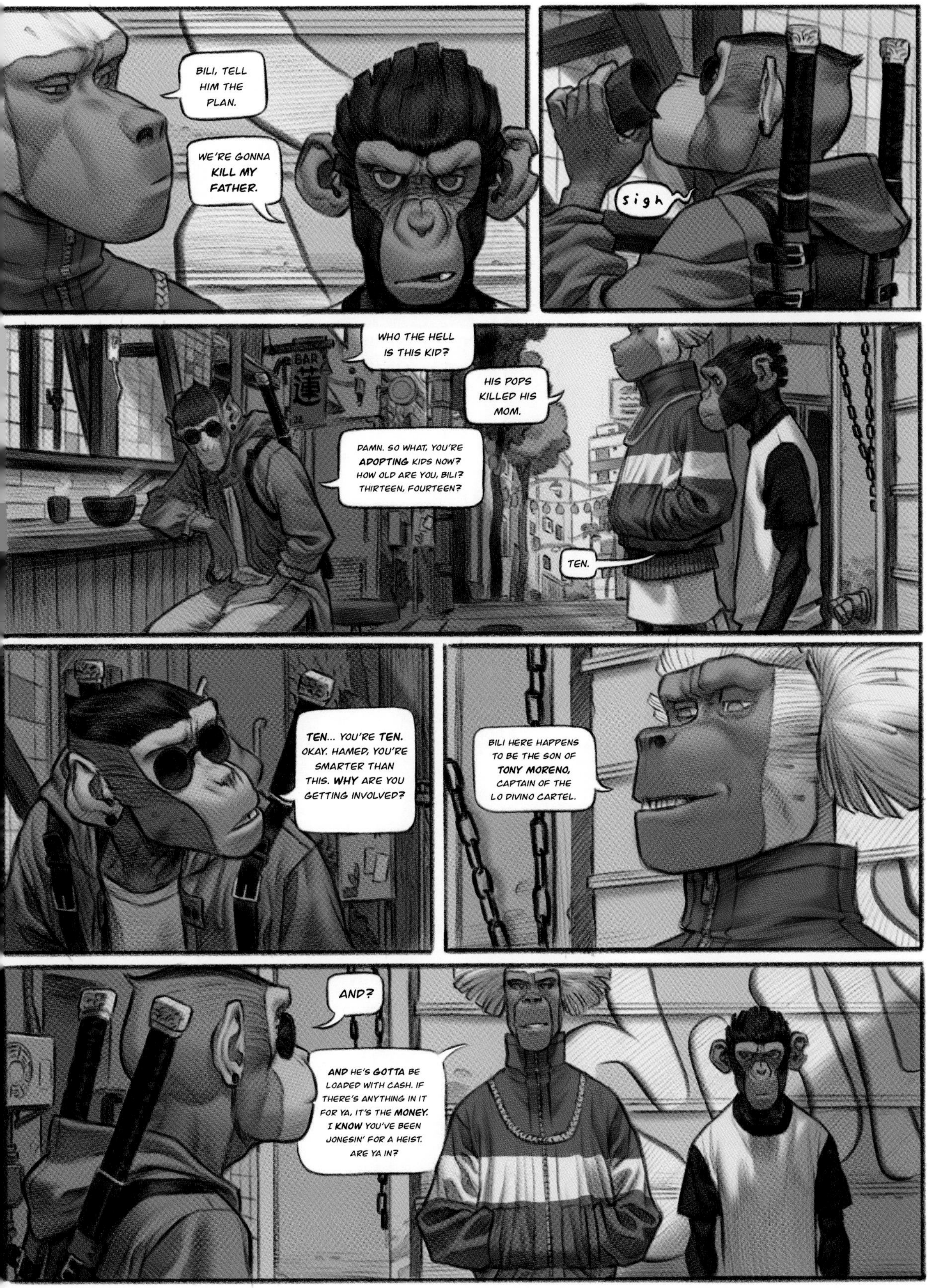
BILI, TELL HIM THE PLAN.
WE'RE GONNA KILL MY FATHER.
sigh
WHO THE HELL IS THIS KID?
HIS POPS KILLED HIS MOM.
DAMN. SO WHAT, YOU'RE ADOPTING KIDS NOW? HOW OLD ARE YOU, BILI? THIRTEEN, FOURTEEN?
TEN.
TEN... YOU'RE TEN. OKAY. HAMED, YOU'RE SMARTER THAN THIS. WHY ARE YOU GETTING INVOLVED?
BILI HERE HAPPENS TO BE THE SON OF TONY MORENO, CAPTAIN OF THE LO DIVINO CARTEL.
AND?
AND HE'S GOTTA BE LOADED WITH CASH. IF THERE'S ANYTHING IN IT FOR YA, IT'S THE MONEY. I KNOW YOU'VE BEEN JONESIN' FOR A HEIST. ARE YA IN?

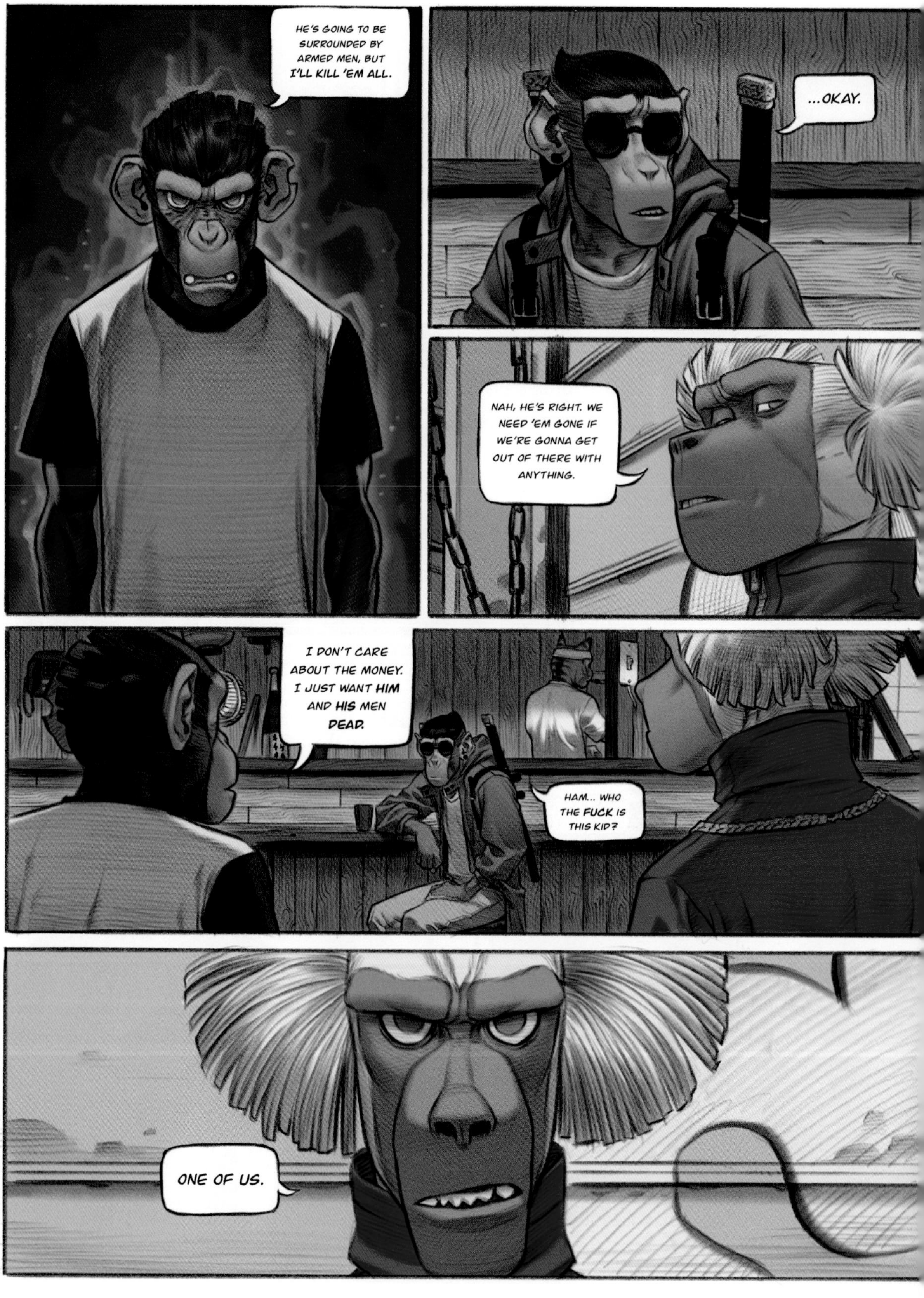

HE'S GOING TO BE SURROUNDED BY ARMED MEN, BUT I'LL KILL 'EM ALL.
...OKAY.
NAH, HE'S RIGHT. WE NEED 'EM GONE IF WE'RE GONNA GET OUT OF THERE WITH ANYTHING.
I DON'T CARE ABOUT THE MONEY. I JUST WANT HIM AND HIS MEN DEAD.
HAM... WHO THE FUCK IS THIS KID?
ONE OF US.

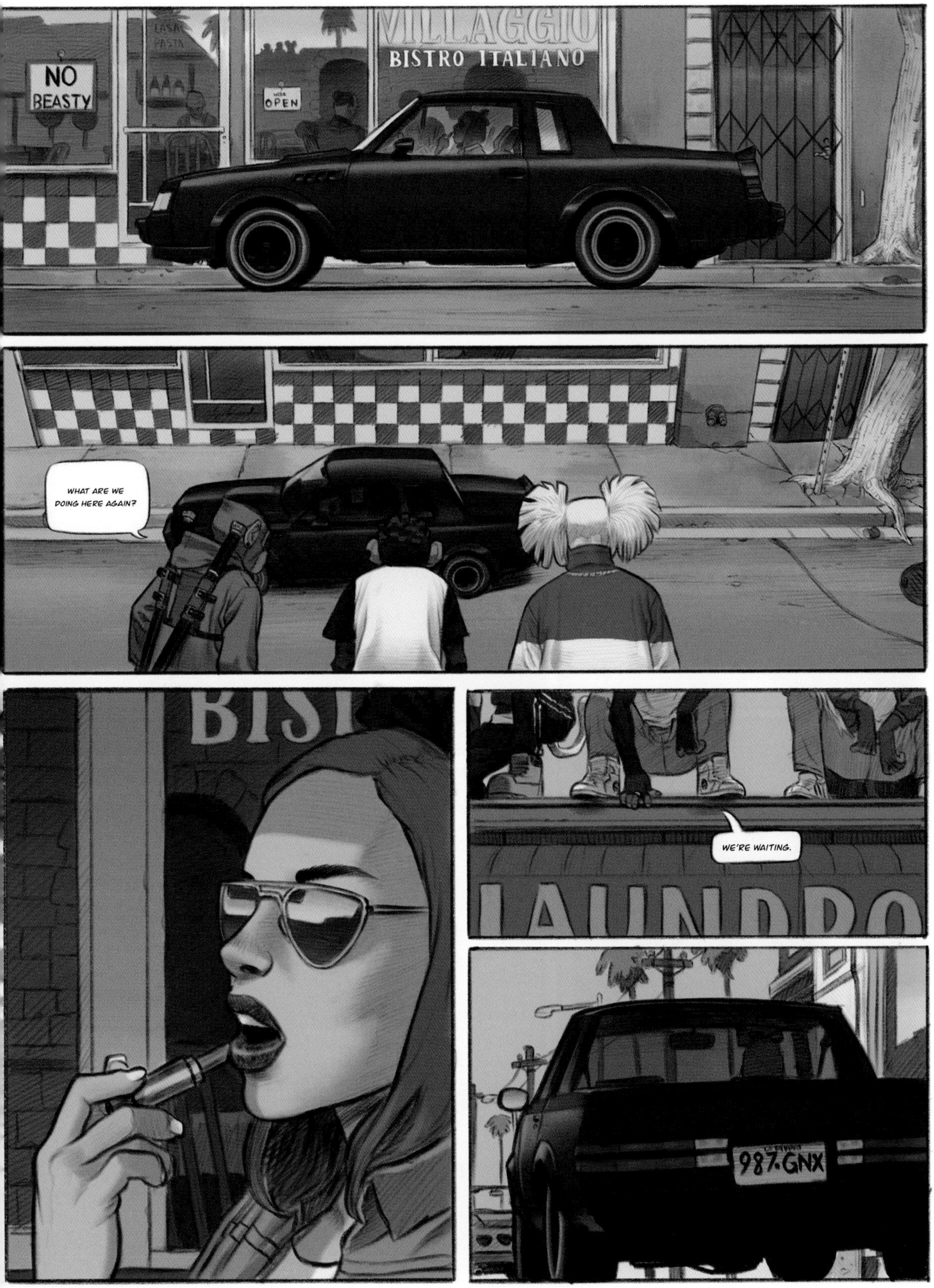
NO BEASTY
VILLAGGIO
BISTRO ITALIANO
OPEN
WHAT ARE WE DOING HERE AGAIN?
WE'RE WAITING.
987·GNX

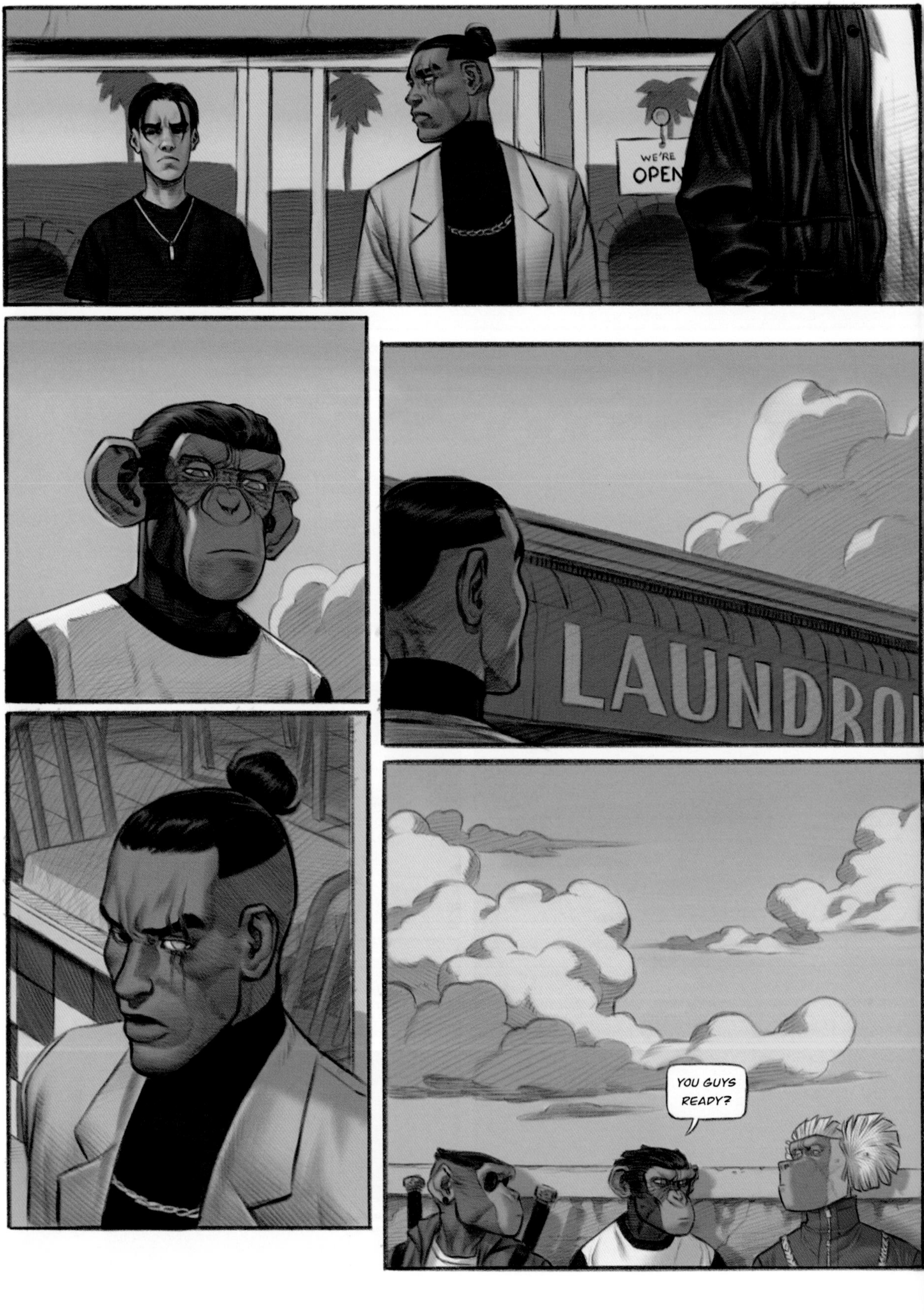
WE'RE
OPEN
LAUNDRO
YOU GUYS READY?

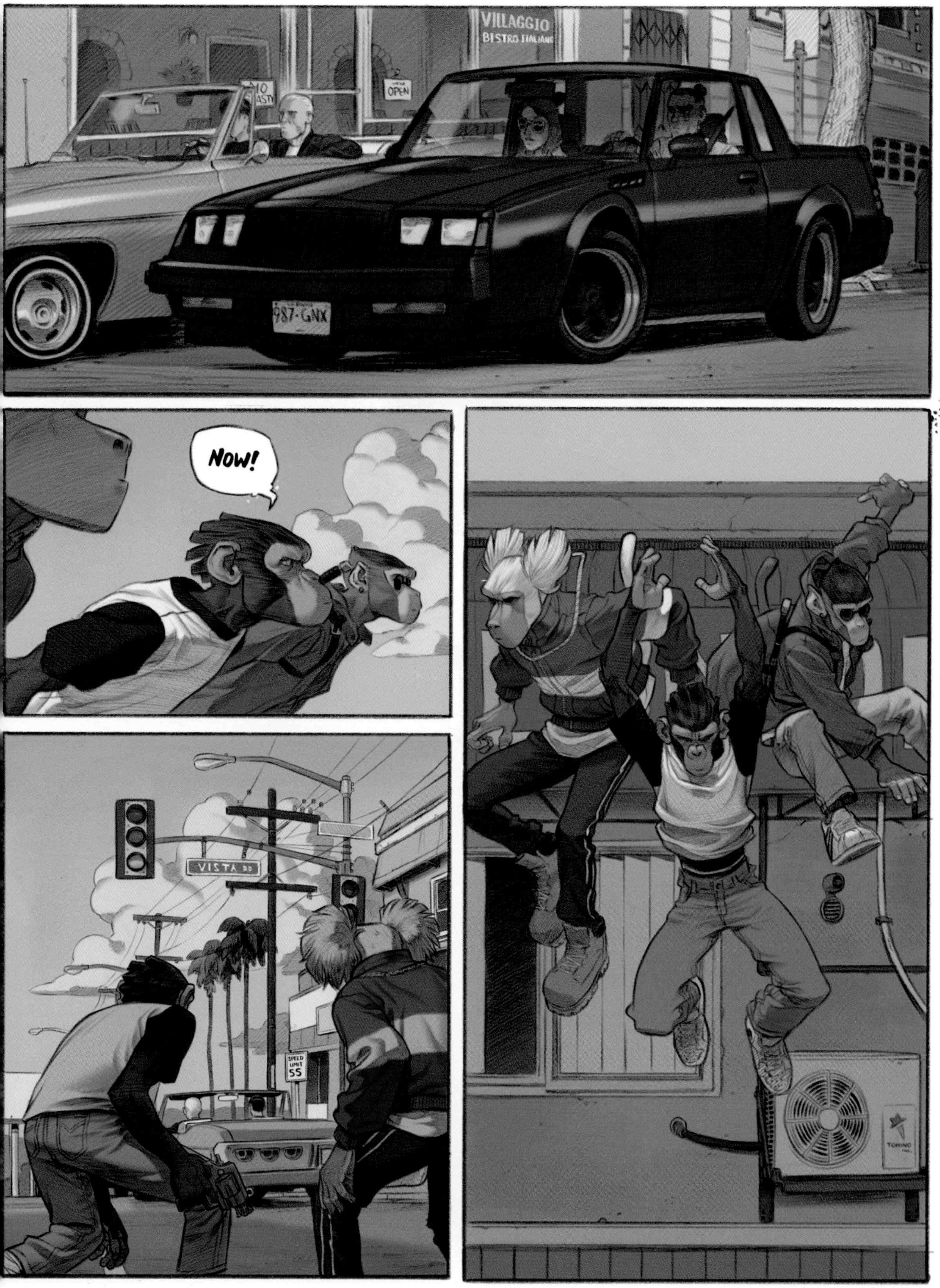
VILLAGGIO
BISTRO ITALIANO
OPEN
987-GNX
NOW!
VISTA RD
SPEED LIMIT 55

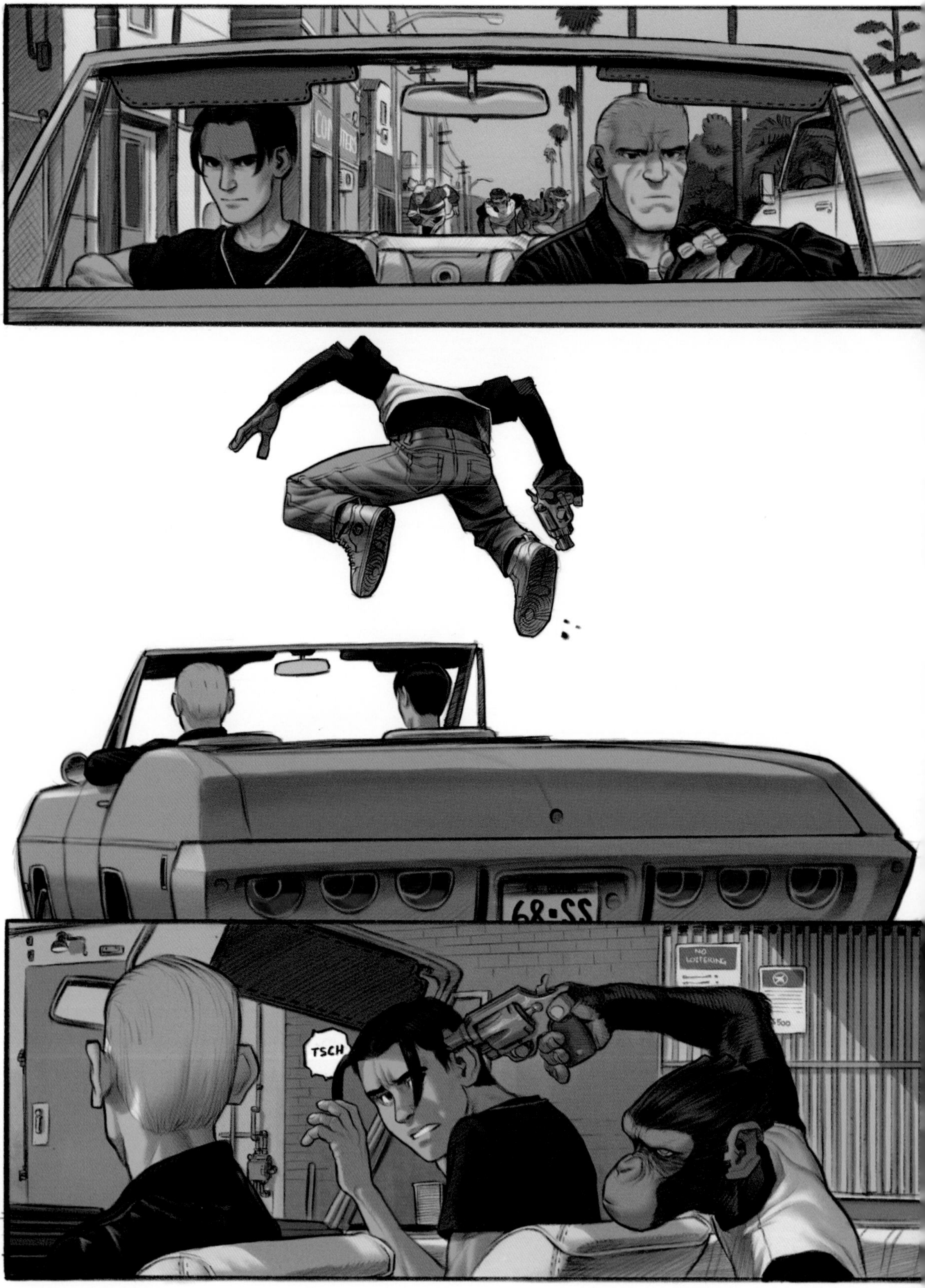
NO LOITERING
TSCH

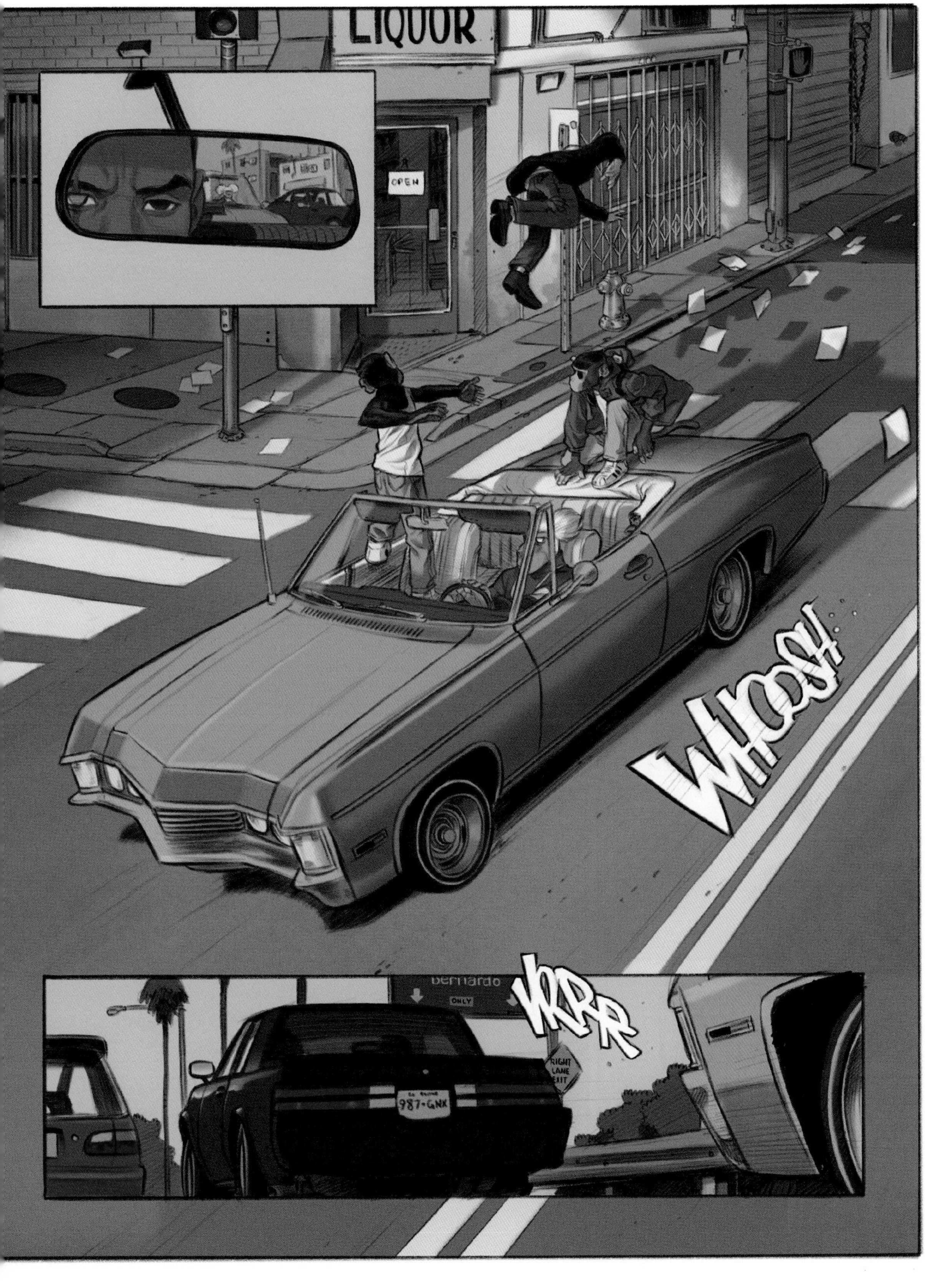
LIQUOR
OPEN
WHOOSH!
VRRR
ONLY
987-GNK

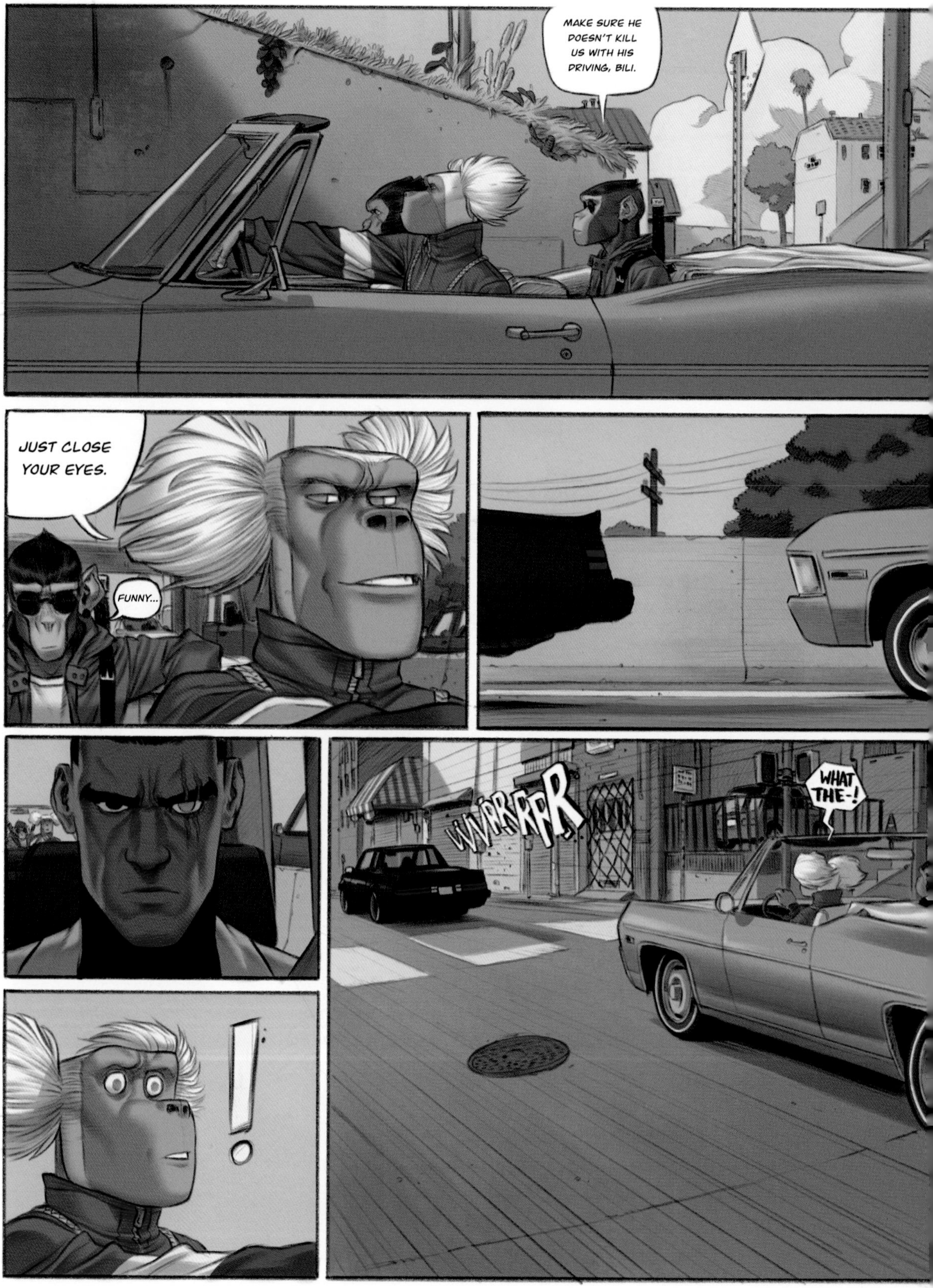
MAKE SURE HE DOESN'T KILL US WITH HIS DRIVING, BILI.
JUST CLOSE YOUR EYES.
FUNNY...
WVRRRR
WHAT THE-!
!

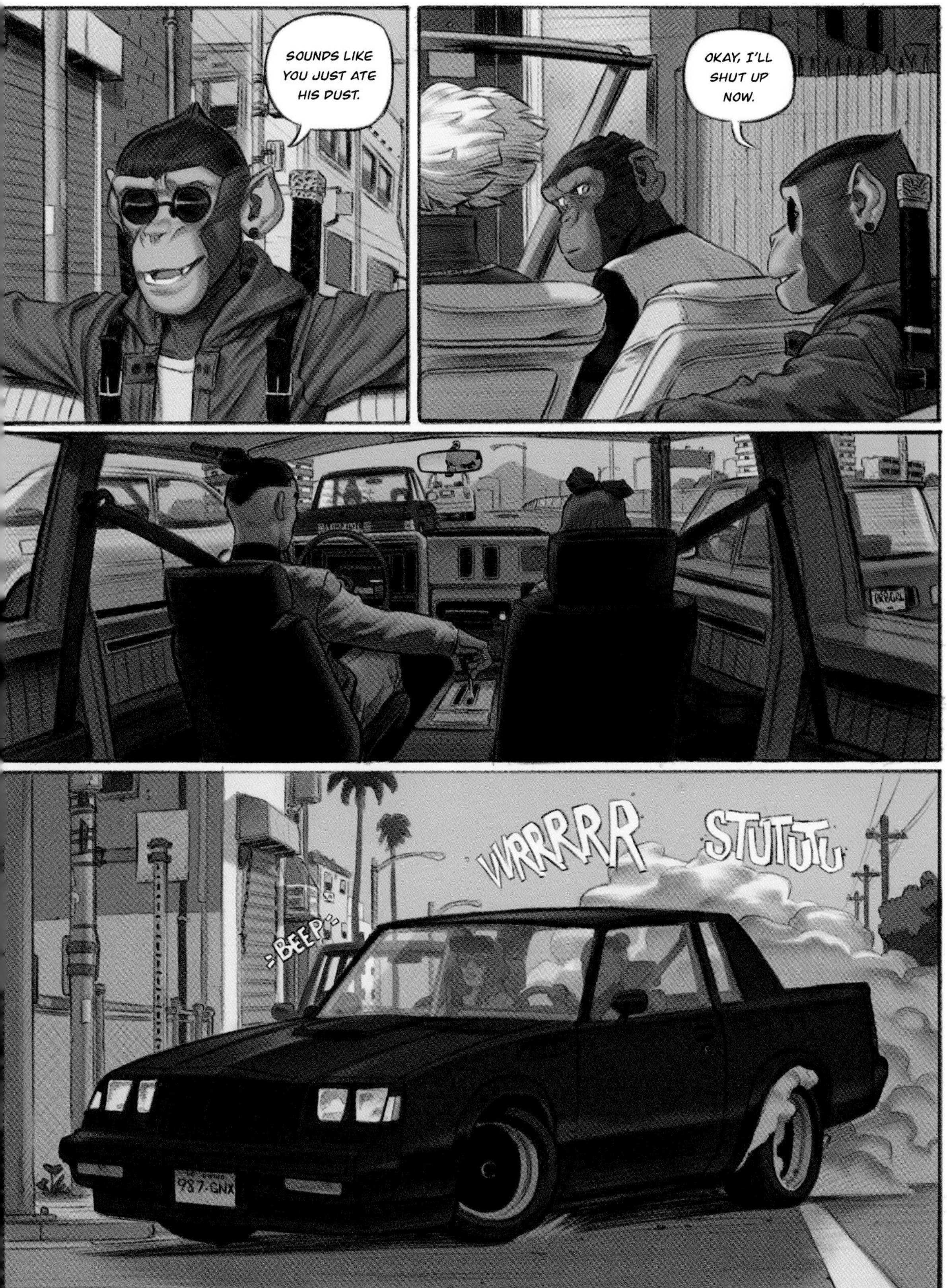
SOUNDS LIKE YOU JUST ATE HIS DUST.
OKAY, I'LL SHUT UP NOW.
VRRRRR
STUTUTU
BEEP
987-GNX

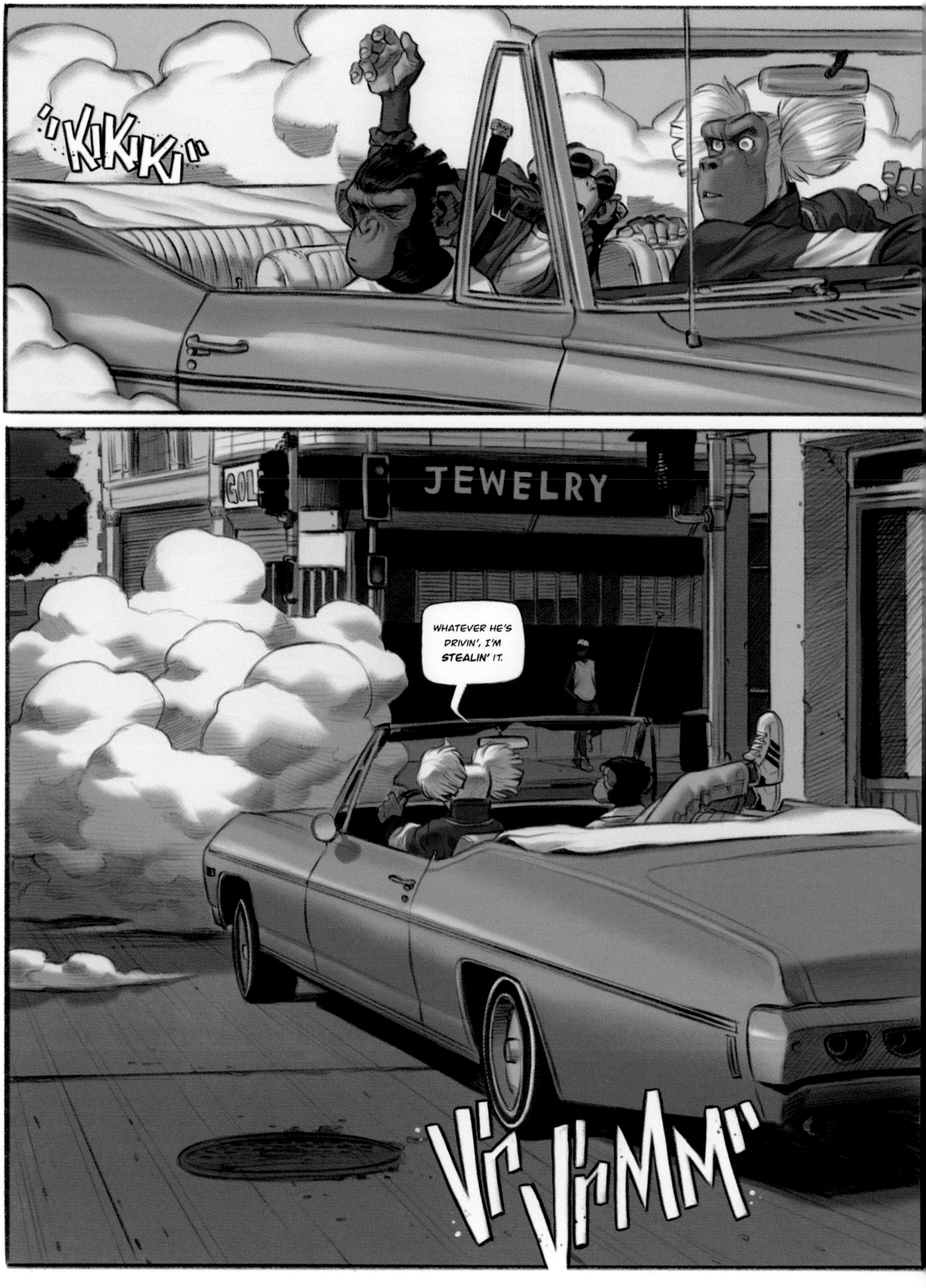
"KIKIKI"
WHATEVER HE'S DRIVIN', I'M STEALIN' IT.
JEWELRY
VRVRMMM

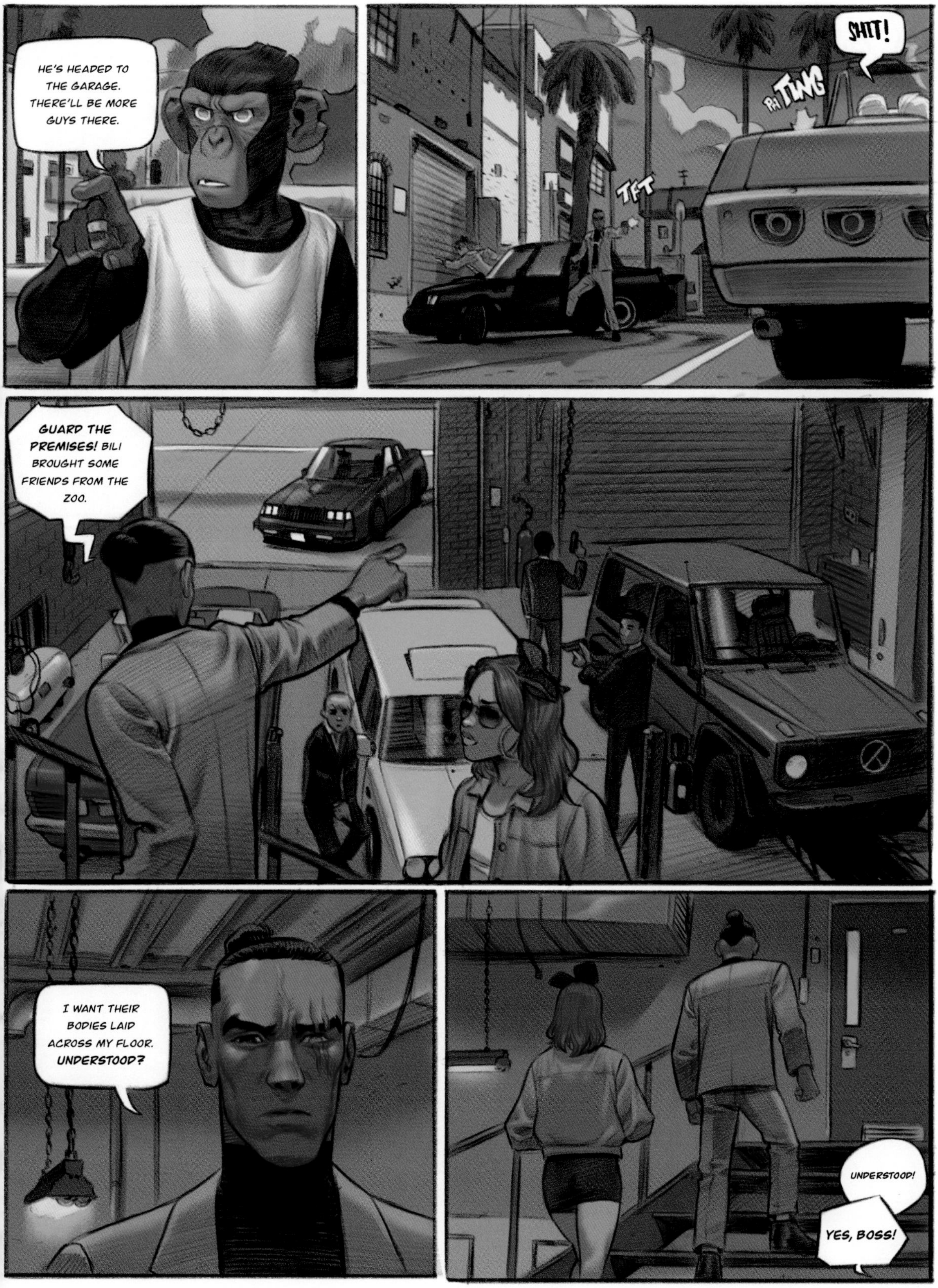
HE'S HEADED TO THE GARAGE. THERE'LL BE MORE GUYS THERE.
SHIT!
PA TWNG
TFT
GUARD THE PREMISES! BILI BROUGHT SOME FRIENDS FROM THE ZOO.
I WANT THEIR BODIES LAID ACROSS MY FLOOR. UNDERSTOOD?
UNDERSTOOD!
YES, BOSS!

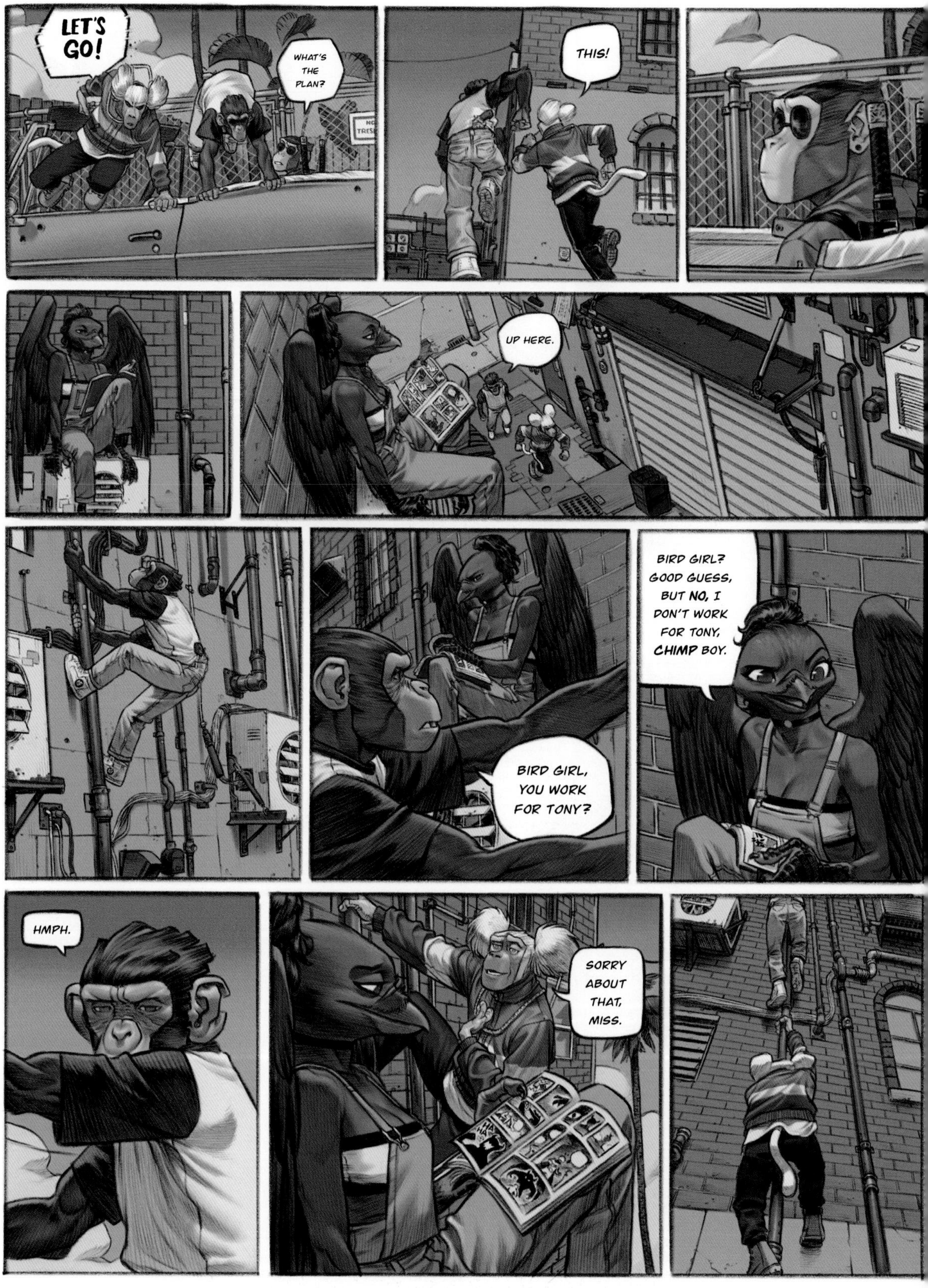
LET'S GO!
WHAT'S THE PLAN?
THIS!
UP HERE.
BIRD GIRL, YOU WORK FOR TONY?
BIRD GIRL? GOOD GUESS, BUT NO, I DON'T WORK FOR TONY, CHIMP BOY.
HMPH.
SORRY ABOUT THAT, MISS.

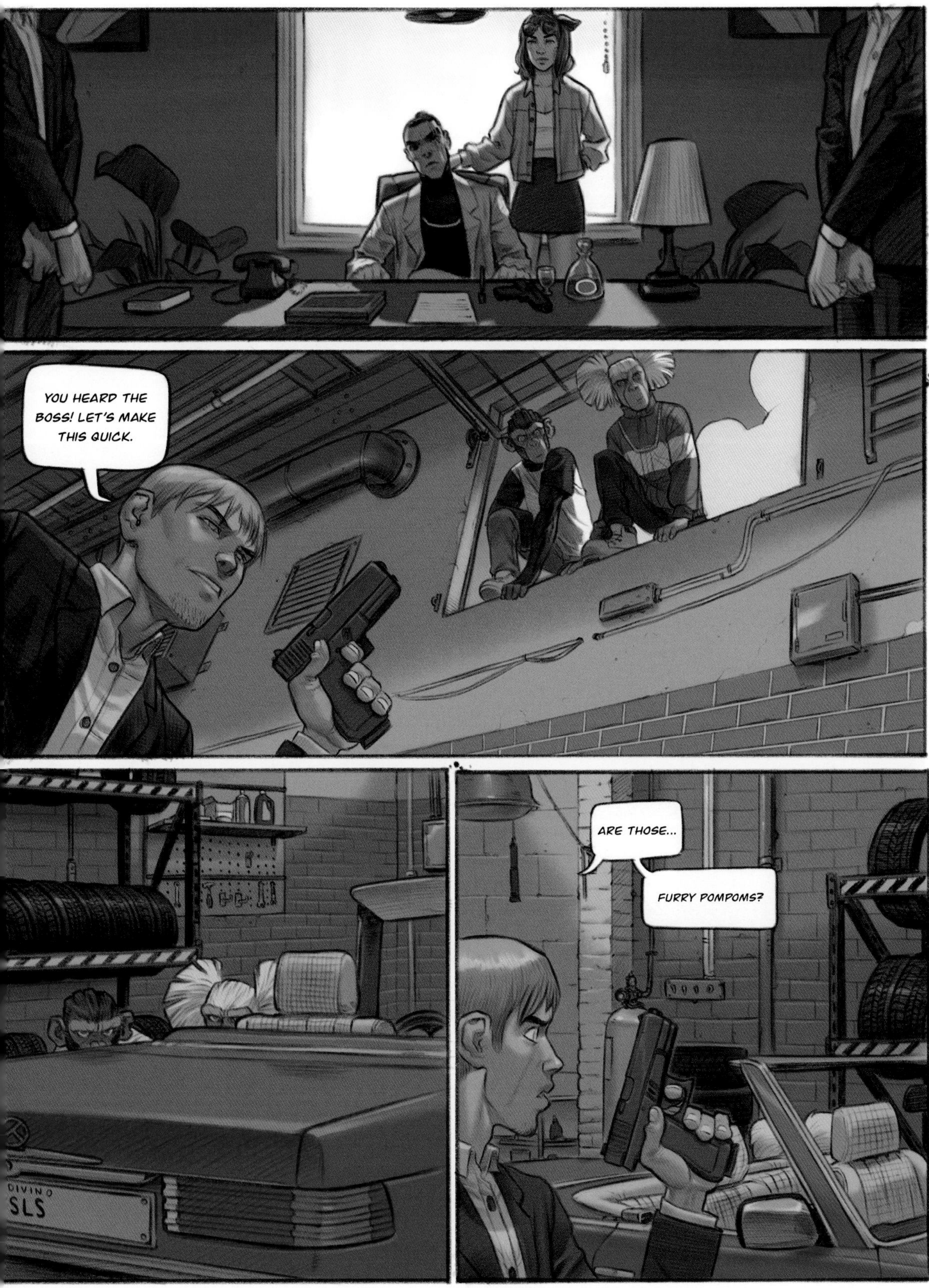
YOU HEARD THE BOSS! LET'S MAKE THIS QUICK.
DIVINO
SLS
ARE THOSE...
FURRY POMPOMS?

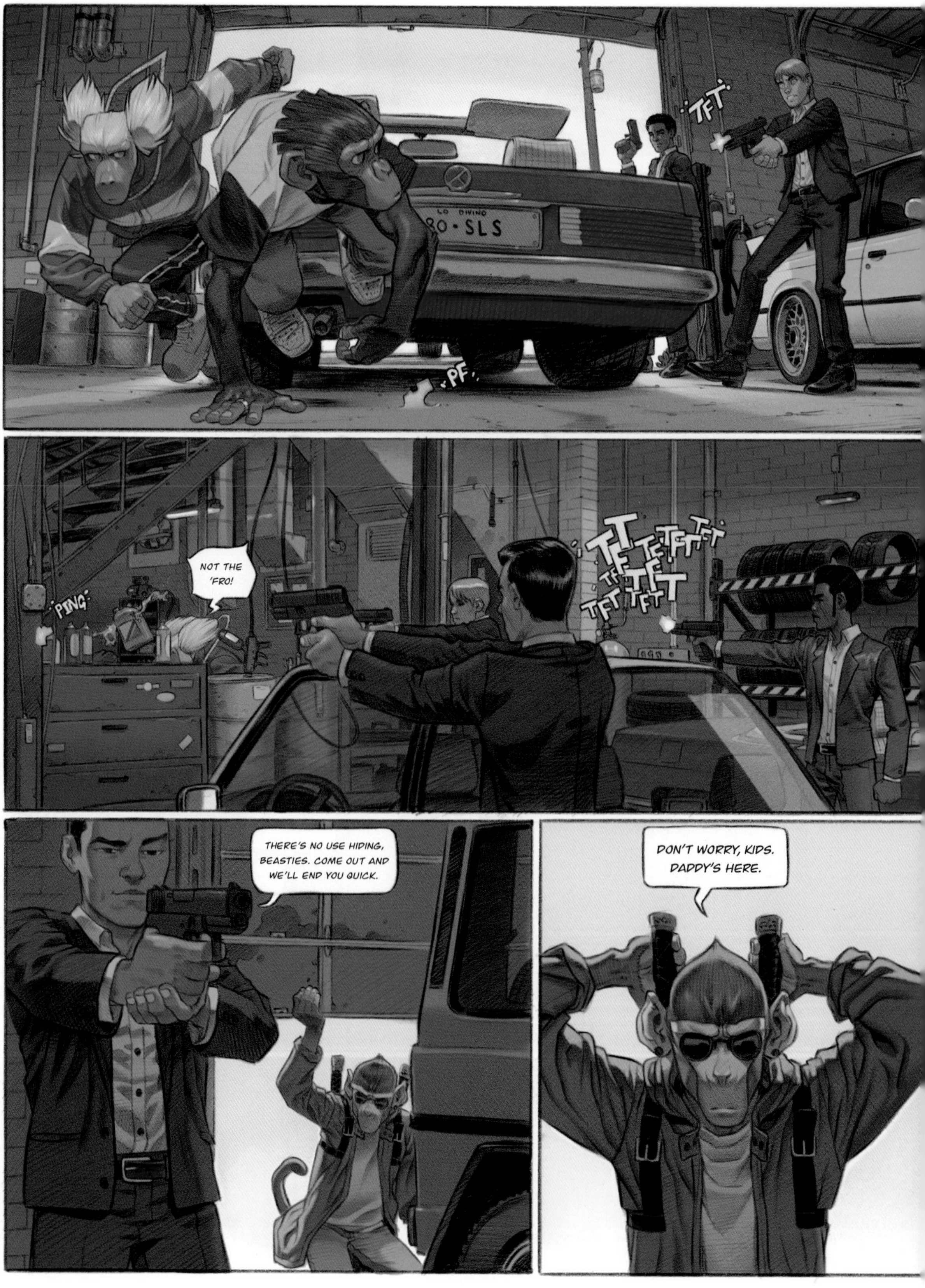

TFT
PF
NOT THE 'FRO!
PING
TFT TFT TFT TFT TFT TFT TFT TFT
THERE'S NO USE HIDING, BEASTIES. COME OUT AND WE'LL END YOU QUICK.
DON'T WORRY, KIDS. DADDY'S HERE.

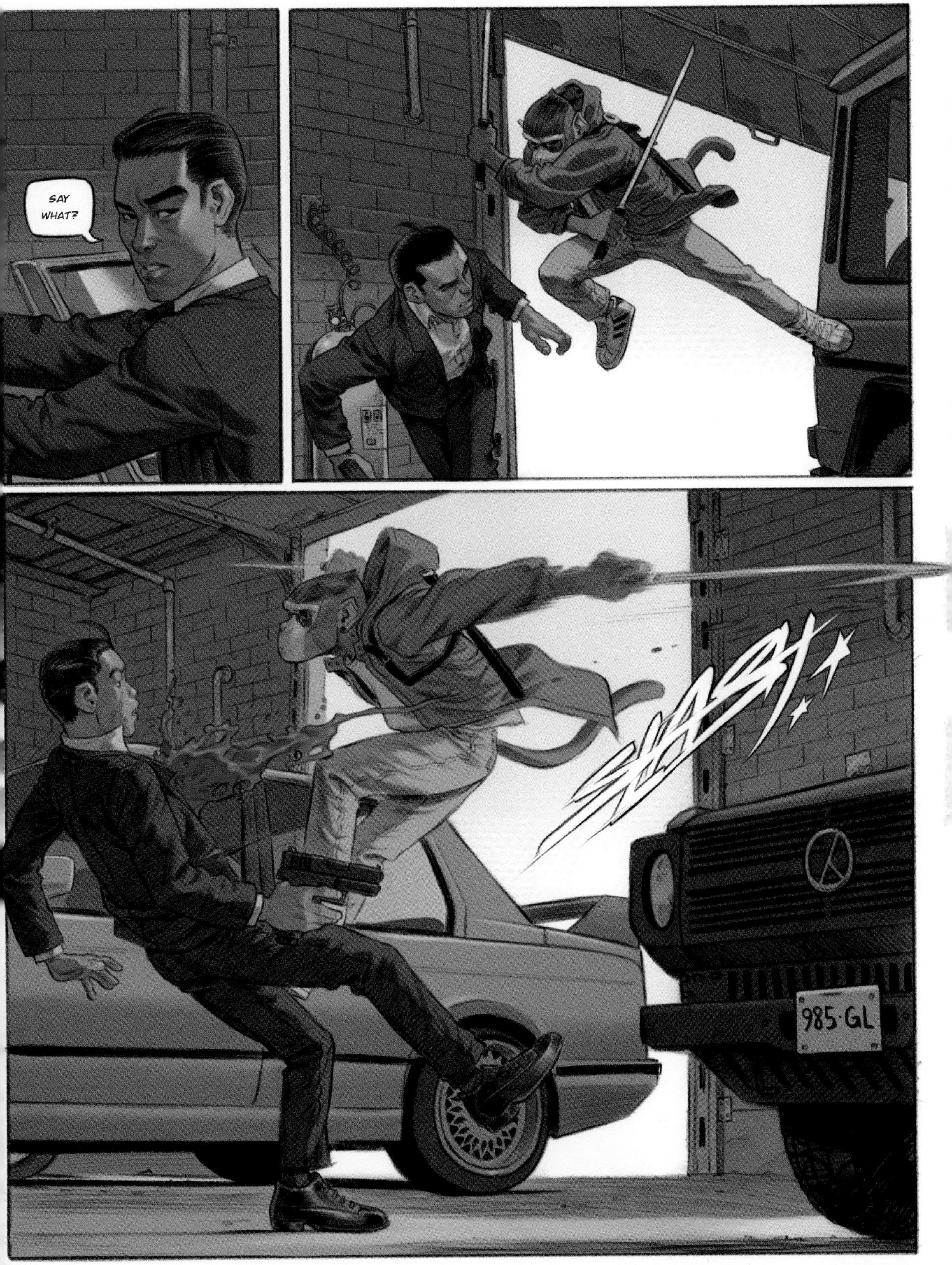
SAY WHAT?
SLASH!
985·GL

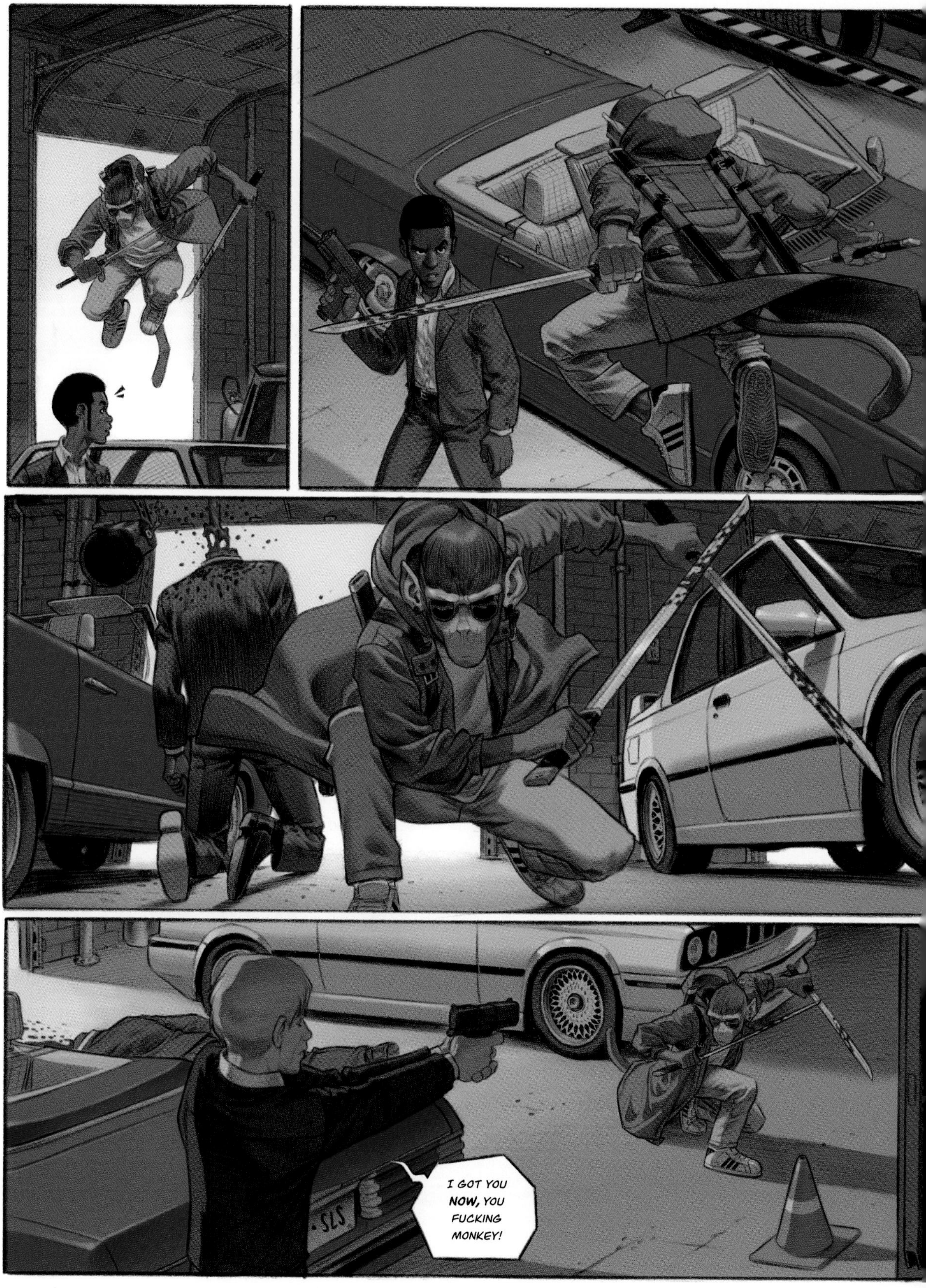
I GOT YOU NOW, YOU FUCKING MONKEY!

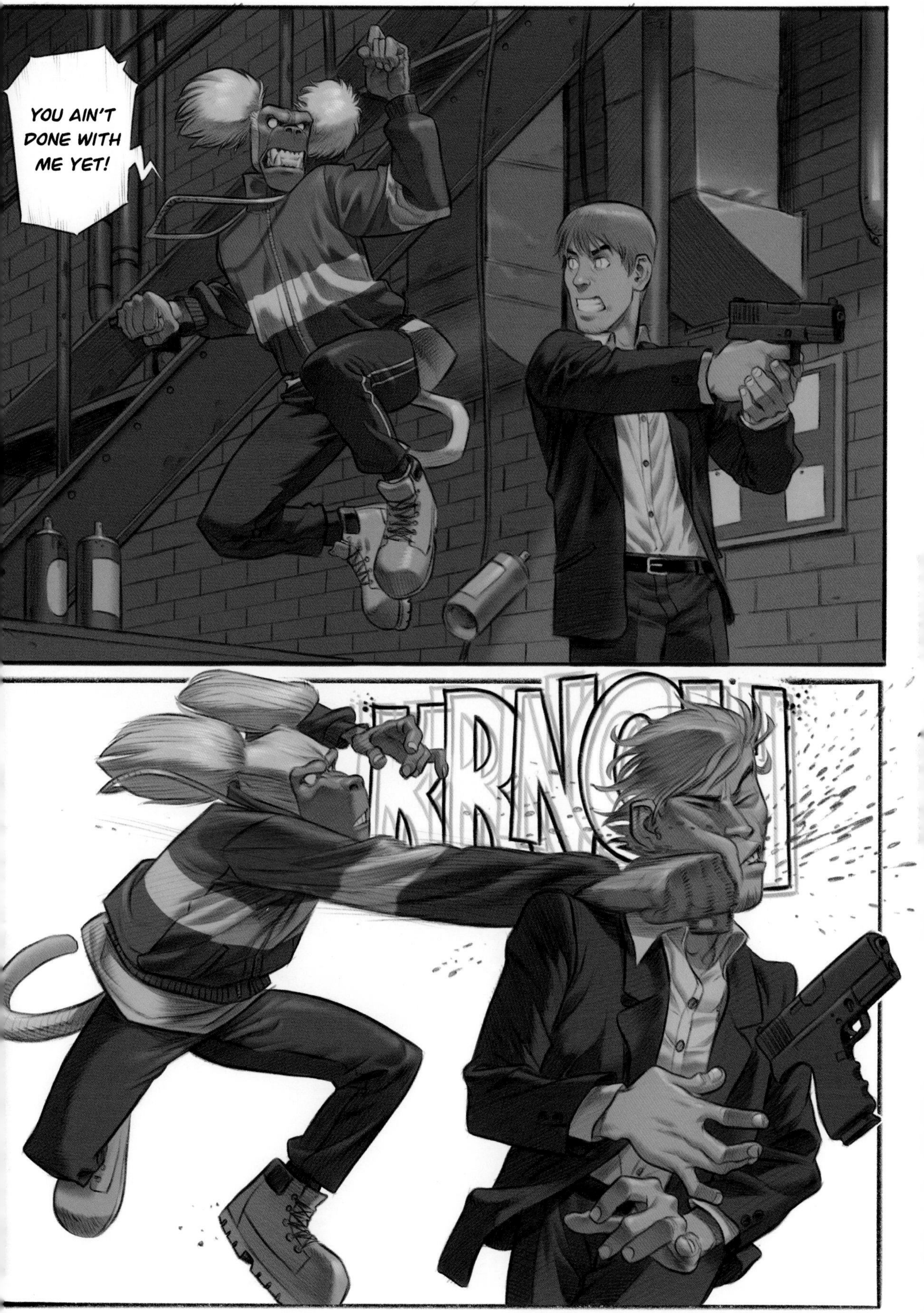
YOU AIN'T DONE WITH ME YET!

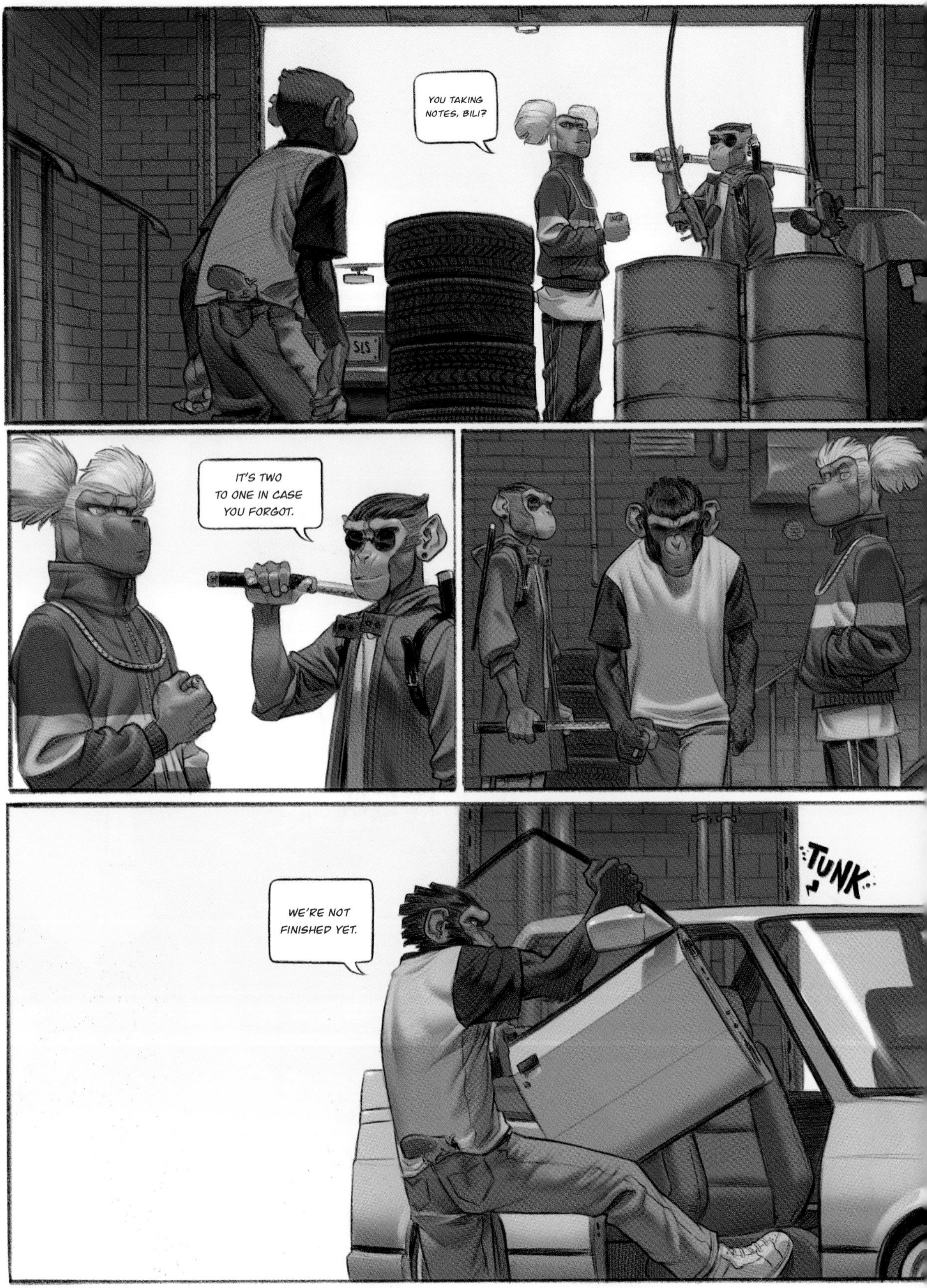
YOU TAKING NOTES, BILI?
IT'S TWO TO ONE IN CASE YOU FORGOT.
WE'RE NOT FINISHED YET.
TUNK

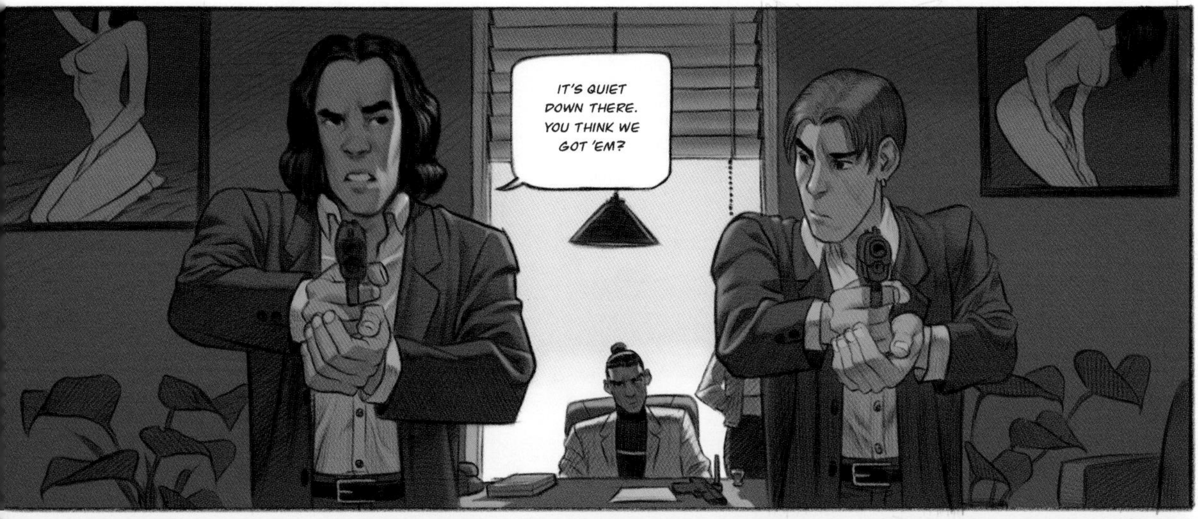
IT'S QUIET DOWN THERE. YOU THINK WE GOT 'EM?

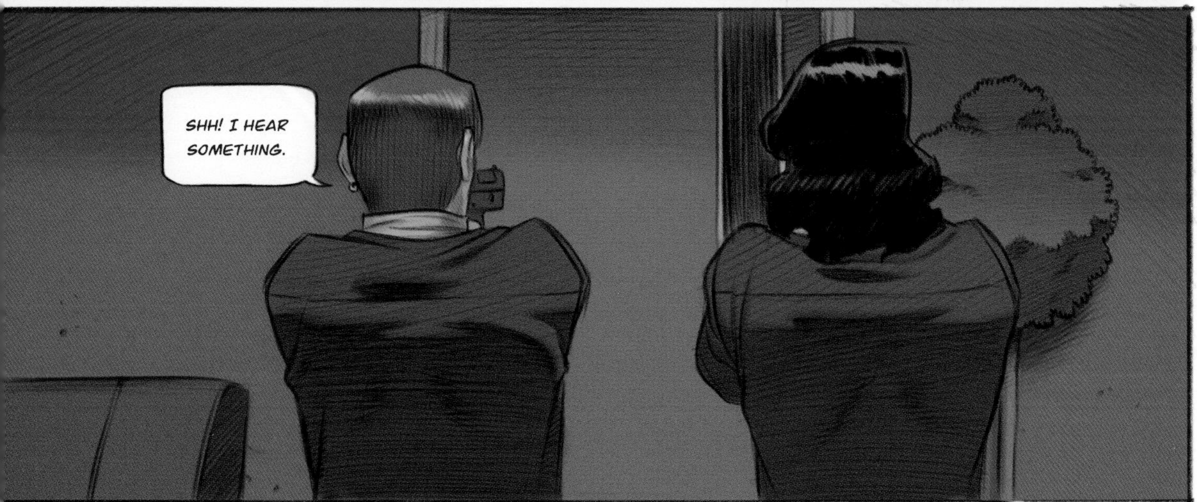
SHH! I HEAR SOMETHING.

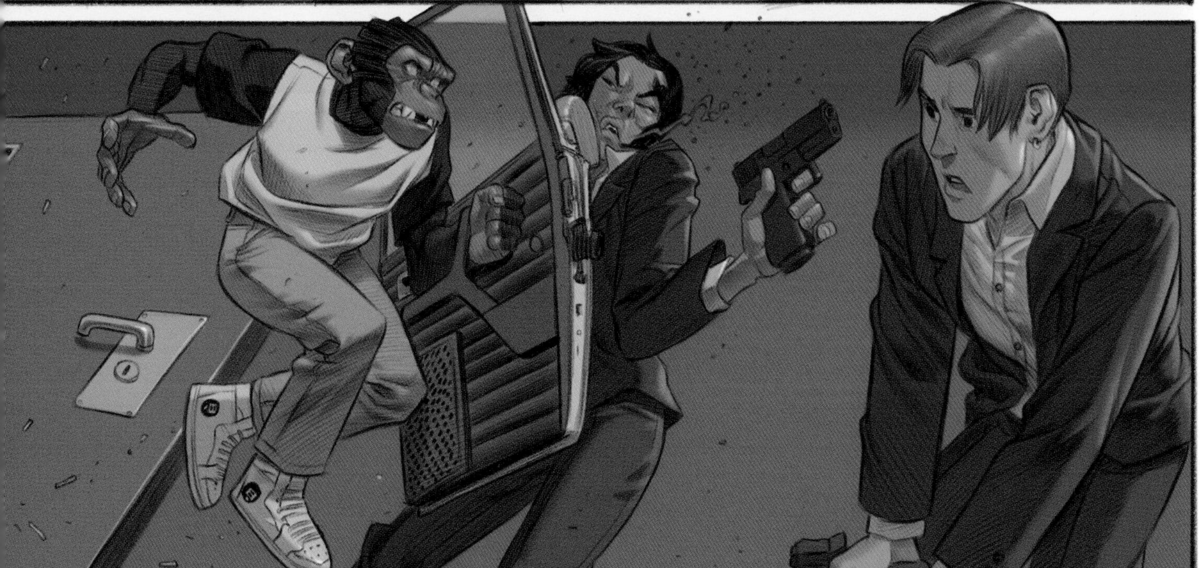

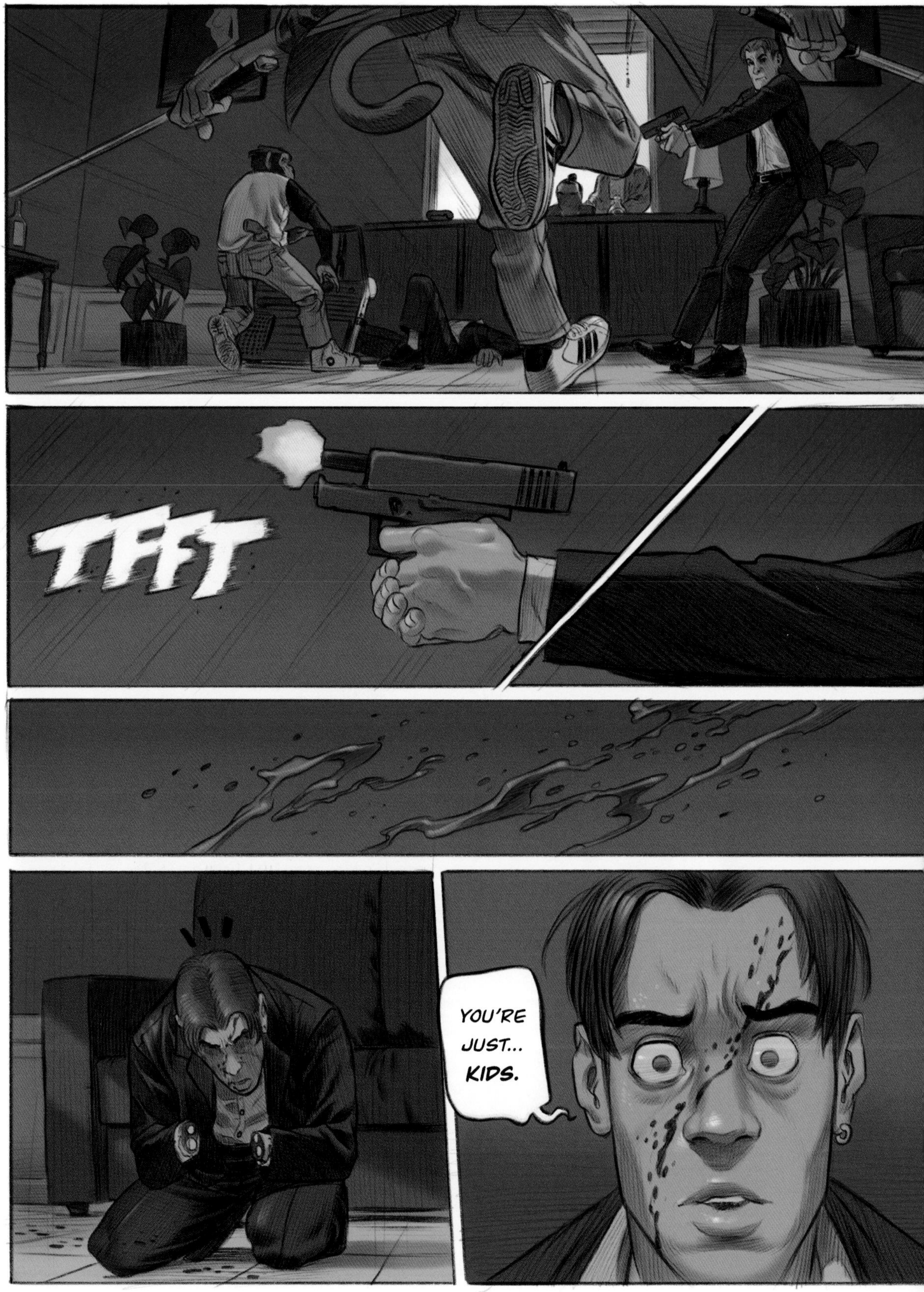
TFFT
YOU'RE JUST... KIDS.

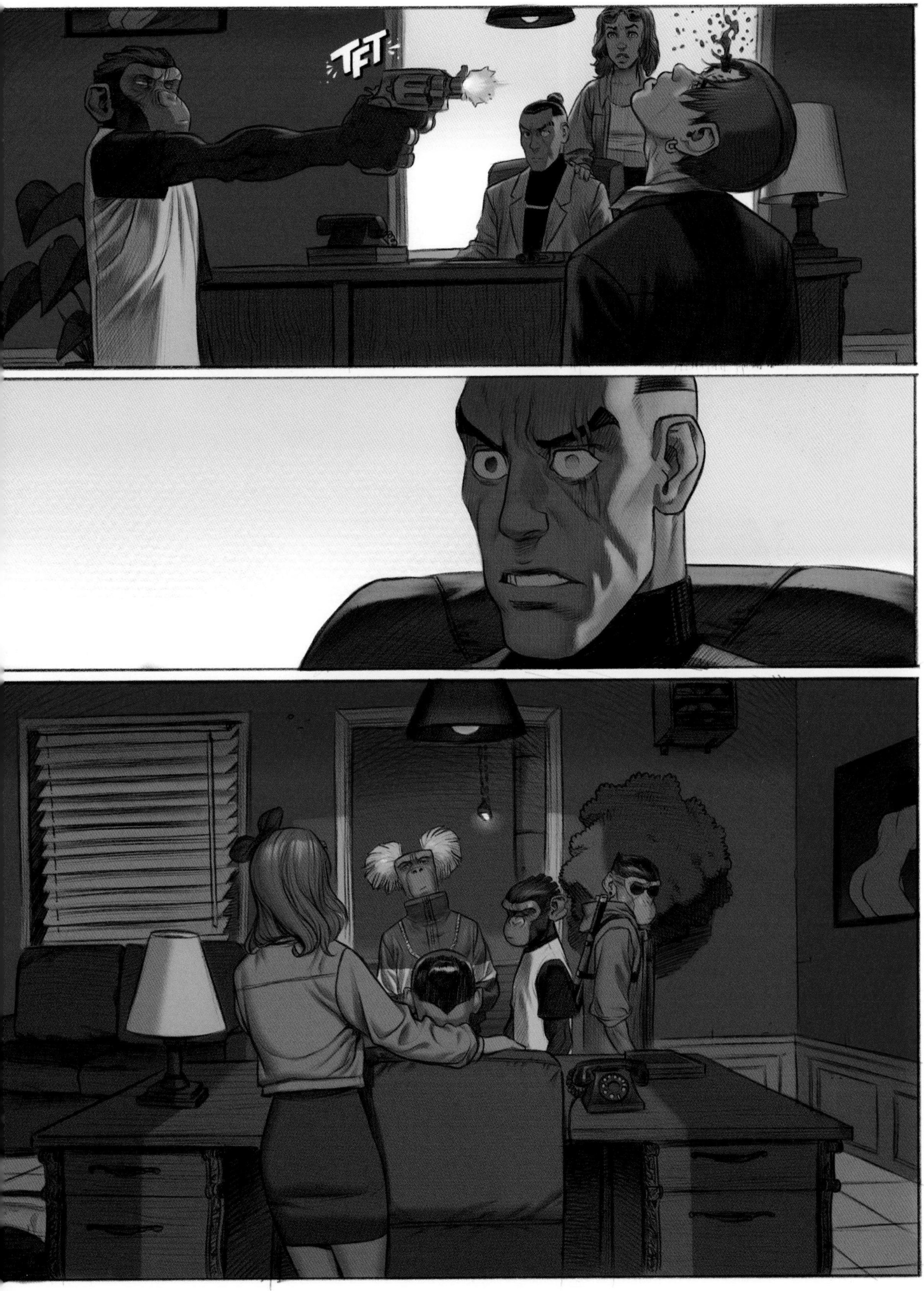
TFT

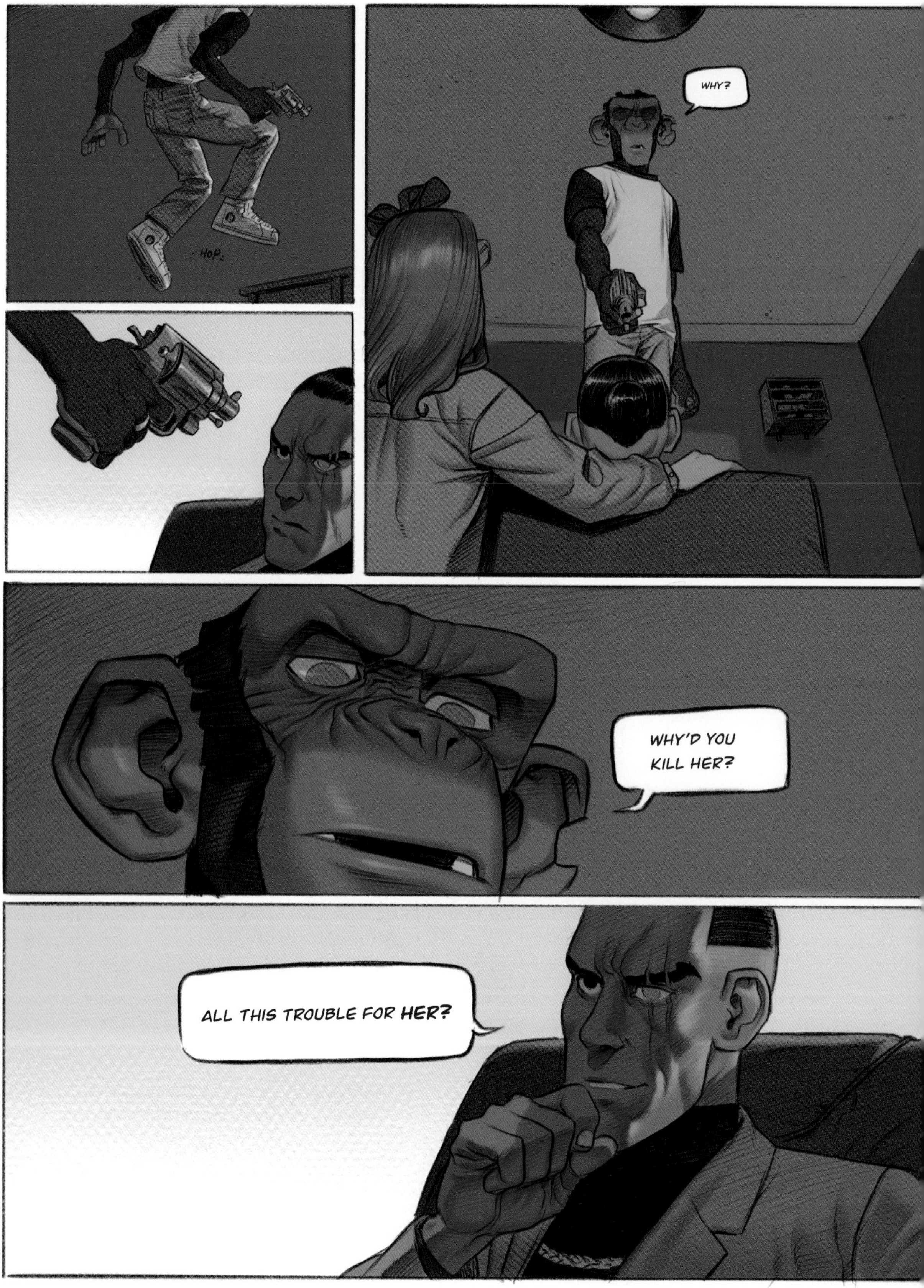
HOP
WHY?
WHY'D YOU KILL HER?
ALL THIS TROUBLE FOR HER?

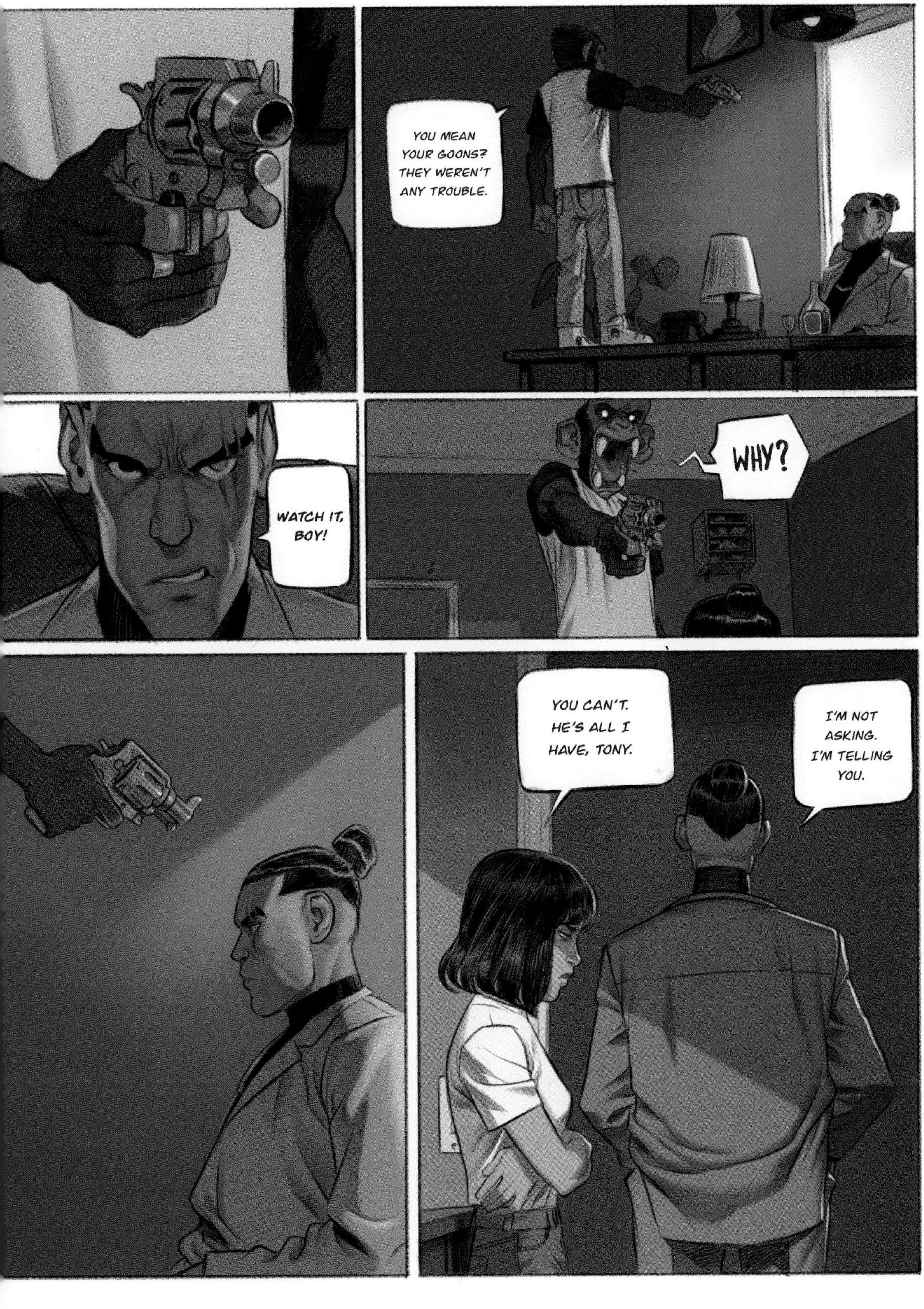
YOU MEAN YOUR GOONS? THEY WEREN'T ANY TROUBLE.
WATCH IT, BOY!
WHY?
YOU CAN'T. HE'S ALL I HAVE, TONY.
I'M NOT ASKING. I'M TELLING YOU.

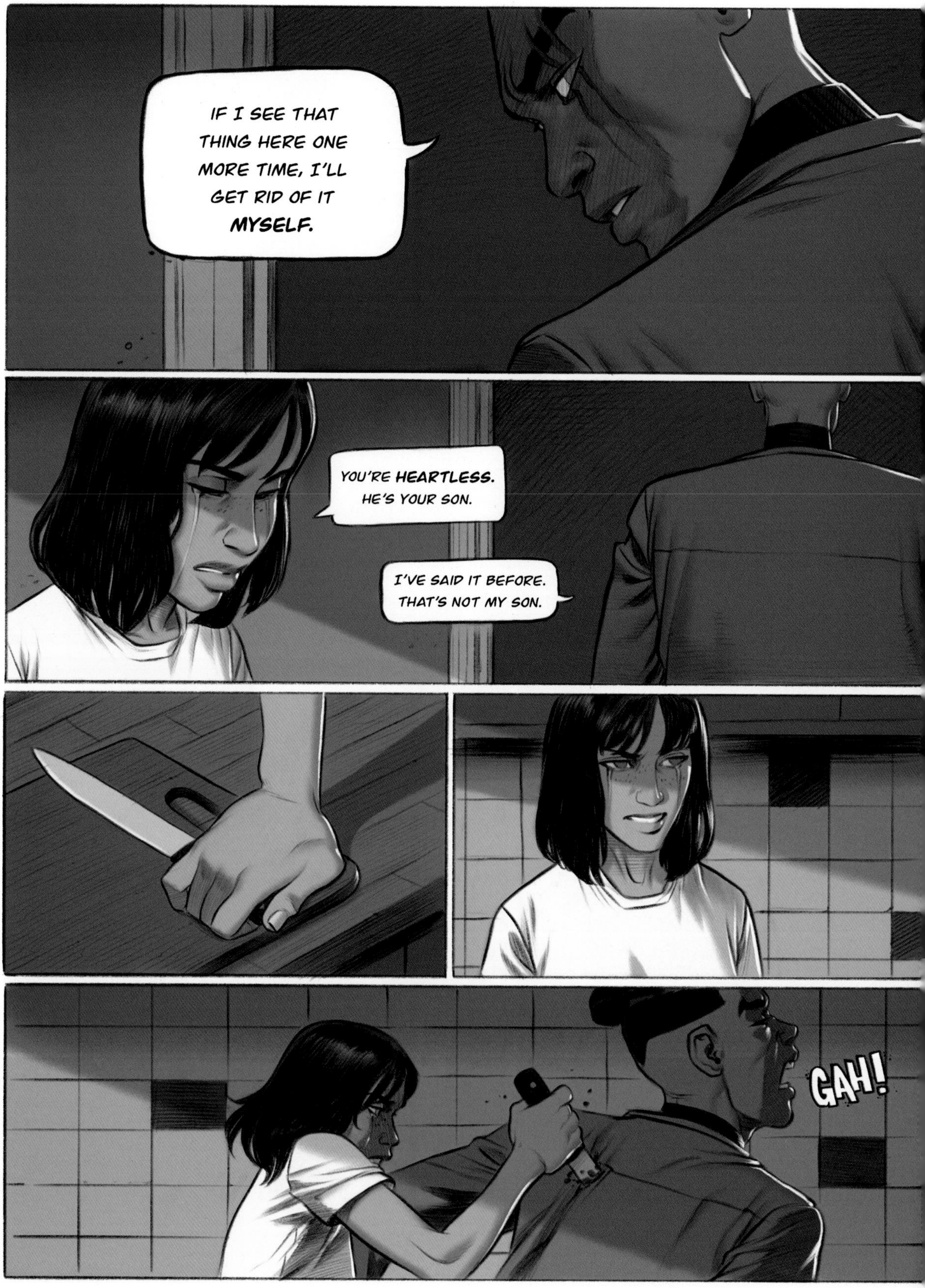
IF I SEE THAT THING HERE ONE MORE TIME, I'LL GET RID OF IT **MYSELF.**
YOU'RE **HEARTLESS.** HE'S YOUR SON.
I'VE SAID IT BEFORE. THAT'S NOT MY SON.
GAH!

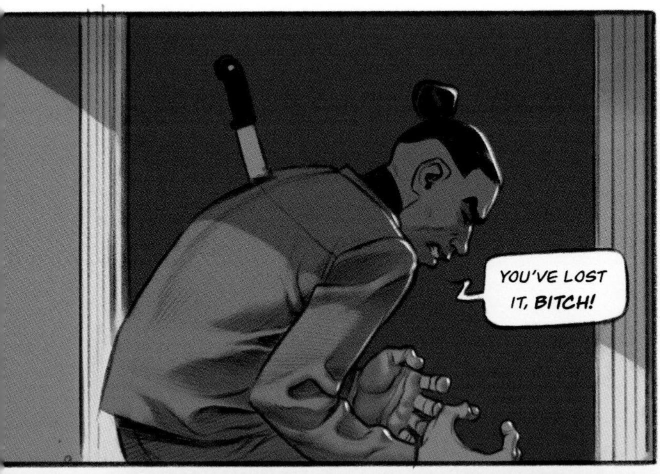
YOU'VE LOST IT, BITCH!

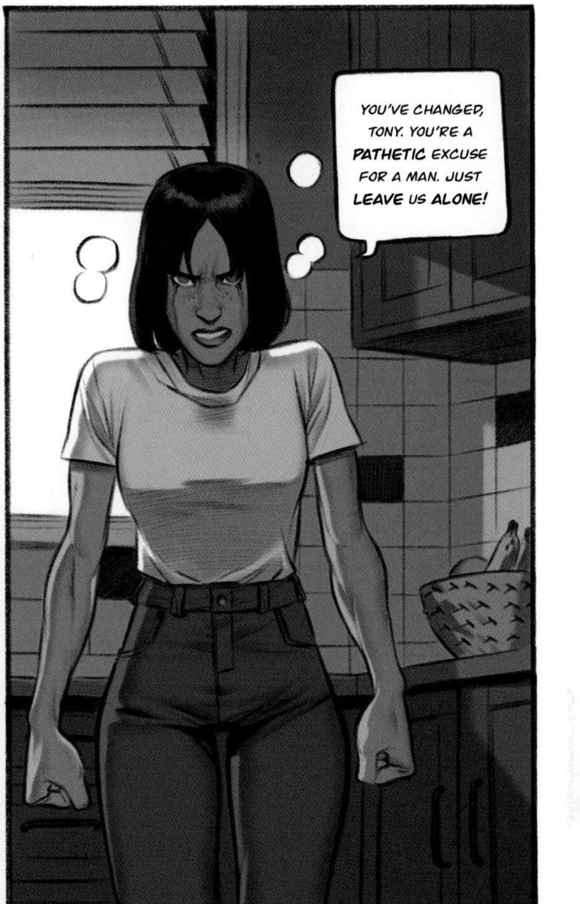
YOU'VE CHANGED, TONY. YOU'RE A PATHETIC EXCUSE FOR A MAN. JUST LEAVE US ALONE!

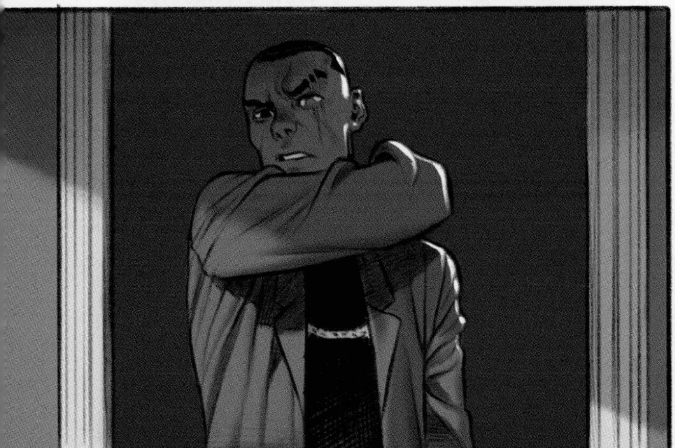

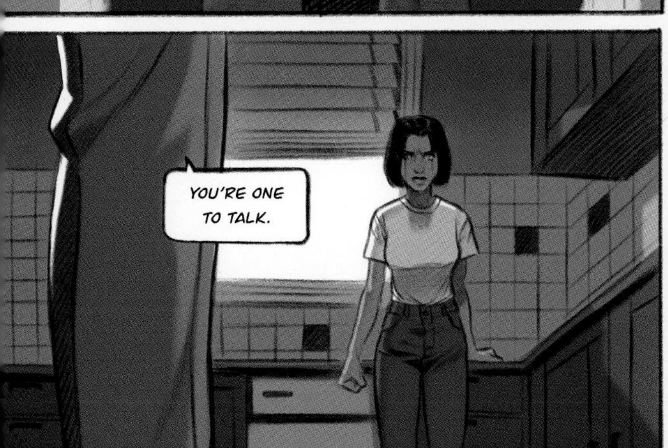
YOU'RE ONE TO TALK.
CLINK

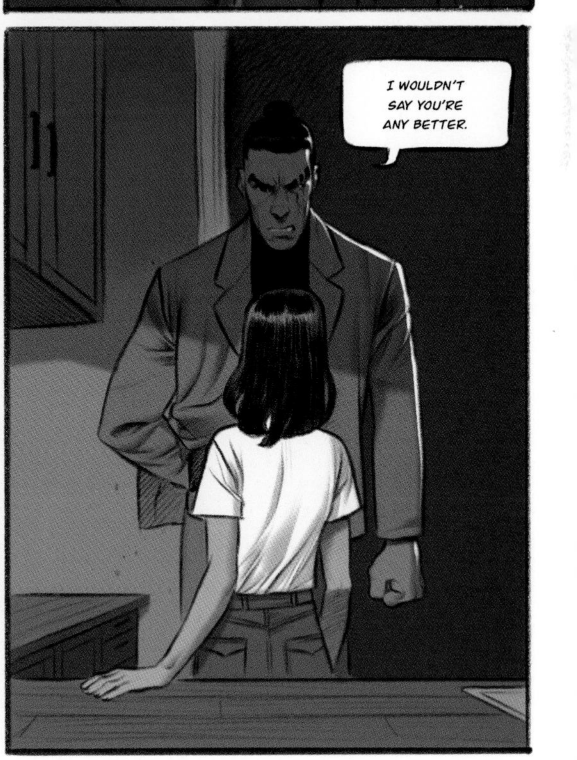
I WOULDN'T SAY YOU'RE ANY BETTER.

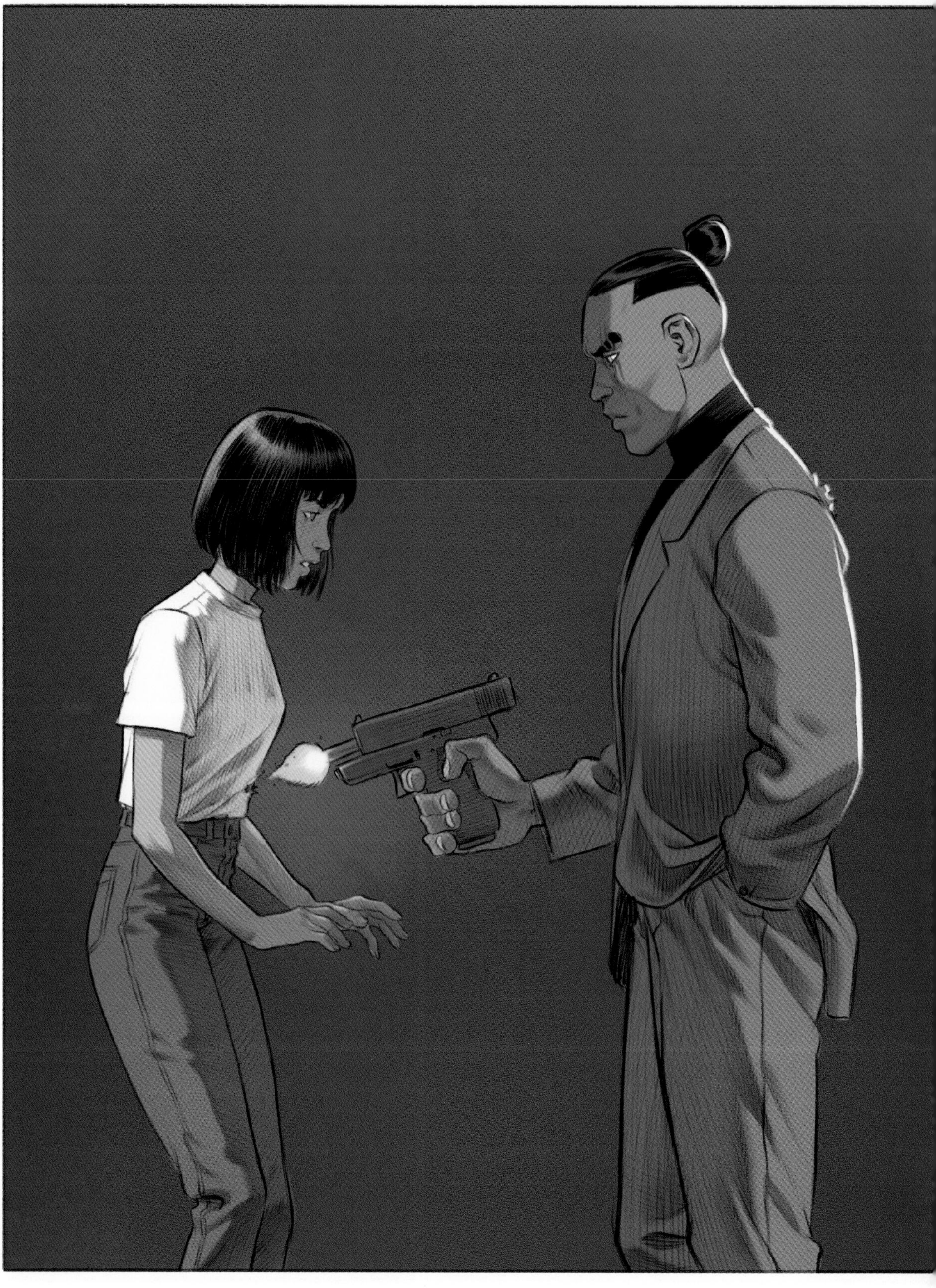

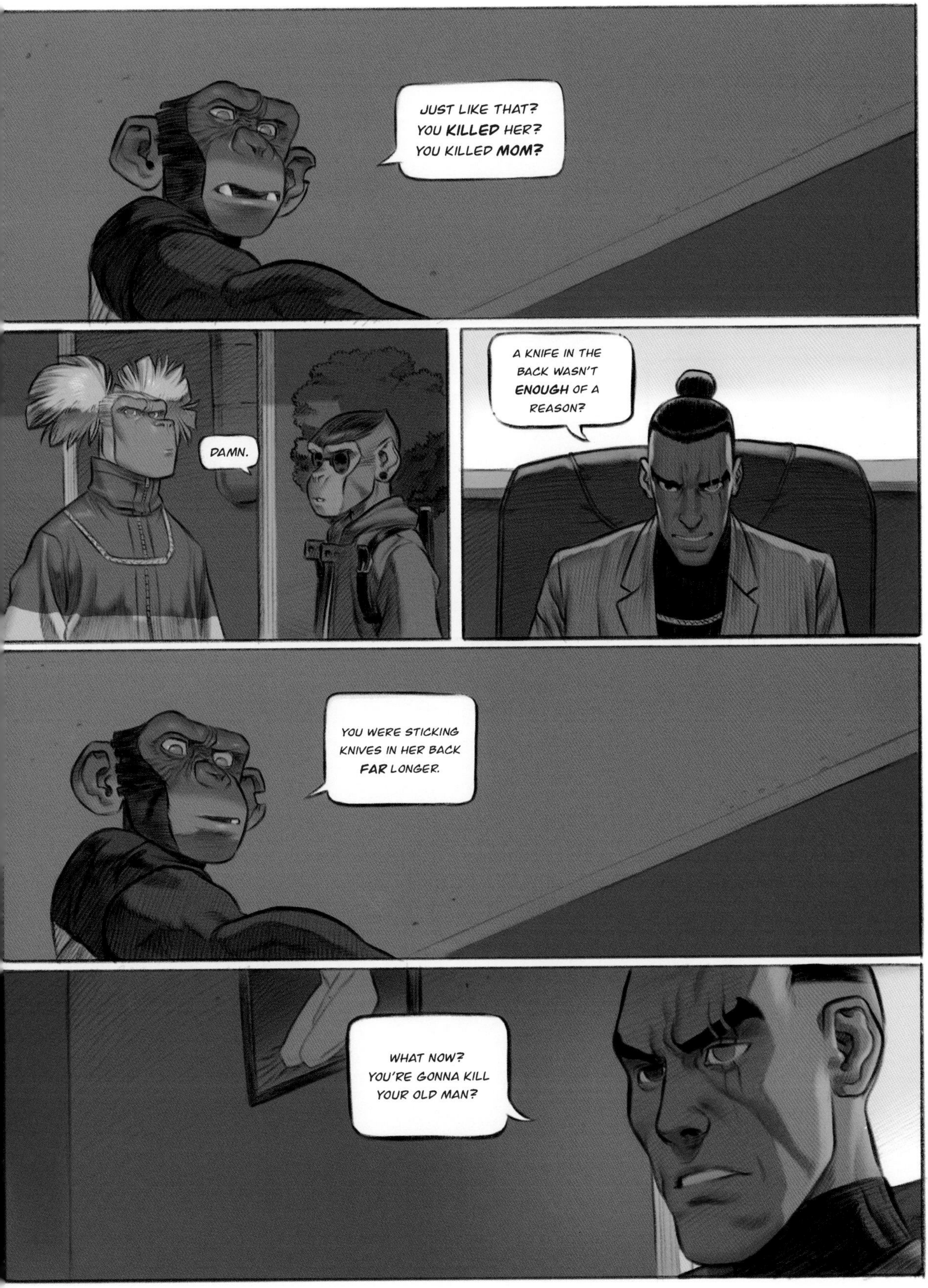
JUST LIKE THAT? YOU KILLED HER? YOU KILLED MOM?
DAMN.
A KNIFE IN THE BACK WASN'T ENOUGH OF A REASON?
YOU WERE STICKING KNIVES IN HER BACK FAR LONGER.
WHAT NOW? YOU'RE GONNA KILL YOUR OLD MAN?

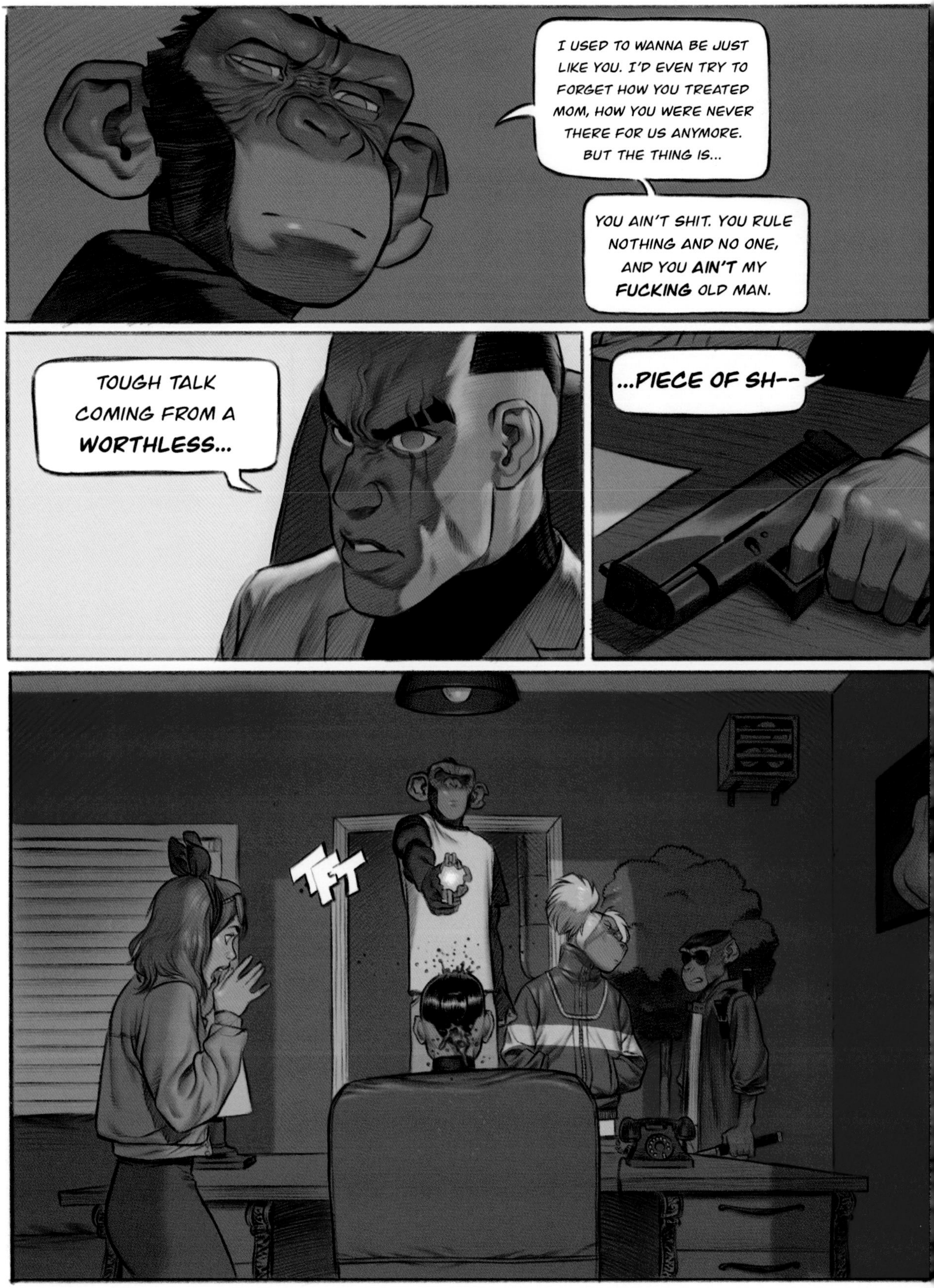
I USED TO WANNA BE JUST LIKE YOU. I'D EVEN TRY TO FORGET HOW YOU TREATED MOM, HOW YOU WERE NEVER THERE FOR US ANYMORE. BUT THE THING IS...
YOU AIN'T SHIT. YOU RULE NOTHING AND NO ONE, AND YOU AIN'T MY FUCKING OLD MAN.
TOUGH TALK COMING FROM A WORTHLESS...
...PIECE OF SH--
TFT

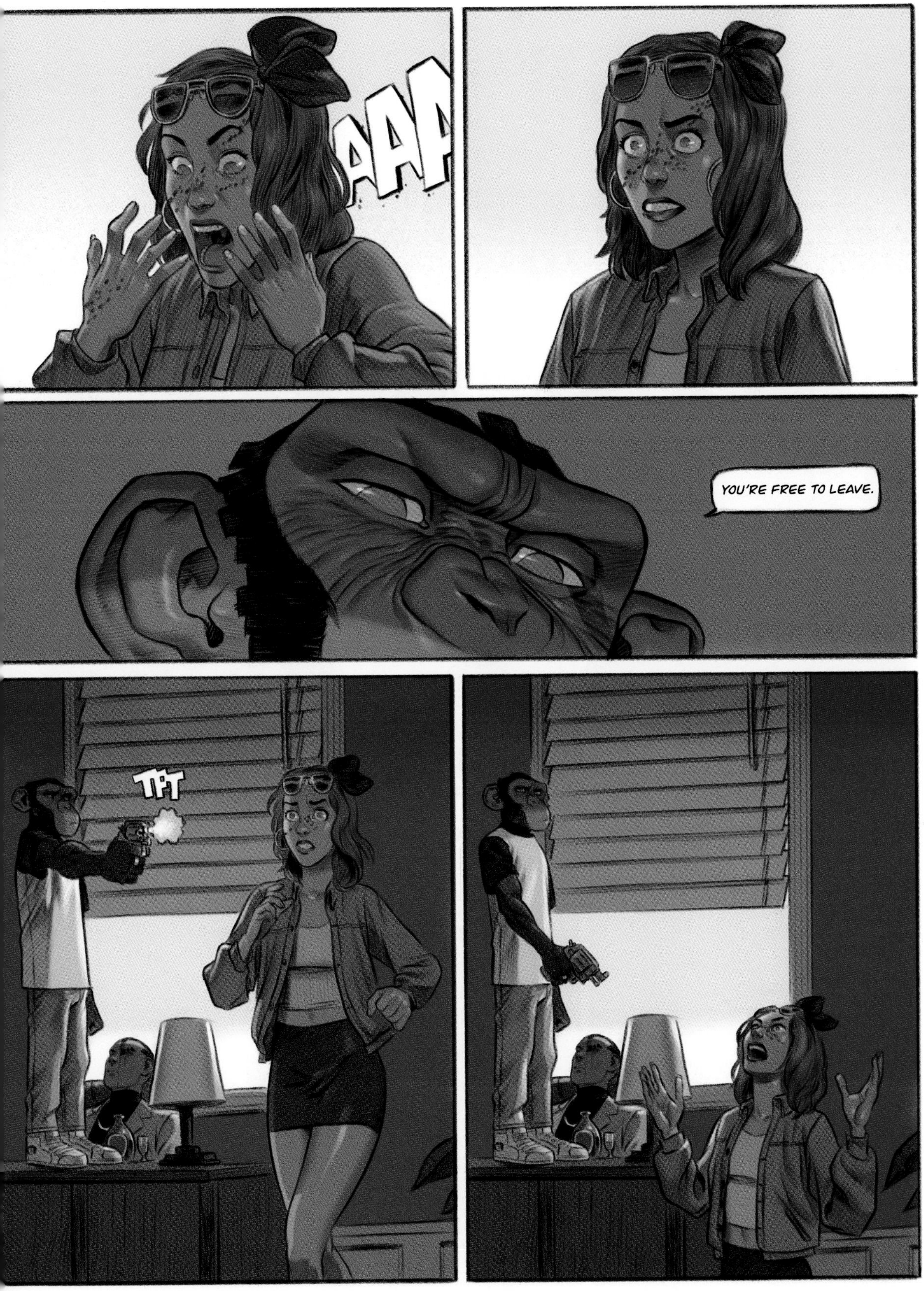
AAAA
YOU'RE FREE TO LEAVE.
TFT

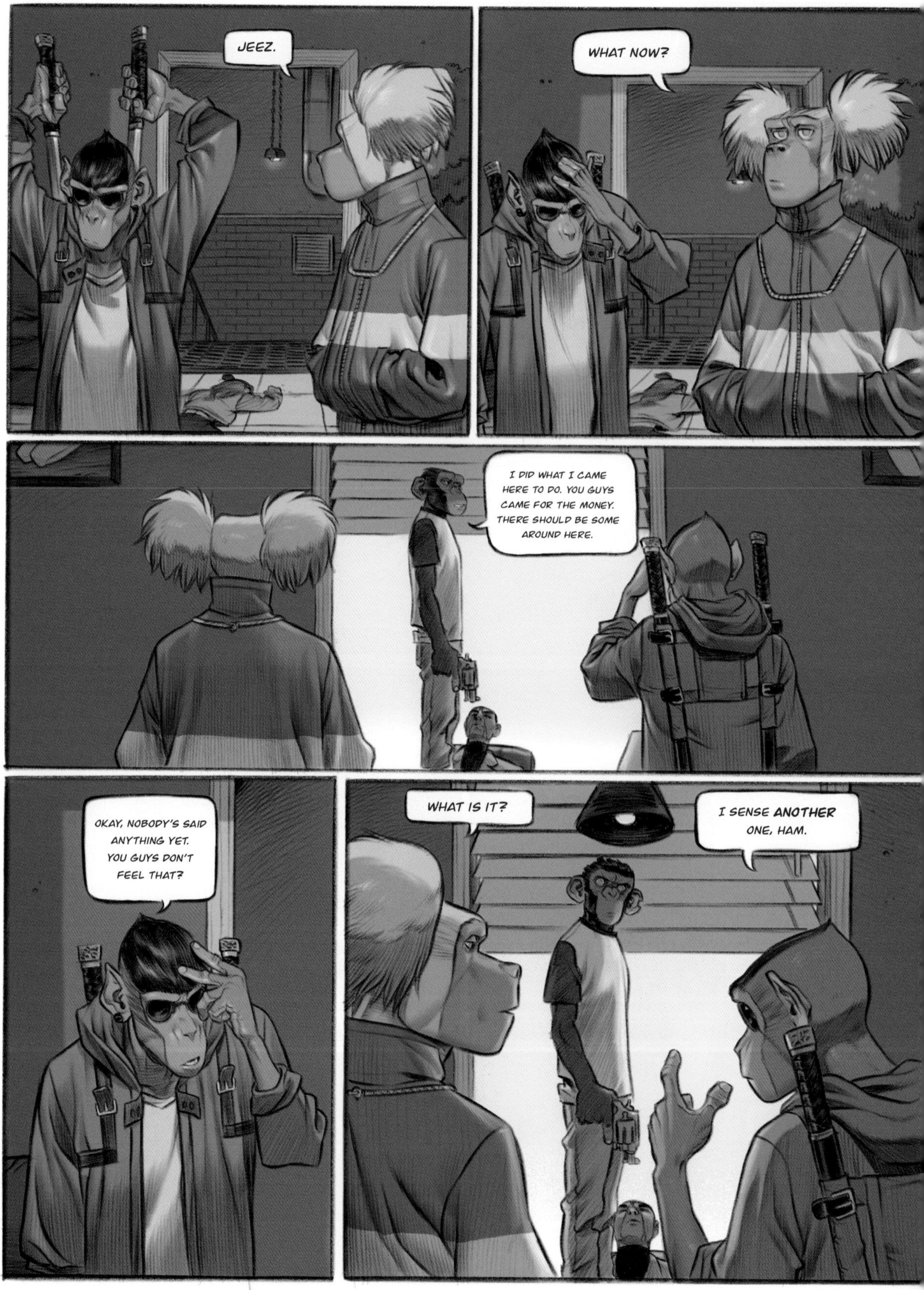
JEEZ.
WHAT NOW?
I DID WHAT I CAME HERE TO DO. YOU GUYS CAME FOR THE MONEY. THERE SHOULD BE SOME AROUND HERE.
OKAY, NOBODY'S SAID ANYTHING YET. YOU GUYS DON'T FEEL THAT?
WHAT IS IT?
I SENSE **ANOTHER** ONE, HAM.

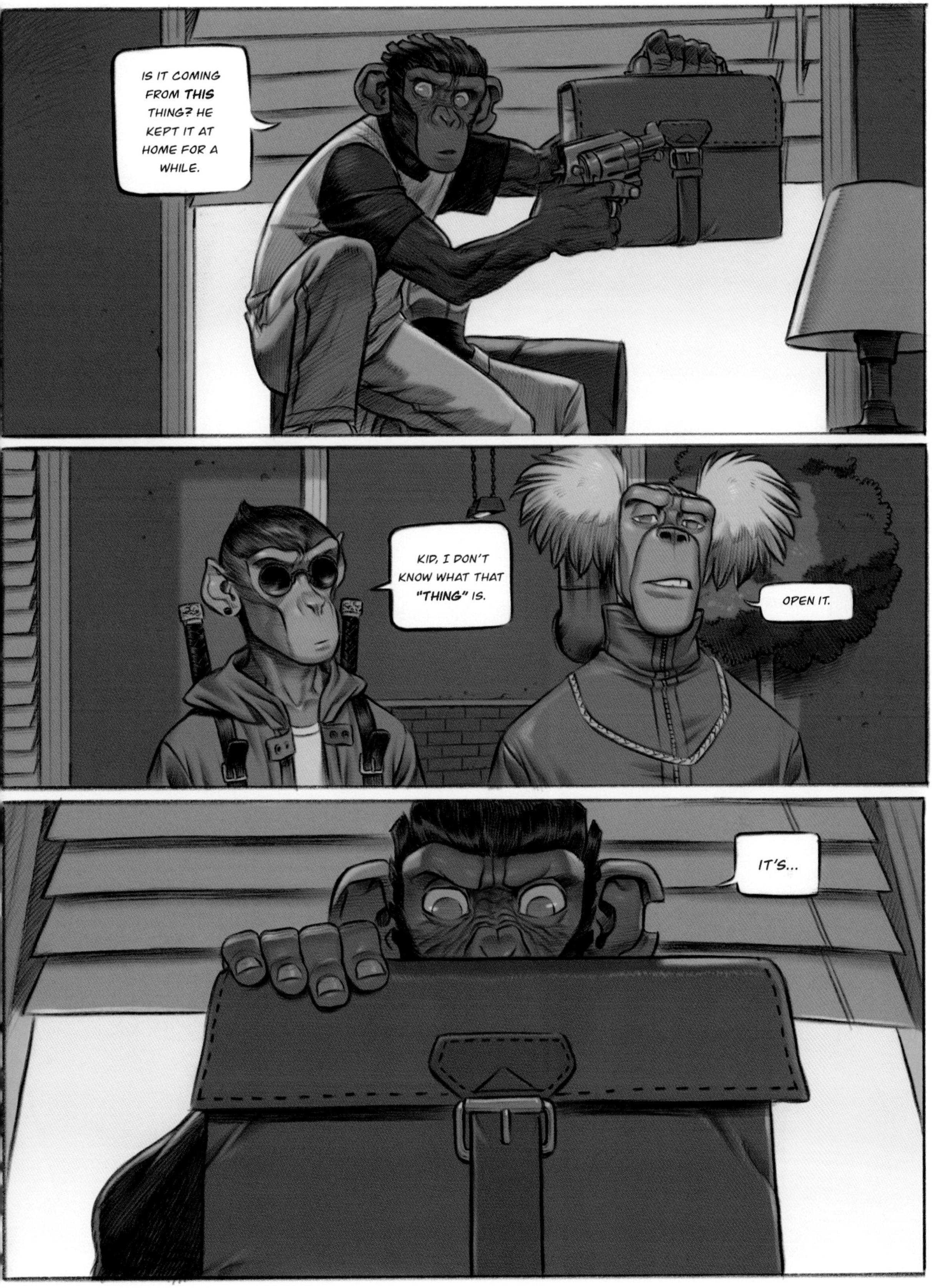
IS IT COMING FROM **THIS** THING? HE KEPT IT AT HOME FOR A WHILE.
KID, I DON'T KNOW WHAT THAT **"THING"** IS.
OPEN IT.
IT'S...

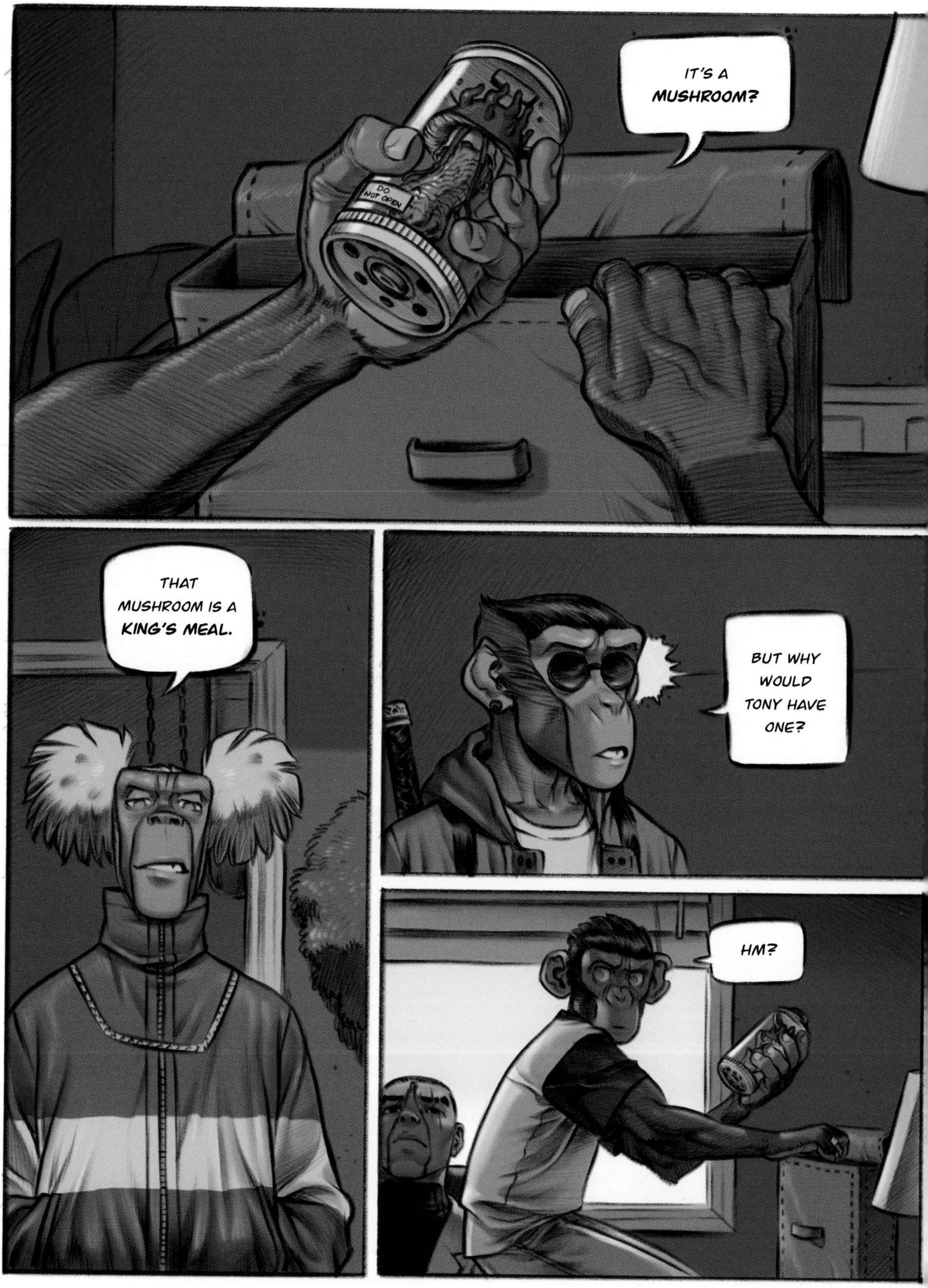
IT'S A MUSHROOM?
DO NOT OPEN
THAT MUSHROOM IS A KING'S MEAL.
BUT WHY WOULD TONY HAVE ONE?
HM?

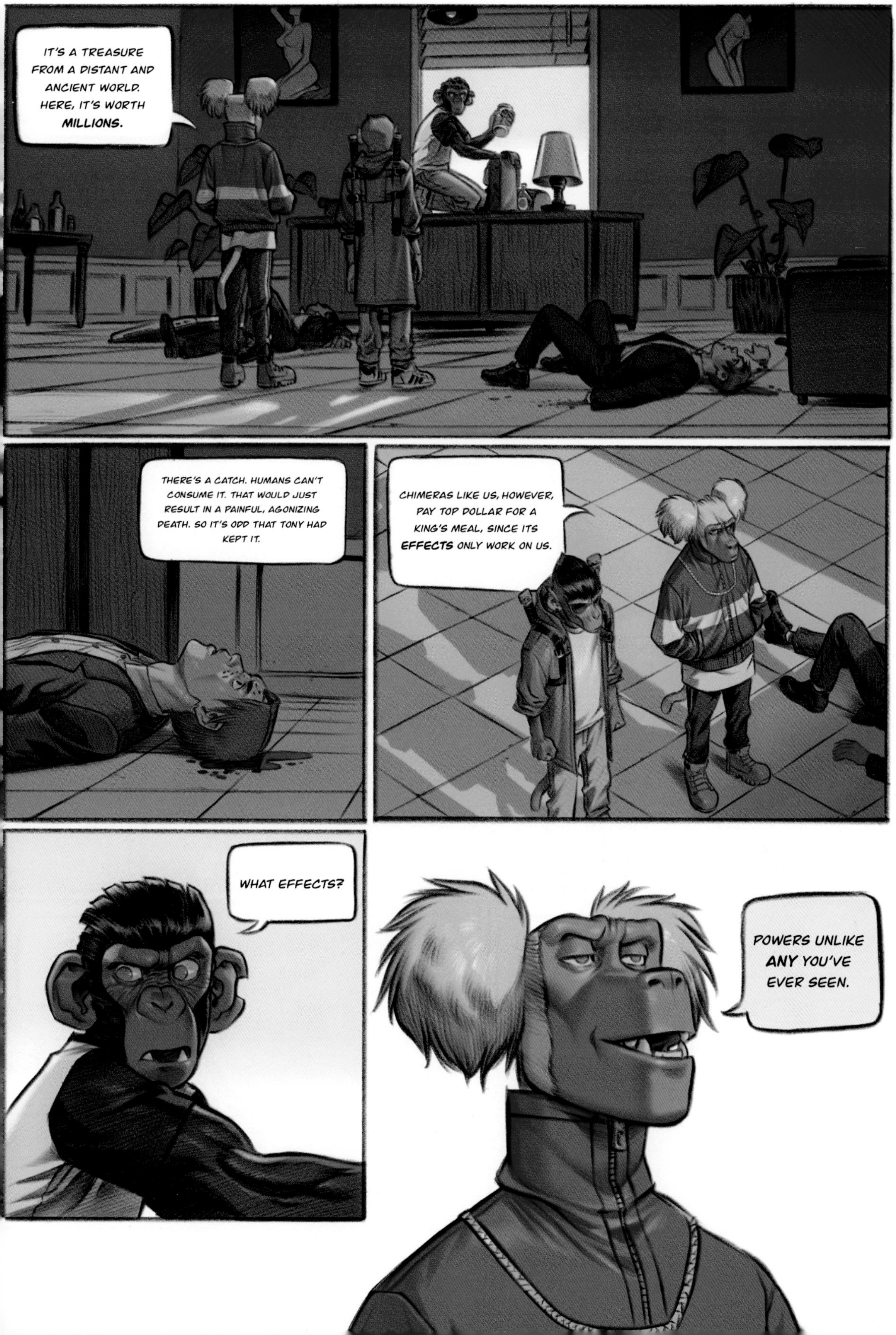
IT'S A TREASURE FROM A DISTANT AND ANCIENT WORLD. HERE, IT'S WORTH **MILLIONS.**
THERE'S A CATCH. HUMANS CAN'T CONSUME IT. THAT WOULD JUST RESULT IN A PAINFUL, AGONIZING DEATH. SO IT'S ODD THAT TONY HAD KEPT IT.
CHIMERAS LIKE US, HOWEVER, PAY TOP DOLLAR FOR A KING'S MEAL, SINCE ITS **EFFECTS** ONLY WORK ON US.
WHAT EFFECTS?
POWERS UNLIKE **ANY** YOU'VE EVER SEEN.

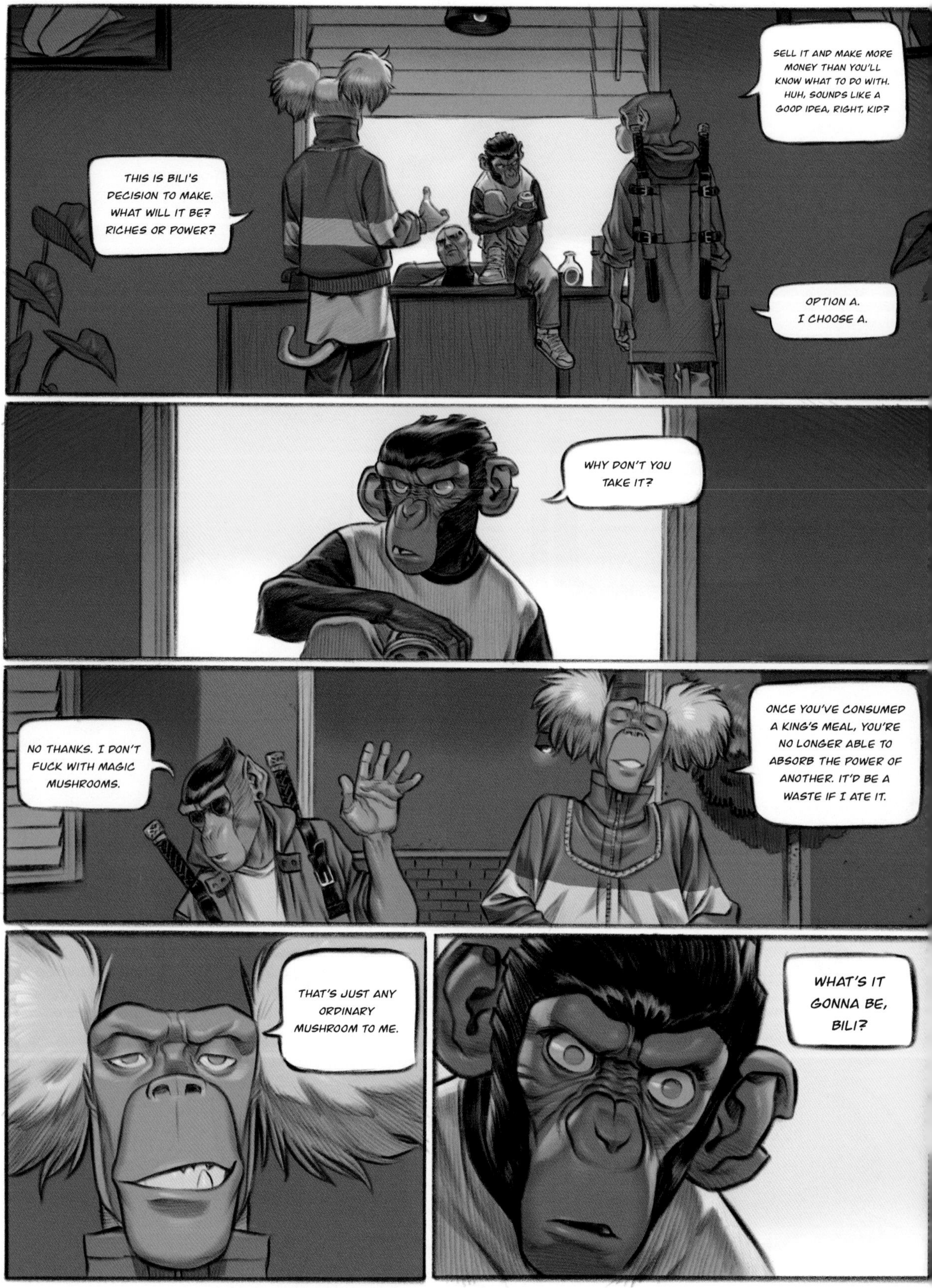
SELL IT AND MAKE MORE MONEY THAN YOU'LL KNOW WHAT TO DO WITH. HUH, SOUNDS LIKE A GOOD IDEA, RIGHT, KID?
THIS IS BILI'S DECISION TO MAKE. WHAT WILL IT BE? RICHES OR POWER?
OPTION A. I CHOOSE A.
WHY DON'T YOU TAKE IT?
NO THANKS. I DON'T FUCK WITH MAGIC MUSHROOMS.
ONCE YOU'VE CONSUMED A KING'S MEAL, YOU'RE NO LONGER ABLE TO ABSORB THE POWER OF ANOTHER. IT'D BE A WASTE IF I ATE IT.
THAT'S JUST ANY ORDINARY MUSHROOM TO ME.
WHAT'S IT GONNA BE, BILI?

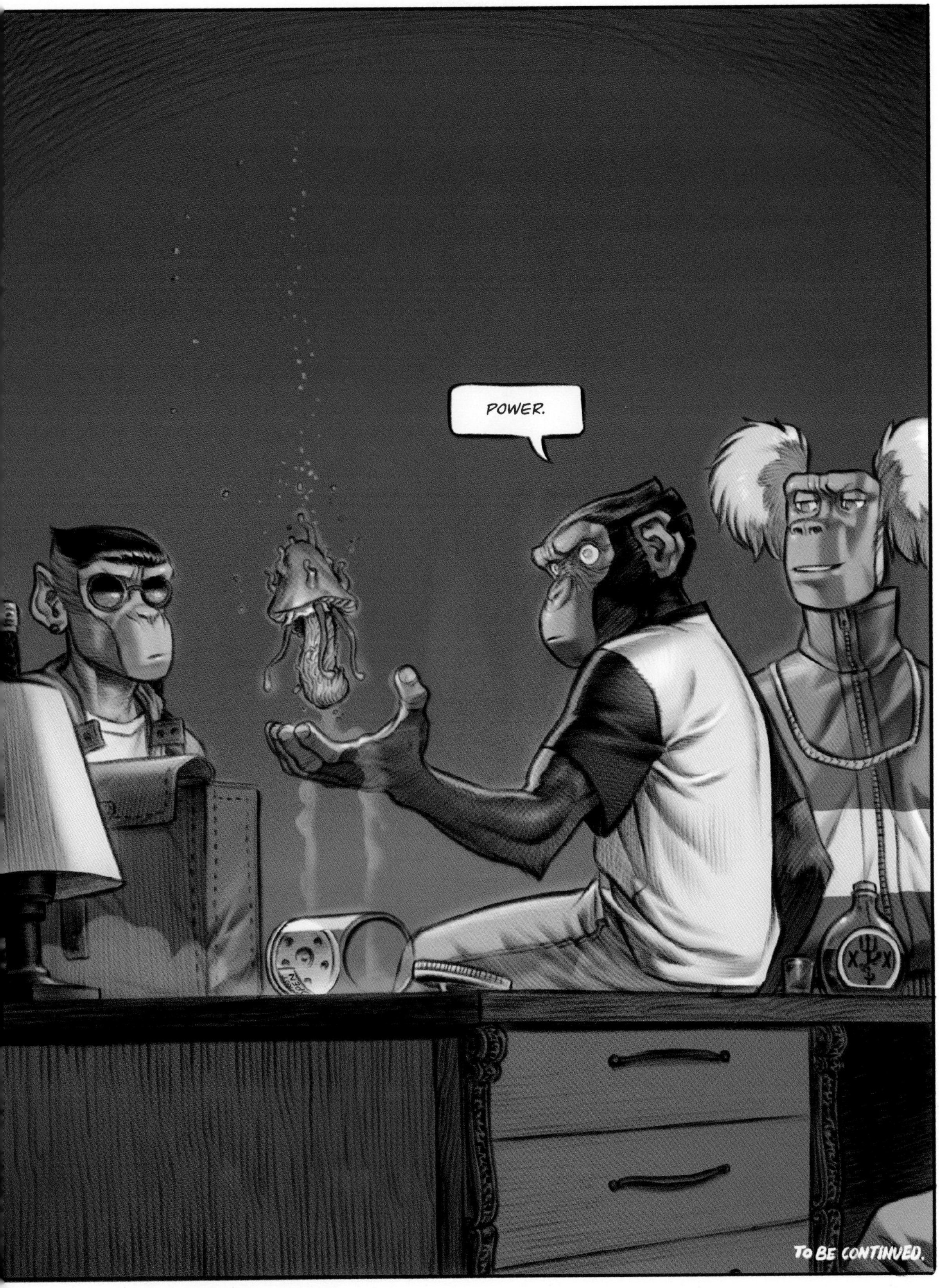
POWER.
TO BE CONTINUED.

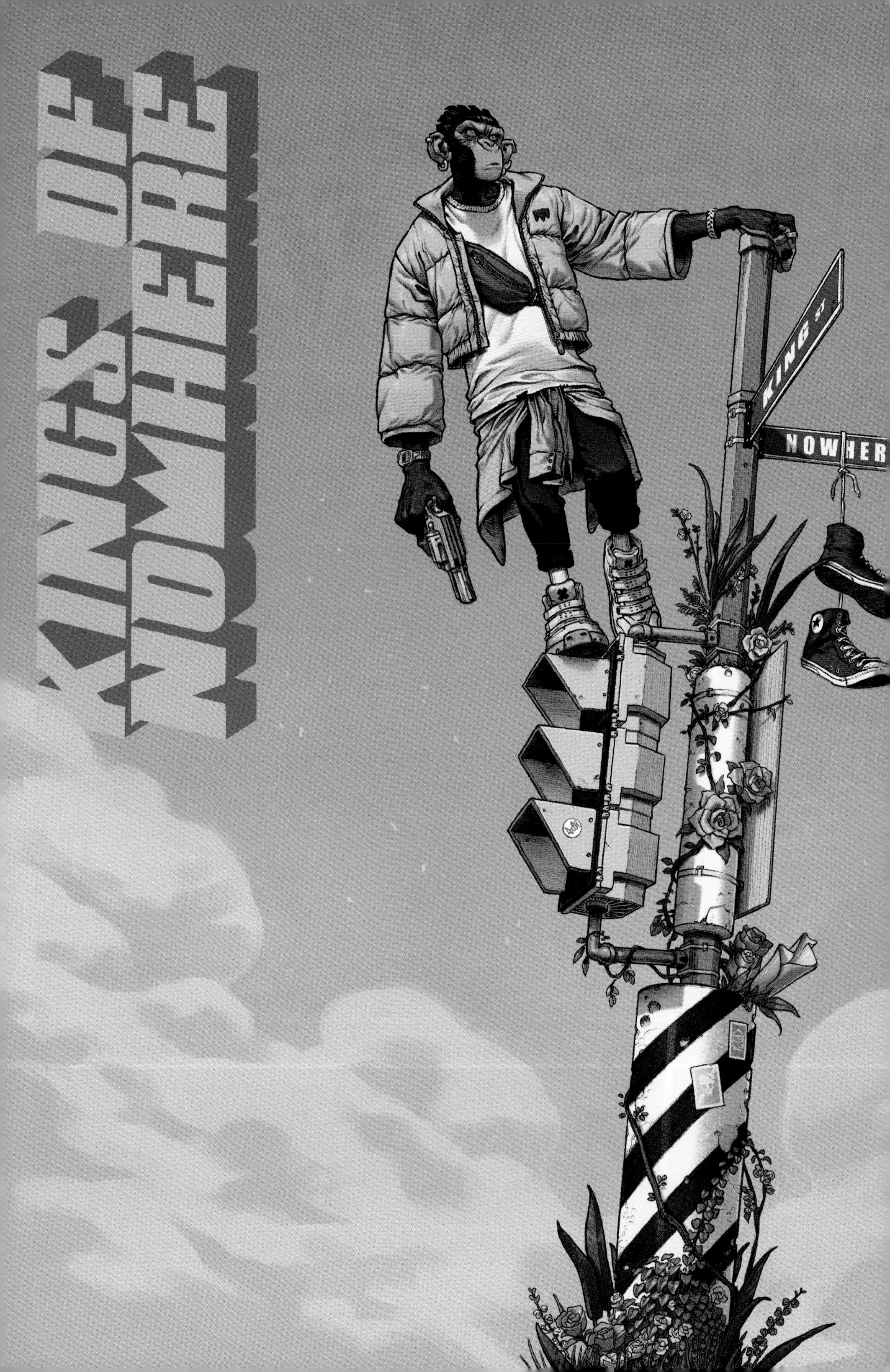
KINGS OF
NOWHERE
KING ST
NOWHER

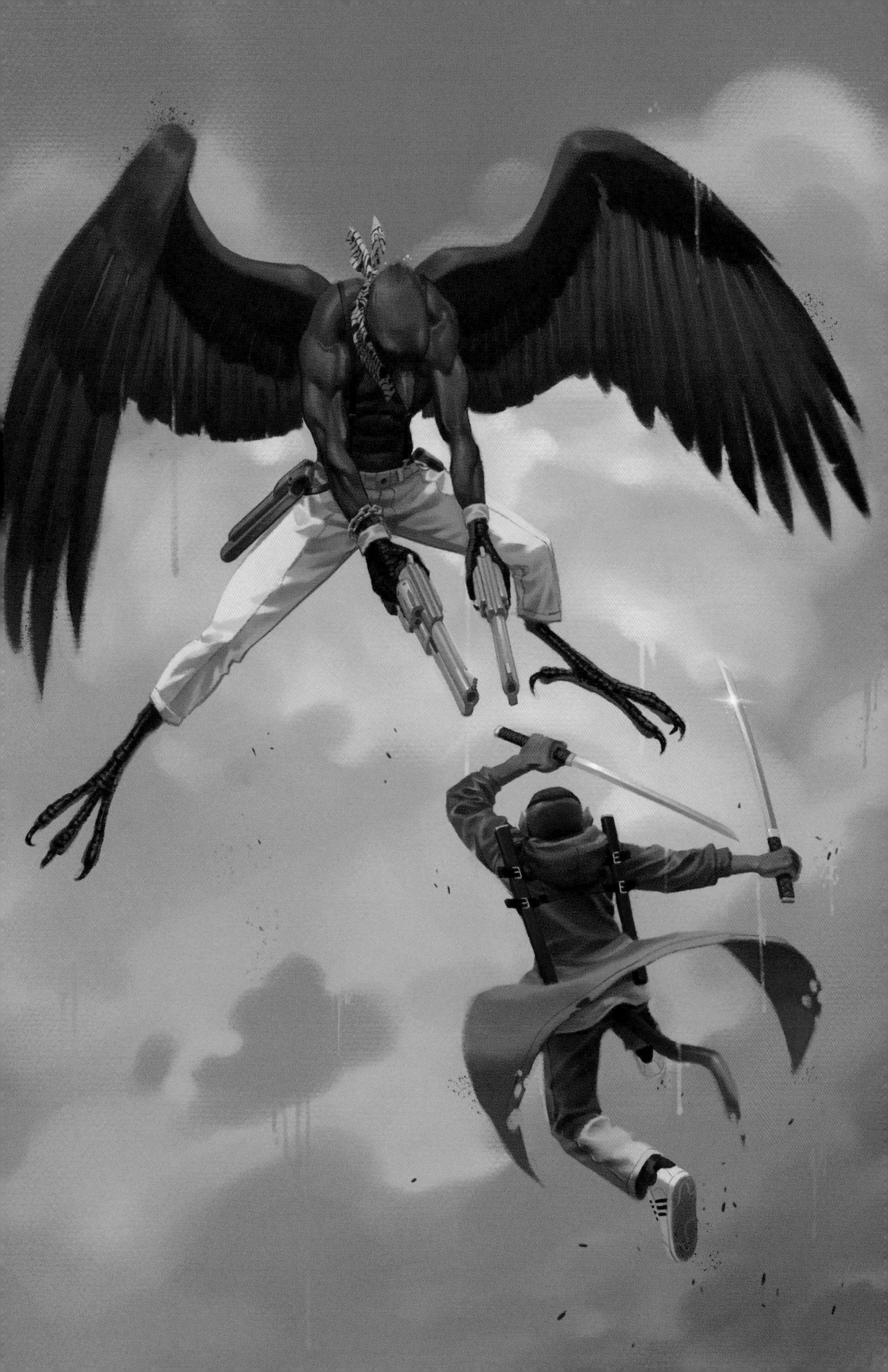

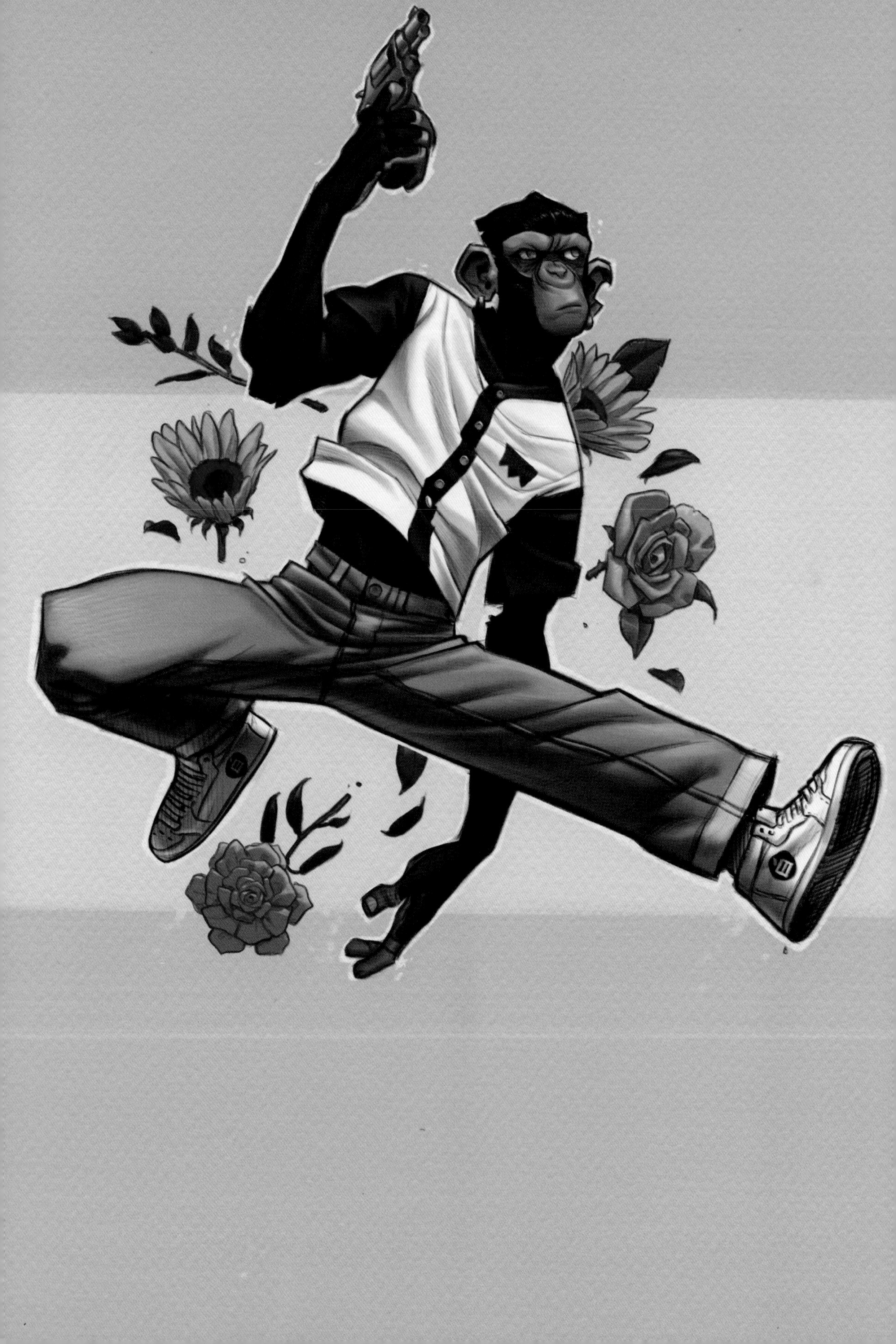

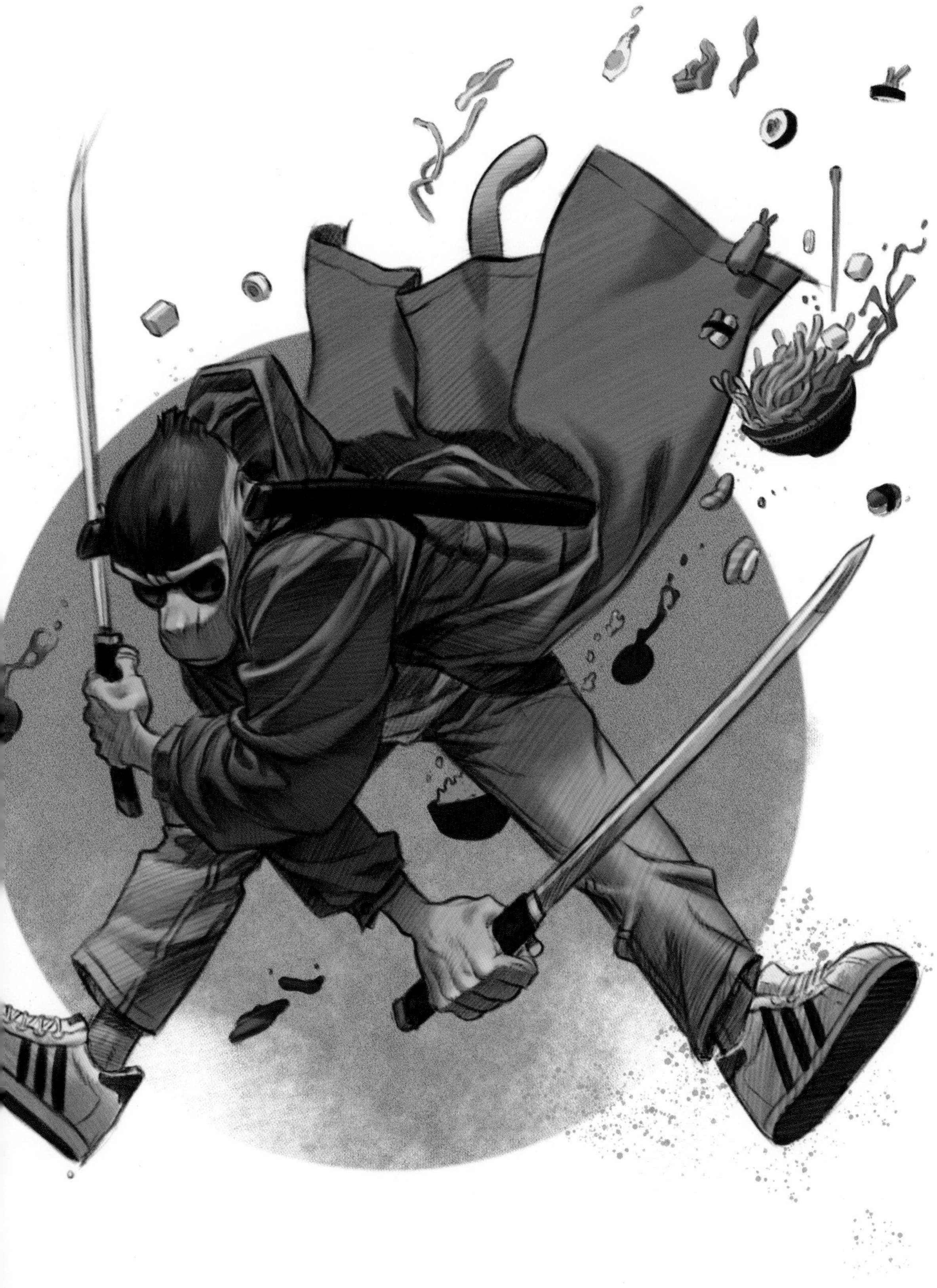

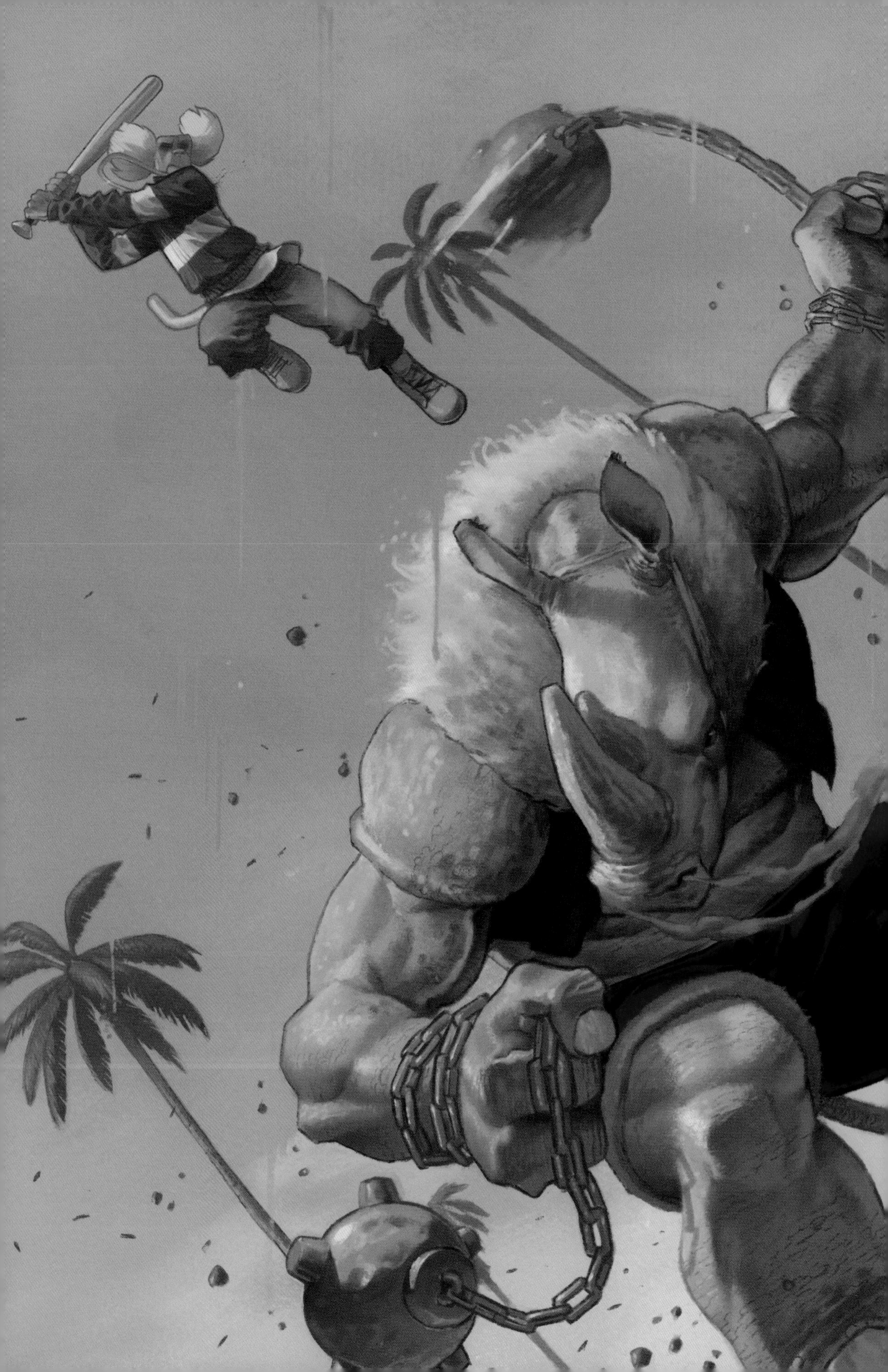

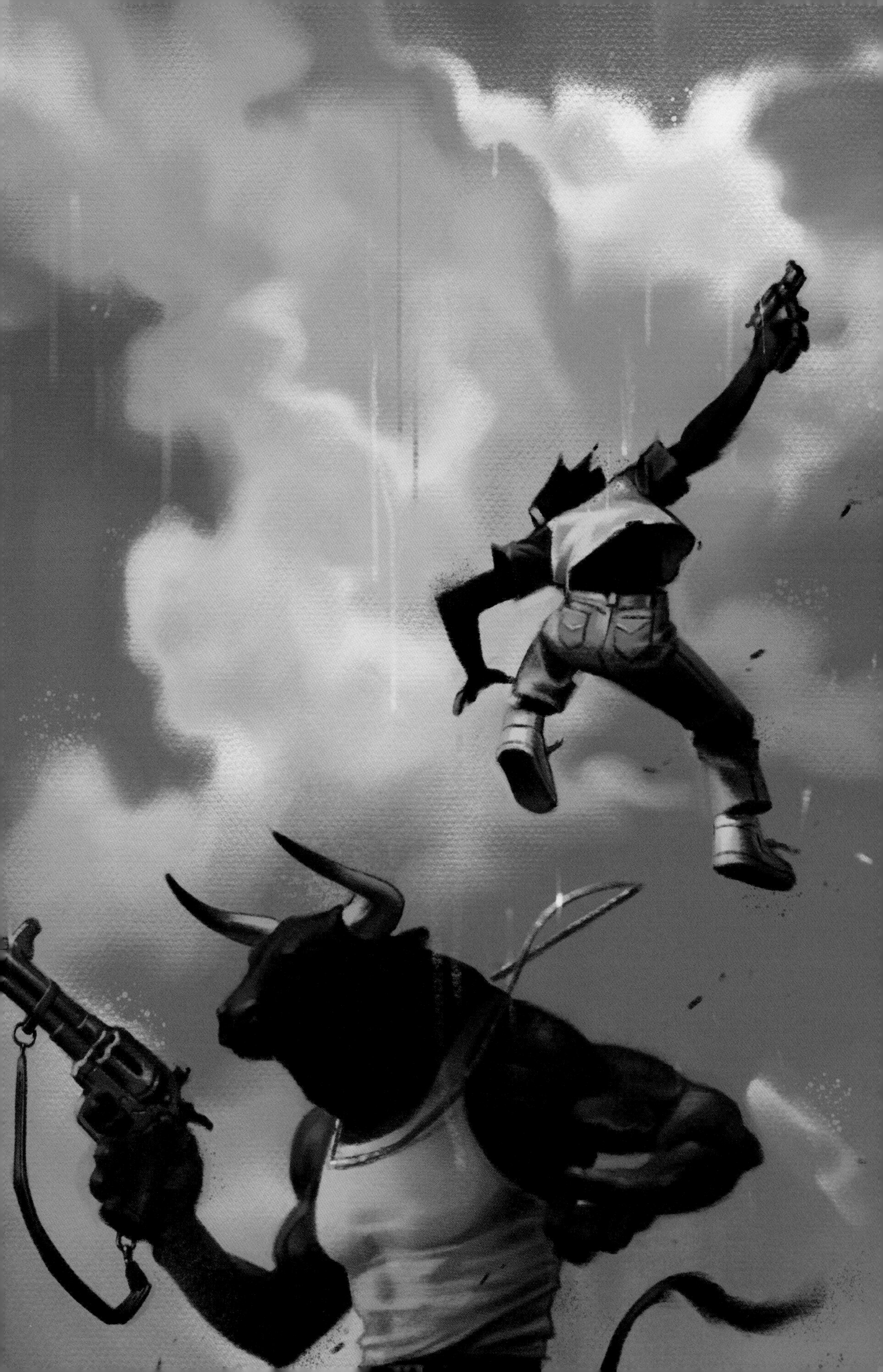

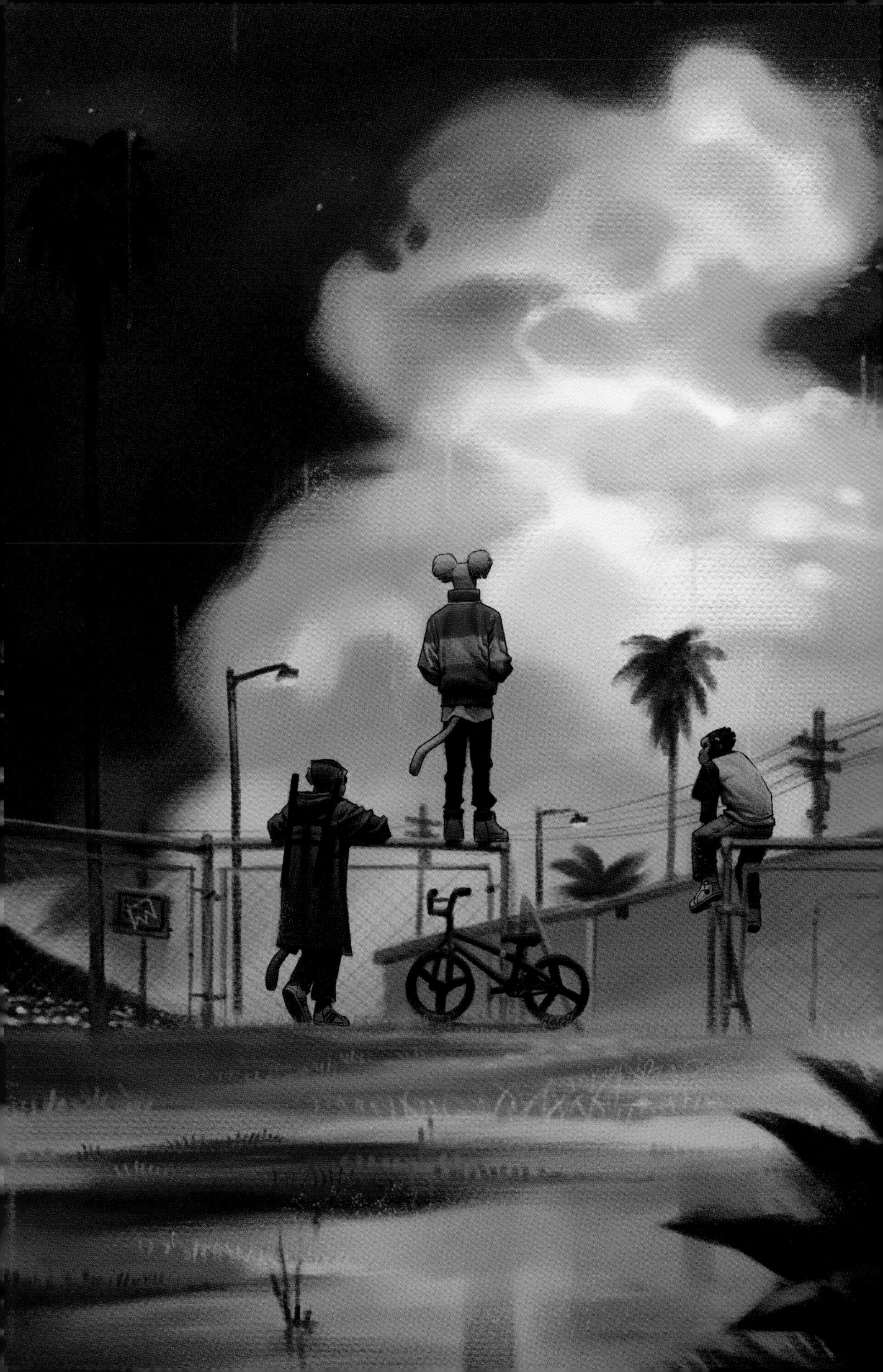

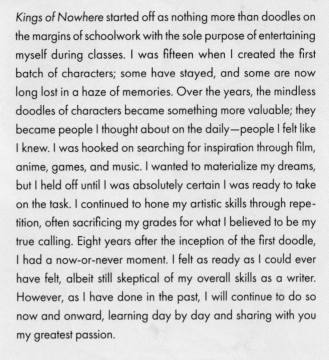

Kings of Nowhere started off as nothing more than doodles on the margins of schoolwork with the sole purpose of entertaining myself during classes. I was fifteen when I created the first batch of characters; some have stayed, and some are now long lost in a haze of memories. Over the years, the mindless doodles of characters became something more valuable; they became people I thought about on the daily—people I felt like I knew. I was hooked on searching for inspiration through film, anime, games, and music. I wanted to materialize my dreams, but I held off until I was absolutely certain I was ready to take on the task. I continued to hone my artistic skills through repetition, often sacrificing my grades for what I believed to be my true calling. Eight years after the inception of the first doodle, I had a now-or-never moment. I felt as ready as I could ever have felt, albeit still skeptical of my overall skills as a writer. However, as I have done in the past, I will continue to do so now and onward, learning day by day and sharing with you my greatest passion.

—Roosh

finished

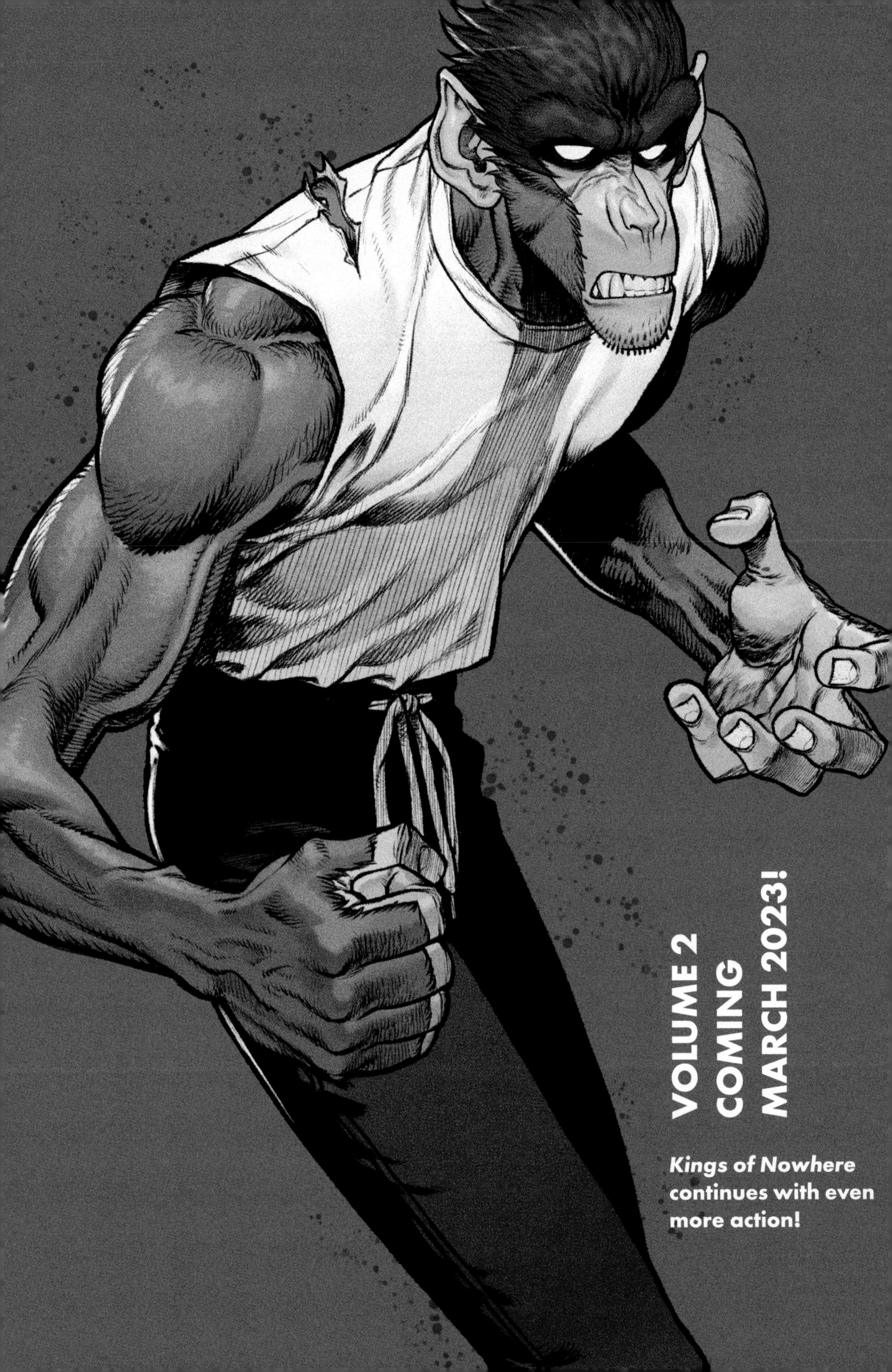
VOLUME 2
COMING
MARCH 2023!
Kings of Nowhere continues with even more action!